THE GIRL I USED TO BE

DEBBIE HOWELLS

B
Boldwood

First published in Great Britain in 2022 by Boldwood Books Ltd.

Cover Design by Head Design Ltd

Cover Photography: Shutterstock

A CIP catalogue record for this book is available from the British Library.

Paperback ISBN 978-1-80415-016-0

Large Print ISBN 978-1-80415-017-7

Hardback ISBN 978-1-80415-015-3

Ebook ISBN 978-1-80415-019-1

Kindle ISBN 978-1-80415-018-4

Audio CD ISBN 978-1-80415-010-8

MP3 CD ISBN 978-1-80415-011-5

Digital audio download ISBN 978-1-80415-013-9

Boldwood Books Ltd
23 Bowerdean Street
London SW6 3TN
www.boldwoodbooks.com

To everyone who's found themselves somewhere they never expected to be.

To live is the rarest thing.
Most people just exist.

— OSCAR WILDE

Only love is real

PROLOGUE

2020

I called you one morning. It was early and I'd gone for a run. Reaching the top of the hill, the sun was bursting through the trees, the air vibrant with the sound of birdsong.

For a moment, I stood there, as suddenly everything was falling into place, answers coming to me, answers that had evaded me for weeks, if not forever. I reached into my pocket for my phone and started texting you.

I have an idea for another book!

As I started walking again, I didn't have to wait long for your reply.

But you're not going to tell me!

It was followed by a smiley emoji. You knew that thing I had, about not telling anyone too soon because the magic went. But this was different. This was the story of me and you, which, until now, I hadn't known how to write.

I'm giving our story an ending! That's all you're getting – for now.

But knowing it was your story just as much as mine, I made you a promise.

But one day, when it's written, I'll send it to you.

PART I

1

MARCH 2019

Anna

As I clear away breakfast, I'm only half listening as a voice on the radio catches my attention.

'*When people know they don't have long, I think it crystallises what's really important. And sadly, so many have regrets – but never about the material. It's about wishing they'd spent more time with family; been more loving, more forgiving.*'

I listen as the interviewer goes on.

'What else do they talk about?'

'*It's usually missed chances. Living the life other people expected them to live, instead of being true to themselves. Not appreciating the small, everyday things... Wishing they'd been happy, chased their dreams...*'

'Things that would serve us all to bear in mind, really.'

'*Yes. When you think how impermanent life is...*'

Rays of sunlight reach into the kitchen as I tune out the

voices, trying to remember the last time I really felt happy. But things happen; life changes you. It's an inevitable part of getting older.

My mobile buzzes and Lucy's face appears on the screen.

'Hi, Luce!' She's been my best friend for almost forever.

'Anna, you're never going to believe this.' Lucy's voice is filled with excitement. 'I've been offered this amazing job, babe. Interior designing a brand-new villa in the south of France! Bloody stunning place – practically on the beach. They want me to start the day after tomorrow!'

I picture white walls contrasted against purple bougainvillea, a sea that's multiple shades of turquoise. 'Wow, Luce. Sounds amazing!' Things like this often happen to my friend; she's never lost her adventurous streak. When her aunt left her the old finca she owned in rural Ibiza, true to the dream she's always had, Lucy sold her flat and moved there. 'How long are you there for?'

'A couple of weeks – but when I get back, why don't you look at flights? Get away from the horrible English winter for a few days.'

'I'd love that.' The thought of some time away is irresistible.

'Think about some dates. It would be so great to see you...'

Remembering the quiet hills surrounding her house, the views of the sea, I don't need persuading. 'It's been far too long... I'll text you.'

Lucy goes on. 'So how are things with you?'

'Good. Work is work...' I try to sound brighter than I feel. 'James is a pain in the arse – but we both know how that goes.'

'What's happened this time?' She sounds resigned.

'He has a week off in May and I wanted to book a holiday. I found a week in Tuscany – out of season, not too busy, as he likes it, but he wants to go to the Algarve to play golf.'

Lucy's straight in there. 'Then let him! You can come here – everyone's happy!'

'Maybe I will. I just wish...'

'You wish he'd think about what you'd like to do. Well, we both know that's never going to happen. Shit. I've just seen the time.' She sounds horrified. 'Sorry, babe. I have to go. My flight's at midday and I've got loads to do before I leave. I'll send you some photos when I get there. And don't forget to text me some dates.'

Ending the call, I turn to get my jacket and my sleeve catches on the handle of one of the kitchen units, snapping the bracelet I'm wearing. It's one James gave me on our anniversary several years ago. Picking up the broken chain, I wonder if it's symbolic, as suddenly I'm craving the excitement of Lucy's life; to be embarking on an adventure, just as she is.

But for most of us, life isn't like that, I remind myself. And I'm not Lucy. I have my job and I'm married to James. A world away from Lucy's multicoloured one, my life is here.

I close the front door behind me and step into the street of Georgian town houses, where the warm ochre of Bath stone is caught in the spring sunlight. It's quiet, the first blossom appearing on the cherry trees. Feeling the breeze pick up, as I whistle to my dog, a noise comes from next door.

Peering through the sparse shrubs, I see my elderly neighbour standing on her doorstep. 'Grace? Is everything OK?'

'Anna, dear.' Her lined face looks puzzled. 'I'm not sure. You see, I can't find Ron.'

'Why don't I help you?' Ron, her husband, is devoted to her. He won't have gone far. By the time I open her garden gate, she's at the bottom of their steps, frail, her face anxious, her elegant dress faded. 'Come on.' I take her arm. 'Let's see if we can find him.'

'I think he's gone, dear.' She looks remarkably serene for someone whose husband's missing.

'I'm sure he hasn't.' I help her inside, Yippy, my dog, trotting ahead of us as I call out. 'Ron? Hello? Are you there?'

When there's no reply, we go through to the kitchen. 'He's probably upstairs. I'll go and look. Why don't you sit down – I'll put the kettle on.'

As Grace sits, Yippy lays his head on her knee. After filling the kettle, to my relief, the front door opens and Ron calls out, 'I'm back, Grace. I'm just hanging up my jacket. I won't be a minute.'

When he comes into the kitchen holding a small bag of shopping, Grace's face lights up. As Yippy trots over and licks his hand, a look of surprise appears on his face as he sees me. 'How nice to see you, Anna. You've time for a cup of tea, I hope.'

'I've just put the kettle on.' I lower my voice. 'Grace was worried – I found her outside. I think she'd forgotten where you'd gone.'

A shadow crosses his face, then he goes over to his wife. Placing his hands on her shoulders, he kisses her tenderly on the cheek. 'I told you I was only going for a bit of shopping,' he says gently, then kisses her other cheek. 'It's OK, love. You don't need to worry. I'm back.'

* * *

Back outside, I'm just about to get in my car, when a shrill voice comes from behind me.

'Anna? Now, just a minute…'

Recognising the voice, my heart sinks. Carol Madison is involved with the Bath Festival. She lives further along the same street but only ever speaks to me when she wants something.

Catching me up, she pins on a high-wattage smile. 'I'm so

pleased I've caught you. I'm rallying volunteers to help with the Jane Austen festival. You couldn't spare a couple of days could you? It isn't until June... We're awfully short of people in ticketing again...'

As she talks, she flutters her eyelash extensions, and I take in hair that's newly coiffed, nails that are beautifully manicured.

I've always helped in the past, but the thought of two days in a stuffy ticketing booth fills me with dread. However, there are times we all have to do things we don't want to. But I'm already regretting my decision as I nod. 'OK.'

'Oh Anna...' For a moment, she almost looks emotional. 'Thank you. I knew I could count on you. I'm having a little coffee morning next month... you must come along. I'll drop you an invite.'

She'll forget – thankfully. I'm not one of Carol's clique, nor do I want to be. But as she gives a little wave and walks away, I'm annoyed with myself. Carol always gives me the tasks other people don't want.

But I'm not going to let her spoil the rest of the morning, and as I drive out of Bath, I feel my heart warm as my thoughts turn to my neighbours again. They won't have the regrets the radio show was talking about. Even after decades together, love radiates from them. It makes me sad that I can't say that about me and James.

Turning off the main road, I take the lane to Dyrham Park. About a mile on, I reach a lay-by where I pull over and get out. Letting Yippy out, I start along the footpath. After a long winter, the countryside is awakening, a haze of green filling the woods from millions of tiny leaf buds. Walking here is my escape, the empty landscape a place I'm free to think. Breathing in the cool air, Millie, my stepdaughter, comes to mind and I make a note to self to call her. Then I think of the book I want to write, the small notebook in which I collect ideas jammed into the pocket of my jeans.

It's one of my precious days off, and as I walk, I revel in the freedom I feel, in the softness of air that's filled with birdsong, the rays of sunlight rippling through the branches; the enduring timelessness of the trees.

Near the top of the hill, the woods thin out. Under a sky of palest blue, I take in the sweeping views. It's as beautiful as it gets in early spring, but as I carry on walking, it's like a cloud hangs over me.

Remember how you used to laugh and dance; the joy you felt at being alive? You should be celebrating each moment of this life, feeling it sparking in your veins, making your eyes bright, your heart beat faster...

I can't begin to remember the last time I felt like that. I stop walking, thinking back to my twenties, when I was left reeling after being diagnosed with a serious illness. After, given a second chance, I promised myself I'd make the most of each and every moment. But too many years have passed in a job that doesn't thrill me, living a life where nothing ever changes. Is this how it is now, for the rest of my life?

As I turn to head back, a restless feeling takes me over. Then up ahead, an escaped lamb emerges at speed from under the trees, its frantic cries echoed by those of its mother from behind the fence. I watch a man stumble into sight, lurching after the lamb, obviously trying to catch it. Straining my eyes to make out his face, even before I do my heart misses a beat, because I know him.

We were teenagers when we met at a party, where he played his way into my soul on a blue guitar. We fell in love and for a year we were inseparable. And if I'm honest, deep down, I've never forgotten him.

JUNE 1995

ANNA

'Anna, come on! Mark's here! We need to go!'

At Lucy's, we were getting ready to go to a party. I took a last glance in Lucy's mirror, checking my hair, adding another coat of lip gloss and a spray of my friend's perfume, before turning to face her. 'OK! Ready!'

We hurried downstairs and went outside. The air was warm, the sun sinking lower in the sky as we walked towards Mark's car. Reaching him, Lucy kissed his cheek.

'To the pub first?' he suggested.

'Where else?' Lucy winked at me.

As we climbed into his car, a zing of excitement raced through me. I could feel it in my bones. It was going to be one of those nights – a really good one.

Reaching Bath, Mark squeezed his car between an old banger and a battered Land Rover. Getting out, the city felt lethargic, the day's heat radiating off the buildings as we turned down the cobbled lane to where the pub was.

Already it was crowded, time flying as we joined our friends. The sun was setting by the time we left a couple of hours later. With five of us crammed into Mark's car, we followed the road out of Bath, before turning into a narrow lane that spiralled into the heart of the countryside.

Reaching the farm, Mark followed the stony track, parking at the end near several other cars.

As I got out, Lucy grabbed my arm. 'Come on.'

The air was heady with the scents of newly cut hay and honeysuckle as we crossed the yard to the barn where the party was under way. Inside, at one end there was a bar, while at the other, a group of people had gathered around a makeshift stage.

'I didn't know there was going to be a band tonight.' Lucy loved live music. 'Do you know who they are?'

'No idea.' Following her gaze, I made out a drum kit set up next to a keyboard, just as Mark appeared beside us.

'Here.' He passed us each a plastic glass of wine. 'This band's good. I've heard them...'

His words were drowned out as the first guitar chord reverberated through the barn and everyone turned towards the five guys climbing a rickety stepladder onto the stage.

As they started to play, I watched, enthralled by the upbeat music, the obvious chemistry flowing between them. Mark was right about them – but he was wrong, too. They weren't just good, they were brilliant.

I watched the lead singer, then the keyboard player who looked as though he was lost in his own world; the drummer and the two guitarists as one of them broke into a solo that made my skin prickle.

As I watched him, there seemed to be something familiar about him. Beside me, Lucy nudged my elbow. 'Amazing, aren't they? The drummer, Anna...' Lucy's eyes were glued to him.

'Behave,' I told my friend. 'You have Mark, remember?'

Much later, after they finished to rapturous applause, the atmosphere seemed deflated; the music of the DJ who took over seeming somehow generic.

'Let's get another drink.' As a few people started dancing, Lucy looked around for Mark. 'Anna, look. I have to go over there.'

I followed her gaze to where Mark was talking to the drummer. There was no point in saying anything – I knew what my friend was like once she'd set her sights on someone.

She read my mind. 'I know – I'm with Mark.' She couldn't take her eyes off the drummer. 'I'm also young, Anna. Mark and I are hardly forever. Come on – let's get another drink. I want to talk to him.'

After buying more wine, as we reached Mark, he nodded towards the drummer. 'Dave, this is Lucy – and Anna.'

'We loved it,' Lucy said instantly. 'Seriously. How long have you guys been together?'

But before he could answer, someone lurched into him, knocking his arm and spilling his drink.

'Man...' Sounding resigned, Dave shook off the beer running down his arm as my heart missed a beat. It was the guitarist.

Close up, he seemed on edge, less familiar and more restless as his eyes roamed everywhere.

'I'll get you another, mate. Anyone else?' His eyes flickered towards Mark, then lingered on me.

As our eyes met, what felt like an electric shock hit me. I shook my head.

'Yes – please.' Giving me an odd look, Lucy broke the moment.

'I'll come with you.' Mark followed the guitarist.

They disappeared over to the bar and I turned to Lucy. 'I'll be back in a bit, Luce.' Leaving her flirting effortlessly with the drummer, feeling suddenly light-headed, I went outside.

Away from the barn, I made my way between the shadowy shapes of cars, the music fading into the background as I took in the outlines of trees silhouetted against a glittering sky.

Standing there, I was lost in the moment; only dimly aware of the sound of footsteps coming closer before someone collided with me.

'Shit. I'm sorry...' The voice sounded suitably chastened. 'Shit...'

'It's OK.' Pain was shooting through my foot, but as the light from the barn briefly caught his face, I realised it was the guitarist again.

'Shit. I mean it. Sorry.'

'It's OK. Really!' I met his gaze. 'Your band was great,' I start to say, exactly as he said, 'Did you like the music?'

We both broke off, as a smile plastered itself across my face. 'The music was great,' I said exactly as he said, 'Thank you!'

Hearing voices coming towards us through the darkness, he held a finger to his lips and grabbed one of my hands. 'Come with me.'

In a moment of recklessness, I let him lead me away from the party, under the silhouetted trees into a vast open field, where he stopped.

The field was bathed in moonlight and following his gaze, I took in the same stars I was looking at earlier, stars that out here, away from the lights in the barn, seemed somehow magnified.

'Is this why you came out here?' I asked.

'Yeah.' He's silent. 'I guess I just like looking at them.'

'It is amazing.' The sky seemed bigger somehow, the world seeming to fade behind us so that it was just the two of us.

Turning to me, he frowned slightly. 'We haven't met before, have we?'

My voice was husky. 'I don't think so.'

Looking up at the sky again, a shooting star arced overhead.

'Wow! Did you see that?' He spoke softly. 'Do you know they're lucky? You're supposed to make a wish.'

As we stood there, feeling the warmth of his arm against mine, I knew what I wanted to wish for. It was to string this moment out, so that it went on and on. He turned towards me again and this time as our eyes met, it was impossible to look away.

Strains of music drifted towards us as he held out a hand. 'Shall we dance?'

'What – here?'

He grinned at me. 'Why not?'

Taking both my hands, he pulled me towards him as we started to dance, picking up tempo with the music, laughing at ourselves, coming closer as the music slowed again; time seeming to stop as he reached towards my face, gently stroking away a lock of hair.

'You're beautiful,' he said quietly. His fingers grazed my cheek as unfamiliar feelings swirled inside me. 'Are you free tomorrow?' Suddenly he looked awkward. 'I mean, you're probably not... Which is fine. I just thought I'd ask... In case you were...'

I couldn't help smiling. 'I might be.'

'Good.' He looked slightly mystified. 'Just so you know, I don't normally do things like this. I mean, I know I can be impulsive, but I don't...' He tailed it off.

'Stand under the stars with a girl you've only just met?' I finished.

'Yes.' He looked at me. 'I'm Will, by the way.'

'I'm Anna.'

A funny feeling came over me as we stood there. I knew I couldn't have said no, but when we'd never met before, I didn't understand how I could feel like this. 'So... you were saying about tomorrow?'

'Oh. Yes.' He grinned again. 'Do you live in Bath?

I nodded.

'Do you like cheesecake?'

I was laughing. 'As it happens, I do.'

'Cool – because so do I! How about we meet on Pulteney Bridge? We can decide where to go when we get there.'

Suddenly I felt shy. 'OK.'

'Good.' Lifting my hand towards his lips, he kissed it.

2

ANNA

The breeze catches my hair as my heart beats faster. I've never seen Will here before, even once. Calling Yippy over, I take in his faded jeans and thick sweater, well-worn walking boots spattered with mud. The lamb continues to run rings around him. As I get nearer, he glances up.

A look of incredulity crosses his face. '*Anna?*'

'I can't believe it's you…' Our eyes meet for a moment. 'Would you like some help?'

He smiles ruefully. 'I'm trying to put it back in its field but it definitely doesn't want to go.' As the lamb makes another dash for freedom, he lurches towards it, too late, landing unceremoniously on the grass. 'Crap.' He glances at me. 'Sorry.'

Trying to stifle my laughter, I notice a section of fence that's come loose. 'Hold on a minute.' Hurrying over, I flatten it just as the lamb leaps over, clearing it with inches to spare, before trotting off to find its mother.

I prop up the fence so that it doesn't fall over again, then turn back to him.

He shakes his head. 'Why didn't I think of that?'

Yippy bounds excitedly towards him, a frenzy of black hair and wagging tail. '*Yippy!*' Ignoring my shouts, he tries to lick Will's face.

'Don't worry! I like dogs.' As Will tries to get up, his face creases in pain.

I frown. 'Are you OK?'

Struggling to his feet, he winces. 'I think I twisted my ankle.' Managing a tentative step, he screws up his face in pain again before sitting heavily, muttering what sounds like 'idiot' to himself.

I crouch down on the grass next to him. Up close, I take in the familiar warm blue of his eyes. 'How bad is it?'

'Not sure yet.' He shakes his head. 'I'll sit here for a bit, see if it eases. I broke it a few years ago. It hasn't been the same since.' His eyes wander towards mine again. 'Don't worry. I'm sure I'll be fine.'

'How did you break it?'

'I, er... fell up a step. Into a pub. After going into a number of other pubs...'

'Ah.' I try not to laugh. Then on impulse, I sit down next to him. 'I can't exactly leave you here. What if you can't walk?'

He shrugs, then reaches in his pocket for his phone. 'I suppose I could call a friendly farmer.' He glances at the screen. 'Crap,' he says again. 'No signal.'

I pull my phone out of my pocket, seeing several bars displayed on its screen. 'You could always use mine?'

He looks at me doubtfully. 'You really don't have to stay.'

I hesitate. 'What if you need help?'

'I suppose if you don't mind hanging around for a few minutes, it might actually be a good idea.' He sounds apologetic, then for the first time, he smiles. 'Thanks.'

'You're welcome,' I say, trying to sound casual. I notice a scattering of greying hair amongst the brown, a slight crinkling at the corners of his eyes. 'I don't need to be anywhere until later. It seems like one of those days.' Frowning slightly, I'm thinking that if it hadn't been for the call from Lucy, then Grace catching me as I left, the chances are our paths wouldn't have crossed.

'Yeah?' His eyes flicker briefly upwards, at the small clouds scudding across the sky. 'I'm on holiday for a couple of weeks. Well, not really a holiday.' A shadow crosses his face. 'My dad died and I'm sorting out his house – he lived in Hinton. I was planning to walk every day – just to get out for a bit.' He glances at his ankle again.

Hinton's a picturesque village just a short distance away.

'I'm so sorry.'

'He was old.' Will shrugs. 'And he'd managed to stay living at home, which was what he wanted.'

We look at each other and our eyes seem to lock, as, for a moment, neither of us looks away.

'I should try to get up.' Will carefully pushes himself to his feet. After a few tentative steps, he seems to loosen up.

'How is it?'

He nods. 'OK, I think.' He hesitates. 'Were you on your way back?'

'I was.'

'You should go ahead. This may take a while.'

I hesitate. 'If you're sure?'

'I'll be OK.' He pauses. 'It's really nice seeing you again.'

'You, too.' Feeling oddly compelled to stay, I start making my way back to my car, aware of him following more slowly behind, as I wonder if our paths will cross again.

* * *

Back home, the house is quiet and the rest of the day passes uneventfully. I switch on the radio and make a pot of coffee, then head to my small office at the back of the house and turn my attention to the book I'm planning to write. But after seeing Will earlier, memories are flooding back – of the party where we met as teenagers, then of the months that followed, as I kick myself for not asking more about him, for not catching up... but I'd been so stunned to see him.

I think back to the long, easy summer I hadn't wanted to end, when Will and I fell in love effortlessly; sweetly. Double-dating with Lucy and Dave after she'd dumped Mark, we'd wander through Bath's characterful streets, or meet up with friends in one of the parks; when it was hot, heading out of Bath in Will's ancient Mini to spend lazy afternoons by the river.

I'd never been so happy. Will's irrepressible zest for life had been contagious, the days filled with fun and laughter. But we'd had quiet moments, too, mulling over the bigger questions in life; about whether or not there was a purpose to our lives.

Back then, I'd wanted to make a difference to the world in some way. Meanwhile, Will was already reaching people with his passion for music. Still young, with bold plans and even bigger dreams, I'd never imagined we wouldn't be together. But as we both found out, nothing lasts.

With James out for dinner, I pull the curtains closed and curl up on the sofa in my old fleece pyjamas. Pouring a large glass of wine, I watch a Bridget Jones film that James would detest, revelling in the bliss of being alone.

Just before the end of the film, I hear his car pull up outside, then his key in the lock. There's no kiss on the cheek, no 'how was your evening', but there never is.

'Do I have a shirt for tomorrow?' Standing there, he frowns at the television. 'Haven't you seen this before? Only I'd like to catch the news before I go to bed.'

'You could always watch on your laptop.' I ignore the question about his shirt. 'There's only another ten minutes, then it's all yours.'

Without responding, he goes through to the kitchen, where there's the sound of a bottle being uncorked before he comes back with a glass of wine, standing there, his irritation obvious.

My film is still playing, but the enjoyment has gone. Switching it off, I get up. 'How was your evening?'

'Average. If you've finished, I'll put the news on.'

I hand him the remote. 'I'm going to bed.'

Hiding my disappointment that this isn't at all how I imagined life would be.

3

WILL

Back at his father's house, Will grabbed a bag of frozen peas before sitting on the sofa, putting his feet up and draping the bag over his ankle as a kind of impromptu ice pack.

Glancing around the room, he took in the familiar furniture, the paintings he remembered from his childhood, the framed family photos arranged above the fireplace, all of it taking him back. The only thing that was new was the feeling of emptiness.

He still couldn't believe he'd bumped into Anna again. But maybe he shouldn't have been surprised. Life had done this to them over the years, crossing their paths at inopportune moments, like this one right now, when he was dealing with a demanding, soon-to-be ex-wife and a house filled with memories.

Talking of which... He reached for the pile of photos he'd started going through. On the top was one of his dad. Studying his face, he felt a wave of sadness. He'd always hoped they'd forge more of a relationship as they'd got older. For as long as he could remember, there'd been an atmosphere of antagonism between them, almost as though his father had resented him. Will had tried his hardest to defuse it, to find a kinder way of being with each other. But his father hadn't responded. And now... it was too late.

Too late... They were the saddest words. However difficult their relationship, Will was grieving, not just for a parent he would always have regrets about, but for the last link to family and his childhood.

Feeling his ankle go numb, Will adjusted his makeshift ice pack, before looking at another photo. His parents looked so young, him and Simon primary school age, with too-big teeth, tousled hair and beaming smiles. Taken in the garden that his mum had loved, it was a time when life had seemed so simple.

Looking at his brother's face, his heart ached. They'd been such different people, yet still close. Losing him had cut Will to the core. Seven years on, not a day passed that he didn't miss him.

Now, out of the four of them, he was the only one left. God, it made him feel lonely. Self-pitying tears pricked his eyes. When he was young, he'd felt so carefree, his head filled with dreams, the world a place of adventure and opportunity. Life had seemed exciting; filled with promise. The party where he met Anna had been a high point, as had the times he'd played in the band, with all the camaraderie that came with that.

He could still remember noticing her that first time. Typically clumsy, he'd sloshed a pint of beer over Dave – not exactly the best of first impressions. When he'd gone outside, he couldn't believe it when he'd found her alone. It had sobered him up pretty much instantly. There had been something about her – the light in her eyes, her infectious laugh, a free spiritedness that had tapped into his. She'd taken his breath away.

He sighed. They'd been so young – too young perhaps, to imagine they might have stayed together. Nothing stayed the same – life taught you that. Will had found that out a year after they met, when his world had been turned upside down.

And now there was Darcey. Years ago, he'd fallen madly in love with her, this beautiful, spirited woman who'd injected colour into his life. But it hadn't taken long for their relationship to start to fray. Having a penchant for the finer things in life, Darcey had found herself a richer man and wanted a divorce.

Will's heart ached for his daughter. Caught in the middle, he had a feeling Darcey was using her for her own ends. The thing was, he knew all too well how it felt to lose a parent. The thought of Flo going through the same was crucifying him.

He sifted through the photos. There were several of him and Simon growing up; one with a Christmas tree in the background. He could still remember the baubles his mum had got out every year; the way she'd stand back to watch him and Simon decorate.

An aching nostalgia washed over him for all those little moments that had gone forever, as he found himself looking at a photo he hadn't seen before. It was of him and Anna – his mum must have taken it. She'd captured the light in Anna's eyes, her gorgeous long chestnut hair. They were looking at each other, their faces animated, one of her hands on his shoulder as she laughed at something he was saying.

He studied the photo more closely. Anna used to have dreams, too. He could remember how they used to talk about them. He found himself wondering what had become of them. But he had no way of knowing what had happened since she married James. And today, he couldn't help noticing the light in her eyes had dulled.

Was she happy? More to the point, was he happy? But with no family left, his marriage on the rocks, a music career he'd given up on, there wasn't a whole lot to feel happy about.

Sitting there, he put the photos down. It felt like he'd lost everyone in the world who'd been important to him – with the exception of Flo, that was. It bore no resemblance to the life he'd once imagined for himself, filled with people, laughter, music. *Love.*

Instead, it had all gone horribly wrong.

4

ANNA

The following morning, James and I barely speak before he leaves for work. I tell myself he's preoccupied about the client calls and meetings that lie ahead; that he's the same man I married – just older, less joyful. But I know what Lucy would say. *More selfish. And for fuck's sake, be honest, Anna. When was James ever joyful?*

But it's easy for Lucy to say – and love changes over the years. Giddy headiness and passion become something more solid, more grounded. And as I keep reminding myself, I have much that is good in my life.

It's still early when I drive towards Dyrham Park, pushing my annoyance about the holiday out of my mind; feeling a weight lift as I park the car then set off through the woods. A holiday's a small thing when so much is going on in the world and with Yippy running ahead, the landscape starts to work its magic on me.

Reaching the top, I notice a man walking towards me; feel a smile spreading across my face when I see it's Will.

He looks pleased. 'We must stop meeting like this.'

I glance at his feet, amused. One leg of his jeans is caught up revealing a garish sock. 'Is your ankle better?'

'Unbelievably it is.' Following my gaze, he straightens the leg of his jeans. 'On a day as lovely as this, it was too good an opportunity to miss.'

'It is, isn't it?' I glance up at the pale blue sky. 'So how's it going?'

'Slowly,' he looks rueful. 'There are so many memories.'

I remember how I felt clearing my parents' house. 'When my mother died, I found it really difficult. Everything in the house seemed to set off a memory. There were all these things that had been there since my childhood...' Even now, as I think about it, there's a lump in my throat.

'Nostalgia can really get you, can't it? I'm lucky, I guess, that I don't feel any connection to the house, but it's the letters and photos. I keep hoping I might stumble across a family heirloom, but no luck so far.' Sounding faintly humorous, he turns to look at me. 'So, do you live nearby?'

'In Bath. My husband, James, works in Bristol.'

'So you've ended up where you started out from,' he says softly.

His words make me uncomfortable. It was never what I'd imagined doing, but for all kinds of reasons, I'd stayed closer to home. 'And you haven't?'

He shakes his head. 'I live in Glasgow.'

It explains why I haven't seen him in so long. A streak of rebelliousness stirs inside me. 'I come up here most mornings. It's my favourite part of the day – before work.'

'Mine too.' He looks bemused. 'What's work?'

'I work in Bath – in a kind of upmarket farm shop. I organise their events – we host quizzes, book launches and cookery classes. It's just off Milsom Street. You probably know it – it's famous locally for artisan produce.'

'I've walked past. Very nice, but way too expensive for me.'

'Too expensive for most people.' It's one of the things I dislike about it. 'I'm trying to persuade the owner to bring in a more affordable range of produce, but she's not interested.'

'She doesn't need to, does she, if she's doing just fine exactly as she is.'

'That's the problem.' I hesitate. When I'll probably never see him again, it doesn't matter what he thinks. 'There is something else I'm working on.'

'Oh?' He looks curious.

'I want to write a book.'

'Wow...' Will looks impressed. 'What about?'

'So far I only have an outline. But it's about people.' Aware of him studying me, my cheeks flush. 'Namely a girl who has a flower shop, and the people she meets. It's funny and sad – about relationships, really. Life, death and everything in between. I want it to be a book that moves people.'

He looks thoughtful. 'A bit like music.'

'Exactly.' I think of the band he was in. 'Talking of music, do you still play?'

'Sadly, no. You know how my dad used to feel about me pursuing a music career. It kind of ruined it for me.'

Remembering the passion he'd had, my heart twists. 'I can't believe he did that.'

'He beat me into submission, was how it felt at the time. But I still have my guitar.'

'The blue one?'

'Yeah.' He smiles for a moment. 'And I have this idea that one day, I'd love to teach kids who are keen but can't afford lessons. But it's just an idea at this stage.'

'It's a brilliant one. You should do it.'

He frowns slightly. 'Maybe. When life feels more settled.'

Meaning at the moment, it obviously isn't, but all I know about him is his somewhat questionable sheep-catching skills. 'So, what do you do in Glasgow?'

'Ah. I work for a marketing company.' He sounds less than thrilled. 'It has its moments – and it's probably the best job I've ever had, but it isn't what you'd call exciting.' He hesitates. 'It's mostly small stuff – not particularly interesting – though I can work from anywhere, which at least makes it easier to come down here. I do miss all this, though.' His eyes glance around, taking in the miles of parkland.

'Is anyone helping you?' It's an innocent enough question with a hidden motive, as I find myself curious to know if he's alone.

He shakes his head. 'There isn't really anyone. I was married.' A shadow crosses Will's face. 'It's a long story. She met a wealthy banker and we're coming to the end of a long and convoluted divorce.'

'Oh, I'm sorry.'

'It's life, isn't it? Nothing I can do about it other than ride it out.' He clearly doesn't want to talk about it, evidenced when he changes the subject. 'You probably won't believe this, but I keep a few sheep at home.' He glances towards the field the errant lamb came from. 'They're pets – I could never eat them. I like to think I'm quite good with them! And my daughter loves them...' He watches my face as I try not to laugh. 'I'm not kidding! Me and my sheep, we're like that!' He crosses his fingers.

'That is quite hilarious.' Thinking of the escaped lamb, I can't help smiling. 'How old is your daughter?'

'Thirteen – going on twenty-five, with this other-worldly wisdom – I've no idea where she gets it from. Darcey, my soon to be ex-wife, is an actor. If you met her, you'd get it, straight away.

She's… theatrical, I think you'd say. They're very different. Flo, my daughter, is a competitive swimmer and wants to be a doctor.'

'Wow.' I know nothing about the world of stage and screen, or competitive swimming, come to that, but I know a little about teenagers. 'I have a stepdaughter. Millie. She's probably the best thing that's ever happened to me.'

'She's James's daughter?'

I nod. 'She was six when James and I got together.' I can't help smiling as I remember her pink cheeks and tangled hair. 'Her mother isn't the most maternal – Millie and I have always been close.'

'Does she live with you?'

'She used to spend a lot of time with us, but she lives in London now. She started a uni course, but she gave it up because she wanted to paint. She's twenty-one – and fiercely independent. When she isn't painting, she works in a café to keep the wolf from the door, but she's happy.'

'She sounds inspirational,' Will says quietly. 'You must be proud.'

'So proud.' Tears prick my eyes. From the start, our relationship has been something precious, like a beautiful flower or fragile bird I've wanted to keep safe, at the same time nurturing gossamer wings that one day, would let her fly. The same wings James has tried to clip. 'How is Flo coping with your separating?'

'It's the single worst part of the divorce, if I'm honest. It's all on Darcey's terms. Darcey being Darcey, there's always a reason for her to be anywhere other than Glasgow – especially now she has Eric and his money. But on the plus side, it means Flo gets to spend a lot of time with me.' He shakes his head. 'Which doesn't make it easy being here. There's more to sort out than I realised. Talking of which…' He glances at his watch. 'I better get back.'

'And I should walk my dog.' As I speak, Yippy's ears prick up.

He smiles, but he's clearly preoccupied and it doesn't reach his eyes. 'It was good seeing you again.'

'You, too.' I stand there a moment before turning and whistling to Yippy, fighting the urge to look back as I walk away.

* * *

When I get home, I catch sight of Ron and Grace, arm in arm as he helps her up the steps, then unlocks the front door with shaking hands. As he stands back to let her in, he catches sight of me, raising a hand in recognition. Waving back, I take in how frail they both are. What either would do without the other doesn't bear thinking about.

As I get ready for work, now and then Will flits into my head – quite often, if I'm honest. For once, I'm early for my shift at the farm shop, and when I arrive, one of the first faces I see is Liza Merrow's. She's sitting in the café with a couple of friends, and when she sees me, she gets up and comes over.

'I was hoping to see you, Anna. I wanted to order some food for a party we're having. It's only for about ten of us – I don't want to spend a fortune.'

Liza's a regular in here and we've always got on well. She's speaking to me so that she can bypass my boss's relentless efforts to make everyone spend more money. 'Let me put my bag away and I'll grab a notebook.' I go over to the desk where Hannah is busy leafing through a pile of orders.

'Hi. I'll be right back – I'm just going to take an order for Liza.'

'I'd stay away from Meredith,' Hannah warns. 'She's in the worst ever mood.'

Meredith, our boss, if not exactly sunny, is usually reasonable enough. 'What's up with her?'

'No idea.' She shakes her head. 'Talk of the devil...' she mutters under her breath.

As Meredith comes over, I smile brightly. 'Meredith. Beautiful day, isn't it?' Seeing her expression, I glance at Hannah. 'I'll be right back. I just have to go and talk to Liza.'

At a quiet table in the corner, Liza tells me she's planning a surprise party for her husband's fortieth. She wants simple food and when she tells me her budget, we quickly put a menu together.

'I'd ask you to host it here – if it wasn't for Meredith,' she says quietly. 'But what she charges for the room is ridiculous – plus you never really know what you're getting, do you?'

'She's not so bad, really.' But as I speak, I'm playing it down. It's no secret that Meredith can be unpredictable.

'I imagine you're used to it.' She hesitates. 'But the way she keeps putting prices up... Have you heard about the new farm shop that's rumoured to be opening?'

'No.' Maybe that's what's got Meredith's goat. 'But competition can only be good.'

'Let's hope so.'

I take the order back to Hannah and pin it to the diary. 'So what's the matter with her?'

Hannah frowns slightly. 'I overheard her on the phone just now – she was having a right old rant at someone.'

But as the day passes, Meredith keeps whatever it is to herself.

* * *

When James comes home from work, I tell him I saw our neighbours this morning.

'It wasn't one of Grace's better days. She was quite confused.'

'Their daughter really ought to think about moving them into a home,' James says unsympathetically, 'rather than expecting strangers to pick up the slack.'

I look at him, gobsmacked. 'It isn't like that. They're our neighbours and I'm fond of them. It's far better for them to stay where they are than be forced into a care home.' I pause for a moment, knowing it would never cross his mind that he could do something selfless and actually help them. 'You should pop round there, James. You might be able to help them out, now and then.'

'Mending dripping taps and finding lost hearing aids really isn't my thing.' James gets a glass, and pours himself a drink without offering me one. 'I don't mean to sound harsh – I'm just busy. I think I told you I'm going to be late tomorrow. I have a meeting up at the golf club.'

'Right.' Suddenly I find myself staring at him, at the expensive suit he's wearing, at the frown that's become permanent. If he mentioned the meeting before, I don't remember. But no matter. All I'm aware of is relief flooding over me at the prospect of another evening here without him.

As I serve up dinner, I cross my fingers as I bring up the subject of the holiday again. 'James, I've been thinking about that week in Tuscany—'

Before I can finish, he interrupts. 'I've already told you. We're going to Portugal.'

Somehow, I keep my cool. 'What about what I'd like to do?'

He frowns at me. 'Look, I have one week off. I work bloody hard and I'd really like to spend it playing golf.'

I'm silent for a moment. 'It would have helped if we'd at least discussed it.' Sensing another row brewing, I let it drop. 'But if you're set on going, that's fine. You can play golf and I'll go and see Lucy.' Picking up our plates, I take them over to the table, inwardly frustrated that my opinion means nothing to him; that after everything we've been through he can be so cold towards me.

The rest of the evening is spent as it always is, James engrossed in some TV series, while I go to my office and search for other writers' stories to publication, fantasising that one day I might actually be one of them. That night, as we lie in bed, I stare at my husband's back, listening to his faint snores, trying to conjure a memory of the man I married, who'd seemed so caring; unable to remember the last time there was any real warmth between us; telling myself, as I always do, that love is different things at different times in your life. Over the years, it isn't surprising the romance disappears.

1995

ANNA

When Christmas came around, Will and I saw each other whenever we could, packing the intensity of our feelings into the short hours available to us.

Having agonised over what to buy him for Christmas, in the end I'd settled on a book. Hard-backed, its pages blank, on the front was an image of a wave breaking on the shore, the words embossed on the front, 'The Adventure Starts Here'.

When I gave it to him, Will loved it. 'I'm going to write all this stuff in it – you know, the stuff we talk about – about life and having dreams, so I never forget.' He paused. 'Thank you.' He kissed me, then reached into his pocket. 'This is for you.'

I took the little box he held out and opened it. Inside was a bracelet into which tiny irregular translucent stones were set.

'I hope you like it,' Will said hesitantly. 'They're moonstones. I got it in the antique market.'

It was breathtaking, each stone different, catching the light, sparkling subtly. 'I love it.' I looked at him. 'It's beautiful.'

As I slipped it on, Will stepped closer and I felt his arms go around me. 'I love you,' he murmured into my hair.

Against the warmth of him, my heart overflowed with joy as I whispered back. 'I love you, too.'

* * *

The days after Christmas flew past as at last I met his parents and his brother, Simon, who was just like Will, only older and far more sensible. Far from being the tyrant I'd imagined Will's dad to be, he was warm and welcoming, as was his mum.

Will had told me his mum was ill. But there was something about her I couldn't put my finger on. It wasn't just her fragility. It was the way she watched her family, as if gathering snapshots of them, storing them away for later on.

At one point I found myself alone with her.

'He showed me the bracelet he gave you.'

'I love it.' I glanced at my wrist, where it fitted perfectly.

'It's beautiful, isn't it?' She paused. 'I'm so glad Will has you. It makes such a difference, knowing that.'

I wasn't sure what to say. But as I gazed at her, a feeling of unease came over me. It was almost as though she knew she wasn't going to be here much longer. 'He has all of us,' I said, slightly anxiously.

She looked as though she was going to say something but then she stopped herself. 'Yes,' she said quietly.

* * *

On New Year's Eve, Will and I wandered into Bath where our friends were gathering. It was a cold night, frost forming underfoot, my hand warm in Will's. A night that promised the start of a whole new year of possibilities, but I was preoccupied.

'How's your mum?'

Will looked surprised. 'I know she's ill but I think she's doing OK. Why?'

I shrugged. 'I just wondered. You don't really mention her.'

He was quiet for a moment. 'I suppose because there's nothing I can do. It's just how it is. At home... we don't really talk about it.'

'It's OK.' I squeezed his hand, knowing I'd said it before. 'If you want to talk about her, that is.'

'Thanks.'

We walked in silence, until close to the centre of Bath, he stopped suddenly. Turning to face me, his eyes were earnest. 'You know everything we've said? About not letting chances pass you by?' Taking my hands, he pulled me against him. 'I want this, Anna. With you.' His voice was getting louder. 'I want everyone to know I love you!'

'Will, stop!' Aware we were being watched, I tried to wriggle out of his grasp.

'I mean it! Let everyone watch! It doesn't matter! It's New Year's Eve and I love you.' As he started to spin me around, I closed my eyes, the biggest of smiles plastered across my face, my heart bursting with joy. He was right. Life was about love; about inhabiting each one of these glorious moments.

'Hey, guys!' Lucy's voice came from behind me.

As Will released me, I turned to see her and Dave arm in arm coming towards us. 'Luce!' As they reached us, I hugged her.

As Will and Dave walked ahead of us, Lucy nudged my arm. 'I've never seen you look so happy, Anna.'

I was buzzing. 'I've never felt like this!'

'You and Will...' She paused. 'You really have something, don't you?'

I smiled at her. 'The best kind of something.'

That was how we saw the New Year in – surrounded by love and friendship, in the city that was home. Filled with the irrepressible belief, that dreams are for chasing; that anything is possible if you want it enough.

5

WILL

Back at the house, Will flung the windows open before putting the kettle on. The truth was, after talking to Anna, his head was spinning – and not in a good way. Everything he'd told her about his marriage, his job, the music career that never was, all of it was true, but as he thought about it now, he felt a failure.

The best things in his life amounted to Flo and his sheep. As the kettle came to the boil, he made himself a cup of tea. On top of everything else, thinking about Flo, he felt racked with guilt for being here when she was in Glasgow. He glanced at the time, knowing she'd be at school, making a mental note to call her later.

Picking up his mug, he then opened the back door and went outside. Listening to the birds, he noticed leaf buds on the trees, the first daffodils coming into flower. No matter what was going on in the world, there was a kind of comfort in the fact that the seasons went on regardless.

But taking a deep breath, he tried to dispel the feeling he had that everything that had happened was catching up with him. A lifetime of living with grief and everything it had triggered. All these years, he'd tried to bury the loss of his mother. It was the only way he could function at the time. But it was still there, knotted somewhere deep inside him.

He allowed his mind to drift back. He still remembered that time, vividly. Her increasing frailty, the pallor of her skin; the way she'd tried to hide it from them. The last time she was moved to the hospice, it had been the most brutal realisation that her days were coming to an end, that this time she wasn't coming home; that he, his father and Simon were going to have to somehow manage to get through a future without her.

Will swallowed the lump in his throat. He'd felt her death physically, viscerally, as if a savage wound had ripped into the heart of their family. A wound that had never healed... He remembered telling Anna that his mum was dying, before making his biggest mistake in pushing her away. But his pain had been too monumental. The funeral had been the most hideous day. Even now, it stood out in Will's mind as a nightmare he'd wanted to run from. Then not long after, his father had decided to move them away – to Yorkshire of all places. OK, so there had been family there, but for Will and Simon, being removed from their lives and everyone they knew, had only multiplied how desolate they'd felt.

Of course, he knew now his father had been on the run – from grief, from a situation he didn't know how to deal with. His behaviour had become more controlling; the battle between them about the music career Will had wanted to pursue escalating.

Will had thought about running away. But, still raw from losing his mother, he'd stayed put. It had been tough, though. Most people that age got to at least give their dreams a go. His father had banged on about his expectations of Will; how he needed to ensure he could look after himself. For Will, the only way out had been the uni course his father refused to stop going on about.

At an all-time low after his mother's death, Will's free spirit had been beaten into acquiescence. Dreams were no more than that – just dreams. Real life was about being responsible, doing what was expected of you. Happiness didn't enter into it.

Meanwhile, he'd written at least a dozen letters to Anna, before screwing them up and throwing them away. He bitterly regretted things ending that way they had, but nothing had felt the same. He couldn't love when he was hurting so much; couldn't smile in a world without his mother in it. Then the more time passed... life was already far too complicated.

Will sipped his tea. He could pinpoint the exact moment when it all went wrong. It had been that sun-baked, blue-sky June morning that he still remembered vividly, when his mother closed her eyes for the last time.

With his free spirit shoehorned into a demanding uni course, even student life hadn't drawn him the way it had other students. Will's passion was channelled into becoming independent; making sure he never had to rely on his father again.

It was hardly surprising their relationship never recovered. And look at him now. The best thing that had happened in a long time was bumping into Anna again. She'd reminded him of when they first met all those years ago, when life had felt like a great adventure unfolding in front of them. Will sighed. It was different when you were young, but even so. He wondered if life could be like that ever again.

6

ANNA

It seems beyond coincidence when early the following day, Will and I meet again. I try to ignore the way my heart leaps when I see him, the way his face lights up.

'No escaped sheep today?'

'Not so far. I'm glad you're here. I was hoping to see you.' Wearing a dark blue sweater and faded jeans, he looks cheerful, buoyed up.

'Oh?'

His eyes hold the warmth I remember so well. 'It's a beautiful day, isn't it? I was just thinking on my way here, how I'd love to be spending some of it with you. And here you are!'

I'm filled with what I can only describe as a kind of lightness – it's so long since anyone's looked at me like this. I know he's coming out of a difficult divorce – while I'm married. But there's a part of me that wants to hold on to this moment. 'Do you want to walk?'

He smiles. 'OK.'

As we start along the path, it's like winding back time as a sense of freedom fills me.

'I found a photo of us the other day – from way back...' Will pauses. 'Before everything got complicated.'

By complicated, I imagine he means his mother's death. 'They were happy days.' It's my turn to smile, remembering the night we met – the music, the sky full of stars, his eyes as they looked into mine, the feelings that blew me away.

'I think my mum must have taken it. You had all this gorgeous hair and you're laughing at me. We used to laugh a lot, didn't we?'

'We did. Life used to be so simple.' Remembering, I shake my head. 'You forget, don't you?'

'It was, wasn't it? But after Mum died, nothing was the same.' Will looks sad. 'I suppose it was inevitable. It really wasn't a good time.'

'It was an awful time,' I say quietly.

But he doesn't seem to want to talk about it. 'Anyway, it's ancient history now. I was going through more of Dad's photos last night. He did a lot of travelling before he bought the house. I've always sort of had this dream – that one day, I'd do the same.' He looks at me suddenly. 'We both used to, didn't we?'

I nod. 'I remember us talking about people our parents' age and thinking how dull their lives had become.'

'And now we are them,' Will says ruefully.

'Don't say that! There are places I'd love to see – if I had the chance.' Even though James would never want to go anywhere without a golf course. 'James isn't interested. I've been trying to persuade him to go to Italy, but he wants to go to the Algarve and play golf.'

Will looks incredulous. 'I never had you down as a golfer.'

'I should think not,' I say indignantly. 'I'm not going with him.'

'What will you do?' He looks surprised.

'Go to Ibiza. Lucy lives there – she moved years ago.' I take in his perplexed expression. 'Ibiza isn't what everyone thinks it is. Most of it's *campo* – countryside – and her house is in the hills. It's beautiful.'

'It sounds wonderful. But you shouldn't let him stop you doing things,' Will says suddenly.

'I know I shouldn't.' I shrug, trying to dismiss the stifling vision in my head, of staying in the same house, growing older with James. 'But it's what happens, isn't it? When you're married? And I guess you're not exactly free either, are you? While Flo is young?'

'Not really.' He shakes his head. 'But one day... When she's older, perhaps. Have you been to Ireland?'

I shake my head. 'No, but I'm thinking green fields and Atlantic waves crashing against cliffs. Mud. And rain,' I add. 'In sheets!'

'You're not wrong,' he says wryly. 'The green is the most amazing shade. You should go – to Baltimore. I spent a long weekend there – it's full of the best people. And pubs, obviously. The Irish are wonderful – you get the warmest welcome.'

I'm imagining cosy rooms and log fires, safely shielded from the raging elements, as a flock of swallows comes into view.

'They're early, aren't they?' I watch them swooping and diving as he echoes my thoughts.

Shielding his eyes, he follows my gaze. 'Tiny, aren't they? It amazes me how every year they travel all the way from Africa.'

'One of nature's miracles,' I say quietly.

'One of many... We're lucky, aren't we?' Will gestures towards the countryside. 'To be surrounded by this?'

It's how I feel every time I come here, and as I turn towards him, our eyes lock, a silent message passing between us.

* * *

'You're quiet.' When I get to work, Hannah gives me a look.

'Am I?' I change the subject. 'Did you get to the bottom of what was needling Meredith the other day?'

'Yes.' She glances swiftly around the shop. 'It was about the new place that's opening – somewhere up Walcot Street. It's going to be very different to this one – proper local and seasonal – like you don't get tomatoes in winter and that sort of thing. And it's going to be a whole lot cheaper.'

So it's more than a rumour. 'About time. Meredith's prices are outrageous. Perhaps now, she'll see that.'

But Hannah's shaking her head. 'Oh no. You see, she's sticking to her guns. She reckons there are enough people in Bath who are happy to be screwed over just so that they can carry their shopping in a posh bag with a fancy logo... She doesn't plan to change a fucking thing.'

'She's an idiot.'

'I've been digging around,' she says quietly. 'I've got the name of the owner of the new place. Do you think we should give it a shot? I mean, it has to be better than selling overpriced produce to people who have too much money.'

I imagine Meredith's face as I tell her I'm leaving. 'I like it. Let's do it.'

* * *

The next day, when I don't see Will, I wonder if he's intentionally avoiding me. The park seems empty, the wind picking up so that it's colder than in recent days, yesterday's fantasy of travelling the world seems suddenly frivolous as I remind myself how absurd it is, at my age, to daydream.

When I get home, I take a mug of coffee through to my office, then switch on my laptop, clicking onto my Facebook feed, where the first post that comes up is allegedly a message from the universe.

Trust in divine timing.
You are exactly where you need to be.

That's all very well, but really? In the past I would have skipped over it, but this morning, the words seem oddly relevant.

Is that what happened when Will and I met again? Was I exactly where I was supposed to be?

1996

ANNA

While I was finishing my GCSEs, Will's mother had moved into the hospice. I was holding on to the hope that like last time, she'd soon be home again, but one scorching Friday afternoon, when out of the blue Will turned up at my house, from his tearstained face, his eyes red from crying, I didn't have to ask.

'Oh, Will...'

He didn't say anything, just came and put his arms around me. I held him, tighter than I ever had, wishing with all my heart I could take his pain away.

'When?' *I asked quietly.*

'Early this morning. I should have been there, but I wasn't...' His body shook.

'Maybe she wouldn't have wanted you there.' Knowing how hard it was going to be, maybe she hadn't wanted her family to witness her leaving this world.

Sitting down, he clasped my hand tightly. 'I don't know what happens now. I don't know anything any more. Dad is heartbroken, Simon...' His voice shaking, he broke off.

'Don't worry about that now. You need to look after yourself, Will.'

His face was ashen under his tears, but as I tried to put myself in his shoes, I knew that to lose your mother was to lose your cornerstone.

It brought home how fragile life was – for any of us, as over the days that followed, I imagined how I'd feel if it had happened to me. I saw Will a few times; watched him as he alternately denied then gave into the grief that consumed him, while in what seemed like no time, the day of the funeral came, one on which early cloud cleared to skies of the deepest blue.

'It's so sad, Luce.'

'I know. I keep thinking how I'd feel if it was me.'

We walked in silence through Bath's streets towards the church. Unsurprisingly, it was packed. Noticing Dave, Lucy and I crept over and squeezed onto the pew next to him.

'Have you seen Will?' I whispered.

Dave shook his head. 'He hasn't spoken to any of us.'

* * *

I saw Will one last time about a week after the funeral, when he told me his father was planning to move away.

Shock hit me. 'What about us?' I whispered, my heart racing as I waited for his answer.

As he turned to look at me, there was a sadness in his eyes I'd never seen before. 'Maybe it's for the best.' His voice was bleak. 'It isn't going to be the same, Anna. Nothing is.'

I was numb as another wave of shock hit me. 'You can't mean that, Will.' It couldn't be over between us.

'I'm going to be miles away.' His face was blank.

I couldn't believe he was saying this. 'We can keep in touch – it doesn't have to be the end.'

As his eyes met mine again, I saw his look of desperation. 'When I think about Mum, it's like a part of me's shut down. I can't feel, Anna. I need time – to get my head around things. But right now...' Getting up, he looked at me sadly. 'I'm so sorry. I never intended it to end like this.'

I sat there, unable to speak as he walked away. Minutes later, my tears started to flow as I heard his car start. It was followed by another sound as my heart broke.

7

WILL

It was like Saturday mornings used to be as Will drove into Bath and parked his car. It was early, the sun low, the streets still coming to life as he started walking towards the centre. Seeing a market setting up under brightly coloured awnings, he wandered over to take a look.

Just as he was about to pay for an overpriced loaf of bread, someone called out from behind him.

'Will?'

Recognising her voice instantly, he was already smiling as he turned around. 'Hello! How are you?'

In a red calf-length dress and suede boots, a woollen wrap wound around her shoulders, Anna looked vibrant. 'Good, thank you.' She lowered her voice. 'You do know you're being ripped off?'

'I'd worked that out – but it was going to be breakfast.' He glanced around. 'Got any better ideas?'

'Indeed – if you have time?' She looked at him questioningly.

Time was one thing he did have. 'I do.' He smiled again.

'Then come with me.' Anna didn't seem the least concerned

about being seen with him. 'It's one of Bath's lesser known secrets – nothing fancy, but the best food...'

After buying takeaway rolls and cups of steaming coffee from a tiny café in a side street, Anna nodded in the direction of the river. 'How about we head down there?'

Crossing Pulteney Bridge, Will was assailed by memories of the many times he'd met Anna here when they were teenagers. It was astonishing how in the years since, so little had changed. 'It's just as I remember it.'

'It doesn't look much different, does it?' In the middle of the bridge, Anna stopped for a moment, her eyes meeting his. 'Remember that New Year's Eve?'

Will's heart missed a beat. He remembered it vividly, standing almost exactly here, holding Anna, spinning her around in circles; the sense of unbridled joyousness they'd felt. 'I've never forgotten it.' He watched her cheeks flush slightly.

'Me neither,' she said quietly. 'Come on. This way.' Anna turned to take the stone steps that led down towards the river. 'Beautiful, isn't it?'

'It's stunning.' It felt peaceful, too. Next to the water, you could barely hear the traffic.

'I've never tired of living here. There's so much going on – and I love how it changes with the seasons.'

He remembered the buzz of summer, the crowded streets; the sense of relief when the quiet of winter came. Will was curious. 'So how come you ended up staying around here?'

Anna looked surprised. 'I lived in London for a while. But I wasn't well.' She hesitated. 'That was why I moved back. My parents were great while I got back on my feet. Then after meeting James, my father died. I wanted to be here for my mother.'

'Sounds like everything happened at once.' Will watched her closely. 'Are you OK now?'

She avoided his gaze. 'I'm fine. It was years ago.'

When it was clear she didn't want to elaborate, Will didn't push her. 'I'd really like to bring Flo here. I spoke to her last night. She was telling me about a project she's doing at school – about how the seasons vary across the UK. She's really into nature – she'd love the countryside around here. It's a pity she can't come and stay for a while.'

'Why can't she?' Anna looked surprised.

'Ah, because that would require Darcey's cooperation.' A frown flickered across Will's face. 'And she is master puppeteer and holder of strings. We dance to her tune, not the other way round.'

'That's insane. And she gets away with it?' Anna sounded shocked.

'If I disagree with her, she turns it into a battle – and Flo's seen too many of those.' Will shrugged. 'She's also a skilled manipulator. I'll be glad when the divorce is settled and we can all get on with life.'

Anna shook her head. 'Life's too short for battles.'

Finding a bench in the sun, they sat down. 'Agreed – but Darcey seems to thrive on them.'

'I'm not sure I could cope with that.' Anna picked up her roll. 'I mean, life springs enough on us without deliberately making things harder.'

'If only she felt like that.' Will unwrapped his roll and took a bite. 'This is really good.'

'Didn't I tell you?' Anna sounded pleased.

Sitting there, it was as if the intervening years had disappeared – or some of them, at least. Will turned to Anna. 'I've often wondered what would have happened – with us – if my mum hadn't died, or if we hadn't moved away.'

She looked surprised. 'I have, too,' she said quietly. 'So many times. But things happen, don't they? And as we get older, we change.'

That much was true. 'I'm quite a good example of that,' he said wryly.

Anna looked thoughtful. 'I think we all are.'

He wondered what she was alluding to but she didn't elaborate. Drinking his coffee, he gazed at the river, taking in its constant flow, the smoothness of the water, the beautiful architecture it was surrounded by. 'Do you ever look at all of this and think about how long it's been here? And how it will still be here long after we've gone? Reminds you how small we are, I always think.'

'So small,' Anna said quietly. 'But people still manage to achieve great things – well, some do.'

'I read this thing a while back about creativity being innate in all of us.' If only Will could harness his. 'I suppose some of us are better than others at exploiting it. Anyway, there's a Warren Buffet quote I really like, about what success really means.'

'Oh?'

'It's about how much you are loved.'

Anna was quiet. 'It's everything, isn't it? Love?' When she spoke, her voice was husky.

He nodded. 'Maybe the single thing that can change the craziness of this world.' For a moment he was silent. Didn't he know better than anyone how empty life was without love? 'It sounds so simple, doesn't it?'

She glanced briefly at him. 'I don't think anything's ever that simple.' She hesitated. 'How much longer do you think you'll be here?'

'I was hoping to stay two weeks, but it isn't going to be long enough. And now, Darcey wants me to go back early. She's decided she has to go to London for a week, which means I need to be there for Flo.' The conversation had left him conflicted. No question he wanted to see Flo, but he felt drawn to stay here a little longer.

Anna frowned slightly. 'Do you mind me asking what happened with you and Darcey?'

'We took our eyes off the ball, I suppose.' Will hesitated. But it was the truth. 'And while her career was taking off, mine was nosediving... Then she landed a role in a BBC series. Overnight, hers became a face everyone recognised. Darcey loves all that – you have to, if you're a performer. I was the same, back in the band days – as you know.'

'So what will you do about your dad's house?'

'It'll wait,' he says briefly. 'But it would be good to get it sold. Darcey wants her share of our money. God knows why when she's with Eric and his millions.' Will felt a shadow cross his face. 'Anyway, it looks like I'll be heading back either tomorrow or Monday.'

'So soon.' Anna sounded taken aback.

As he looked at her, Will's head filled with things he wanted to say, while he still had time. 'These last few days... They've made me think – about all kinds of stuff. But in particular about what I'm doing with my life.'

'Only the small stuff then.' Her eyes were teasing him.

'I'm serious. It's reminded me of how I used to feel – in a really good way.' He paused, not wanting to overdo it. It had reminded him of what he'd lost, too. 'It's been great seeing you again.' He tried to read her face, wanting to know if she felt like he did, that it had been an escape, one he didn't want to end. But his real life was pulling him back.

Sadness flickered in her eyes. 'It's been the same for me.'

As she'd spoken, Will had felt his heart turn over. But then she was getting up, wishing him a safe journey, while he wished her good luck with her book; after that searing moment of connection, as if they were nothing more than two polite strangers again.

8

ANNA

On Sunday, James is up early. In the kitchen, he makes coffee then flicks through the paper, his usual prelude to a day of golf. Normally he's away by 9.30, but half an hour later, he's still here.

'Aren't you playing golf today?'

James glances at his watch. 'Not until later. Duncan's tied up until midday. Something to do with Carol's mother.' Without looking up, he turns the page of his paper.

I stand there for a moment. Maybe this is the chance I've been waiting for. 'James?' I watch as he carries on reading. 'Can we talk?'

Glancing up, he looks surprised. 'What about?

I sigh, not sure where to start. 'I suppose, you and me.' Pulling out a chair opposite him, I sit down. 'I've been thinking about it a lot lately. We don't really do much together any more, do we?'

He interrupts. 'It's you who doesn't want to come to the Algarve.'

'Golf isn't my thing. You know that.' My heart sinks. It isn't a row I want, it's understanding. 'But that's part of it – don't you see? We don't want the same things. We don't laugh any more... And we don't talk, James – about things that matter, like life and love, or what's happening in the world.'

He looks at me as though I'm mad. 'Jeez, Anna. We got that out of our systems when we were teenagers. Or at least, I did.'

I sigh again. 'If something doesn't feel right, what am I supposed to do? Stay silent?'

'This is hardly constructive, is it?' he says coldly.

I have to say it, while I have the chance. 'I thought that after coming so close to breaking up, things would be different between us. That's all.' I rarely bring up the affair he had, that he dismissed as a mistake, but the fact is, ever since, nothing's been the same. 'I stayed because you wanted me to. But to be honest, it doesn't feel like that.'

'Are you ever going to let that go?' His eyes are blazing as he looks at me.

'I wasn't the one who had the affair, James.' Determined not to get upset, I keep my voice calm.

'But you were hardly blameless, were you?' He sounds angry.

'What?' I look at him in shock. 'You're blaming me for you having an affair?'

Realising what he's said, he backtracks. 'I'm sorry. I didn't mean it like that. It came out in anger. I don't blame you – of course I don't.' He sighs. 'I just want us to move on – and when you keep bringing it up, it doesn't help.'

'You seem so angry with me.' I gaze at my husband. 'Don't you ever wonder if maybe too much has happened? If it's too late for us?'

'I've told you, I don't want us to break up,' he mutters.

Not for the first time, I wonder why he's so hell-bent on us staying together. 'But what about the future?' I persist. 'Because if it's like this, it isn't enough, James.' At last admitting what I've been trying to ignore; this cavernous, fundamental difference between us.

When the conversation goes no further, an uneasy silence falls between us. But it's like blinkers have fallen away as I see what I've never acknowledged before. We loved each other once; we used to want the same things. But we're not the same people any more. Life has changed us.

* * *

After James goes out, I pick up my phone and call Millie.

'Hey, Anna!' Her voice is bright. 'How are you?'

I bury my frustration with James. 'Really good! How are you? How's the commission going?'

'I've nearly finished this one, but they want a second.' There's excitement in her voice. 'It's amazing, Anna... You know how much I hoped this would work – I can't believe it's actually happening!'

'Of course it is – you're talented and brilliant, Mills, and you've worked so hard. You deserve this!'

'Try telling Dad that.' Her voice is flat for a moment.

James was a wonderful father when Millie was small and he's only wanted what he sees as best for her. But Millie has a creative soul that he wanted to shoehorn into academia. After battling with him, she'd caved in and started a degree in European History, before leaving at the end of the first term – to James's disapproval and my unwavering support, something she's always been grateful for.

'Your dad loves you, and he's coming round. He just wants you to be happy.' In many ways it would have been easier for Millie to cave in, but with sheer determination, she's resolutely followed her heart. 'He may not have said so, but I think he realises how gifted you are, and meanwhile, I will keep reminding him. Can you send me some photos?'

'Sure! Are you coming to London anytime soon? I could show you them for real.'

Smiling, I reach for my diary. 'In that case, let's make a date.'

After pencilling in potential dates, I'm still smiling as I let her go. But I know what I'm doing – reaching out to the one good thing James and I still share, hoping to find a reason to stay. But is it enough...

A few seconds later, my phone pings with a photo of Millie's commission, a contemporary piece in her trademark soft bright shades. Not for the first time, I'm thankful that she's strong enough to be her own person.

It's dark by the time James comes home. As he opens a bottle of wine, I show him Millie's photo.

He studies the image. 'Millie painted that? It's very good.'

I'm so glad he can see that. 'She did. She's amazingly talented. Shall I forward it to you?'

He nods. 'Thanks.'

A quiet evening passes during which James drinks too much red wine before falling asleep on the sofa. When my efforts to wake him fail, I go to bed alone. Lying there, my mind churns relentlessly as I drift off to sleep before awaking again a couple of hours later.

Gazing at the ceiling, none of this is what I want, I tell myself in the quiet reaches of the night. Not a husband snoring downstairs, who doesn't have a kind word to say to me; the avoidance of any kind of intimacy. But when he refuses to talk about things, there is no obvious way out.

* * *

On Monday morning, I awake early to find James asleep next to me. When I get out of bed, he stirs slightly. 'It's only six. I'll bring you a cup of tea,' I whisper. Hearing his grunt in reply, I tiptoe downstairs and put the kettle on.

By the time I return with a mug of tea, he's snoring again. Knowing it won't be long before his alarm goes off, I dress quickly and hurry downstairs again, where Yippy is bouncing madly around the kitchen. 'Walk, Yippy?'

Reaching Dyrham Park, for the first time in ages, I forget about everyone else, even Will. However wonderful it is that he's come back into my life, this morning, more than anything, is about what I want, and what I'm craving most is freedom. Jogging through the woods, reaching the fields at the top, I run hard, the wind behind me, my feet pounding on the grass, my dog bounding happily beside me.

Slowing down, I breathe in the cold air, feeling my heart thudding from running, my blood pumping in my veins. No matter what else is going on, as I gaze across the fields then up at the sky, I feel a surge of gratitude for being alive.

9

WILL

For the life of him, Will couldn't work out what was happening. Arriving in Hinton to his dad's empty house, it had been every bit as cold and damp as he'd been expecting, every corner crawling with memories. Then amongst the gloom and nostalgia, that morning had happened, when Anna appeared, blazing like sunlight into his life.

It had felt as effortlessly easy as when they were teenagers – and there was nothing wrong with that. Except that here he was, a week later, in a state of confusion. Dragged down by the past as he went through his dad's stuff, fielding Darcey's calls, not to mention dealing with the divorce, the time he'd spent with Anna had invigorated him.

But that was the problem. Things were already complicated enough and Flo needed him – in Glasgow. Even without taking into account that Anna was married, any flights of fancy he had that this was going anywhere were utterly pointless.

It had been a week of glorious contrasts – and difficult memories, not only of his father, but of Simon. His brother's death was still too painful a loss for Will to linger on. But as he'd spent more time with Anna, the weight of his grief had lifted slightly.

He'd even seen shades of his old free-spirited self again.

The last time he'd seen Anna, though, he'd felt torn. As well as planning to go to London, Darcey was having problems with Flo – a thought that filled him with angst. Darcey and Flo were such different people. And Flo was a kid – she needed her parents. Meanwhile, what was he doing? Gadding about in Bath as if he were a teenager again.

Typically, after winding him up, it was Darcey who'd presented the solution. Will had been packing up his things when she'd called him. Sounding calm and lucid, she told him her mother was coming to stay. He didn't need to hurry back.

He shouldn't have been surprised. It was how it had been with Darcey almost from the get-go – Will twisted around her little finger, and, while under her spell, he'd let her. He'd loved her, or so he thought, this goddess of a woman who lit up every room she walked into, who for reasons he couldn't comprehend, had chosen him. But Darcey's love was the kind that varied according to his bank balance, he'd realised cynically, far too late. But he had to take some responsibility for that. From the start there had been warning signs, but he'd chosen to turn a blind eye, seen what he wanted to see. Now he was having to live with the consequences.

After spending the rest of the day sorting out clutter for a charity shop, the next morning he'd gone for a walk, hoping Anna would be there. Walking further than usual, he'd watched the early morning mist lift, but as the sun climbed higher, there'd been no sign of her. Regret had filled him. In this world that felt so uncertain, Will was sure of only one thing. More than anything he wanted to see her.

It hadn't stopped him trying again the next morning. As he

drove along the lanes, the landscape was ethereal, trees looming through the layer of mist that had returned overnight, but when he reached the park and Anna's car wasn't there, he felt his heart sink. Then as he walked through the woods, he felt it lift, beating wildly for a moment as a familiar dog came bounding up from behind him. Then when he turned around, there she was.

'So you're still here?' Calling out, her voice was muffled by the mist.

His face creased into a broad smile. 'Looks like it.'

'How about Flo?' As she reached him, Anna seemed guarded.

'Problem solved – Darcey's mother is staying for a while. Flo gets on really well with her.'

'That's good, then – for you. Are you on your way down or up?'

He wondered if something had happened. This morning there seemed a new sense of purpose about her. 'Up.'

As they walked together through the trees, Will glanced at Anna. 'I came up here again yesterday. I was hoping to see you.'

'I was here really early yesterday. It was wonderful.' Her eyes were shining. 'Yippy and I had the whole place to ourselves!'

'Hey, none taken.' Pretending to be hurt, Will stopped. 'I'll just turn around and head back,' he joked.

She nudged his elbow. 'I didn't mean it like that. But while I was here, I had this amazing sense of freedom. I can't remember when I last felt like that.'

Will was silent. In his life, freedom hadn't existed for a long time.

Anna went on, 'It's made me think – I really need it, Will. Freedom, I mean.'

'From anything in particular?' He wasn't sure what she was saying.

'From anything that holds me back.' She looked lighter somehow. 'I'm working on the details. I think I need to feel free to be myself – whatever that takes.' She paused. 'I suppose I'm realising how much has changed over the years.'

A flash of the teenaged Anna came back to him, a girl whose eyes shone, who laughed infectiously, had a passion for life that was irresistible, as Will felt a heaviness deep inside him. Oh, for a few minutes of that feeling she'd just described. But with the passing of time, too much of life had chipped away at him. 'It isn't always that simple, is it? I mean, things happen that are out of your control.' Look at him: he'd lost his mother, his brother, his father. There was nothing like grief to cast a veil over everything.

Anna was silent for a moment. 'They do. That's life, but it doesn't have to stop me feeling like me again.'

It made him think of Simon, again. His brother had always been very much his own person. Suddenly, he realised Anna probably didn't know. 'I don't know if you know, but a few years ago, Simon died.'

Out of the blue, Will was choked, his eyes wet with tears. Embarrassment filled him. Where the hell had that come from?

'Simon?' Anna sounded shocked. 'I didn't know. I'm so sorry, Will. You must really miss him.'

Wrestling to keep control, Will spoke quietly. 'All the time.'

'When did you lose him?'

'Seven years ago.' For a moment Will couldn't speak.

He felt her hand on his arm. 'It's OK.' Beside him, her voice was quiet. 'But losing your brother…'

Will took a deep breath. 'Is heavy shit.'

'The heaviest.'

As the remaining mist thinned out the sky above them was a cloudless blue. Will was distracted by a high-pitched whistling sound before a white aircraft shot past over their heads.

Will shook his head. He'd forgotten there were gliders around here. It had unlocked another memory, of how as a child, he'd been fixated on the idea of flying one. It had seemed the most magical thing to watch them soar, like birds.

'When I was a kid, I was obsessed with learning to fly. I thought it would be like being a bird... you know, catching the wind and having that view of the world... I found this advert in one of the local papers for trial lessons at the local gliding club. So I started saving my paper round money.'

'Did you do it?' Anna sounded intrigued.

'No.' Will was silent, remembering. 'My dad...' He shook his head. 'He said I shouldn't waste my money on something I wouldn't be any good at.'

'God.' Anna sounded stunned. 'That's brutal.'

'You know what he was like,' Will said briefly. 'But he was probably right.'

'He should have encouraged you.' Anna sounded outraged. 'Think how amazing it would have been – even if you'd only ever done it once.' She paused. 'You should still do it. It isn't too late.'

But it was yet another of those dreams that Will had long lost sight of. 'You've seen what I'm like catching sheep,' he joked. 'Can you imagine me at the controls of an aircraft?'

He felt Anna's arm against his. 'So tell me about Simon. Obviously, I remember him, but I never really knew him.'

The lump in his throat was back. 'He was one of those people who everyone described as a really good guy... As brothers go, he was the best.' There were memories of happier days locked away with his grief. 'He was someone who made you feel better just for being around him.'

'After losing your mum, though... To lose Simon too...'

Will made a heroic effort to pull himself together. 'We all lose people.' He shrugged. 'But sometimes, if we're lucky...' He glanced at Anna. 'We find them again.'

She was silent for a moment. 'Weird, isn't it, seeing each other again?' Her eyes met his.

As she spoke, Will felt something click into place. What if this time, their timing was right? If this was different?

'Nice weird,' he said softly. 'Are you working today?'

'No! I have a whole glorious day off to write.'

Will was smiling. 'So, before you get started, can I persuade you to have breakfast with me?'

Anna smiled back. 'OK!'

* * *

Later, back at his father's house, as he started clearing out yet another cupboard, Will's thoughts were all over the place. The difference in Anna today had been tangible. Meanwhile, here he was, still treading water. Since giving up music, there'd been no passion in his life, a reality he'd put down to getting older, to the weight of responsibility on him.

But what if he was wrong? If he was settling, letting life pass him by? While the prospect of change might be daunting, the thought of things staying the same left him with a feeling of discomfort, but maybe that was the point. A sign that it was time to change things – to find a better job, start playing music again. To get the divorce sorted, so that he could move on and start living again.

JULY 2000

WILL

'Here we go!' Will placed the tray on the table, slopping beer over the sides of the glasses. 'And here's to many more – though honestly, mate, you are sure about this, aren't you?' A few beers were making him far too honest as he shook his head sadly at Ricky. 'You're too bloody young to get married, my old friend. It's not too late to change your mind.'

Ricky sat there smiling, completely unfazed by his best-man-to-be. 'One day, William Anderson, when you meet the love of your life, I will ask you the same question.'

'I've already met her,' Will said sadly. 'And I fucked it up.' Ever the entertainer, he held out his hands in mock despair, hiding the ache he still felt deep inside when he thought of Anna. 'A question of bad timing. But who am I to fathom the workings of the universe?'

'I'll drink to that.' As laughter rippled around the table, Ricky raised his glass. 'Cheers!'

Several pints later, Will was on his way back to the bar when he cannoned into someone. 'Shit. Sorry.' Looking up, he froze.

'Will?' Anna looked stunned.

Actually, she looked stunning, Will couldn't help thinking. In skinny black jeans, her skin was tanned and her hair longer than last time he'd seen her. 'Hi.' He felt dazed. 'I can't believe this. What are you doing here?'

'I'm here with Lucy.' Anna glanced over her shoulder to the table where Lucy raised a hand in his direction. 'We're celebrating!'

Wishing he hadn't drunk so much beer, Will tried to focus. 'What are you celebrating?'

'Lucy's finished her interior design course!' Looking at him, Anna paused. 'So how've you been?'

'I'm... excellent, actually.' Will was trying not to slur his words. 'Really very good. We're on a stag do.' He nodded towards the table where his mates were engaged in rowdy conversation. 'I'm sorry. I really am a bit pissed. I keep telling him he's too young to get married, but he doesn't listen.'

A smile played on Anna's lip. Sexy lips he couldn't take his eyes off, that he wanted to kiss.

'I guess he knows what he's doing.'

Will nodded emphatically. 'Yes. Absolutely.' He leaned closer to Anna. 'I miss you,' he said quietly.

She started, 'Will...' Her eyes darted around the room.

'Look, can we meet up? For a coffee? Or lunch?' he added hopefully.

As Anna hesitated, one of his friends called over.

'Oi. Will... Come on, man. We're moving on.'

'Sunday?' Through an alcoholic haze Will was trying to think. 'Covent Garden? There's a wheelbarrow of flowers when you come out of the Tube. How about I meet you there?

'OK.' Anna was smiling again. 'Why not? What time?'

'Midday?' Glancing at the table where his mates were waving at him, for a moment Will was torn. 'I suppose I should go.'

'You probably should! See you on Sunday, then.' She stood there for a moment. 'Have fun.'

Anna looked slightly dazed, he couldn't help thinking. He hoped it was a good sign. 'You, too.'

He turned to make his way back to his friends – reluctantly. Now that he'd found her again, Will didn't want to leave her.

* * *

On Sunday morning, he awoke early, lying in bed for a moment, smiling to himself as suddenly he remembered he was meeting Anna. Getting up, he whistled his way to the shower. After pulling on a clean T-shirt and jeans, he put the kettle on, checking the time. When this moment had been such a long time coming, no way was he being late to meet her.

With an hour in hand, he was about to head out. Better to be early than risk missing her. Picking up his keys, he heard the phone start to ring. He hesitated. It wasn't the time to get drawn into some convoluted conversation. But when it rang again, he answered it.

'Hello?'

Listening to the unfamiliar voice telling him there'd been an accident, Will's heart missed a beat as he felt his blood run cold.

10

ANNA

As change filters into my life, I buy spring flowers for my office, trying not to dwell too much on James, while more messages from the universe keep popping up on Facebook, however bizarrely, oddly resonant:

There are many ways to find happiness.
Trust in miracles.
Have the courage to follow your truth.

As always, they get me thinking. What is my truth? I don't have the answer, but in the background of my life, I'm aware of a sea change rippling, turning to waves.

***

The following morning, the rain is relentless. When I get to work, the streets are quiet, the shop empty.

'Thank heavens for this rain – the weekend was manic.'

Unlike me, Hannah works full time. 'And Meredith's having a spa day, so it's just you and me, babe! Coffee and cake?'

'Definitely!'

I cast my eyes around the shop. It's Meredith's version of rustic, with a stack of apple boxes on one side on which Cath Kidston linen is neatly folded, terracotta pots of herbs and succulents on the scrubbed wooden tables in the café that's lit by the warm glow of a wood burner.

It should be a place that welcomes everyone, but somehow it never feels that way.

'Here.' Hannah places two mugs of coffee on the counter next to a plate on which are slices of cake.

'Love your hair.' Newly tinted shades of lilac, the front strands are loosely plaited.

'Thanks.' She tosses it back. 'I fancied a change.'

I take one of the slices of cake. 'Talking of which, have you thought any more about applying for a job at the new farm shop?'

She frowns slightly. 'I have.'

'You don't sound sure.' I look at her quizzically.

'This place pays the bills. As long as fucking Meredith stays out of my hair, that's really all I care about.'

'Sure.' I hesitate. While Hannah's a single mum with a six-year-old son, I started working here to help Meredith out with events. And while I can't imagine giving up work forever, I could manage without for a little while, long enough to figure out what I want to do next. 'Perhaps we should check it out.' I remember what Will and I talked about. 'Sometimes change can be a good thing.'

But as I realise Hannah would rather stay where she is, it comes to me that I have choices.

* * *

The following morning, a feeling of restlessness fills me as I look around our lovely home; think of Millie, who I'd do anything for. But I have a job that's meaningless, a marriage that grows ever more distant, while meeting Will again has reminded me of the girl I used to be.

Why am I working in Meredith's frigging shop? I don't even get on with her – she caught me at a point when she was desperate, and being me, I couldn't say no. But I don't want to work in this new shop, either.

When I used to want so much more, life is passing me by, and just as I've let it happen, I'm the only one who can change it. Suddenly, I don't want to wait. I have an hour before my shift is due to start. Sitting at my laptop, I compose a short letter of resignation before printing it off and signing it.

After getting changed, I blow Yippy a kiss. 'Wish me luck.'

As if he understands, he comes over and licks my hand.

* * *

'Hi.' Hannah glances up from the computer screen. 'I'd keep your head down if I were you. Meredith's on the warpath. She wants blood.'

But having made my decision, I'm not allowing myself to be sidetracked. 'Is she in her office?'

Hannah looks uncertain. 'Yes, but, honestly, I wouldn't go there. Anna…'

Going to the back of the shop, I follow the passageway to Meredith's office. Knocking once, I push the door open.

She doesn't even bother to look up from her desk. 'I'm busy, Anna. Whatever it is, just deal with it, will you?'

'Not this time.' I put the envelope on the desk in front of her. 'My resignation, Meredith. I only came here to help you out, and

I've been here five years. Five years of my life – you don't pay us nearly enough, by the way. I'll work the rest of the month, but after that, you'll have to find someone to replace me.' Turning towards the door, I hesitate, glancing back at her. 'And if you want to keep Hannah, I suggest you increase her salary. There are other opportunities out there – as you know.'

She's speechless as I walk out. I close the door behind me and a sense of liberation fills me. I've never spoken to anyone like that before, and given how shabbily Meredith treats us, it feels good.

When I go back, Hannah looks puzzled. 'What's going on?'

'I've handed in my resignation.' My smile fades, because I've always liked working with Hannah. 'I'm sorry to be leaving you alone with her. But I'm here till the end of the month – and, by the way, I've told her she needs to pay you more.'

Hannah's eyes are like saucers. 'Fuck.' Her look of disbelief gives way to a smile. 'To be honest, I never got why you put up with Meredith's shit. I mean, I don't have much choice, but you do.'

'Mostly because I worked with you,' I tell her honestly. 'I've just reached a point where I need something different in my life.' I pause. 'Actually, you do have choices, Han. For a while, I forgot that.'

* * *

At home, as if in agreement, when I switch on my laptop, the universe sends me another of its messages.

Life is filled with possibilities.

One of which, I've already decided, is to dedicate time to writing my book.

When James comes home that evening, I cook his favourite dinner and open a nice bottle of wine, but he barely notices.

'Duncan's buying a new car,' he says between mouthfuls. 'A new Mercedes. Thought I might go and test-drive one.'

His old one is barely a year old. 'Really? I gave in my notice today,' I say casually.

His fork stops momentarily in mid-air. 'I never really understood why you worked there.'

Unsure what to make of that statement, I go on. 'Anyway, I'm thinking about what to do next.'

'And?' He tops up his wine glass.

'I'd like to do... something that makes a difference in some way.'

James frowns at me. 'What do you mean?'

'I don't know yet. I need to think about it. Possibly some volunteer work – I could even volunteer abroad.' I'm thinking out loud, ideas suddenly coming to me. 'There are places all over the world where help is needed.'

'That's hardly going to work, is it?' James's face is black. 'With me being here alone in this house? What do I say to people? My wife's having a mid-life crisis and she's taken a gap year?'

'Would that really be so terrible?' I stare at him. 'And honestly, what anyone else thinks is irrelevant. Anyway, I'm not even talking about a year. I'm not talking about anything definite. I'm just thinking – and you asked.'

He shuts the conversation down. 'That steak was overcooked.'

'Can you pass the wine while there's still some left?' I say pointedly.

He passes the bottle and we fall into another of those uneasy silences that are growing all too familiar, until I break it.

'I wish you'd understand how I'm feeling,' I say gently. 'Like you say, I'm lucky that I didn't need that job. At this point in my life, it gives me choices.'

He's quiet for a moment. 'To be truthful, I'm surprised you'd even consider the idea of going away. We're married, Anna. One of us doesn't go off to do their own thing.'

Touché, I want to say, thinking of his affair, realising as he speaks how powerful his words are; how they tap into something I'm already craving, viscerally; something that my marriage curtails.

Freedom.

* * *

There's a stony silence the following morning, and when James leaves for work, I feel a weight lift. Even more so, when Meredith texts me to say she doesn't need me today. Heading for Dyrham Park with Yippy, I wonder if I'll see Will.

As chance would have it, my arrival coincides with his, and reaching the lay-by where I park, I see him get out of his car.

'Morning!' I call out.

Looking up, he smiles. 'Hi.'

When he comes over, there are flecks of white in his hair. 'You've been painting?'

'Ah.' Following my gaze, he runs his fingers through his hair. 'I measure my days by the walls I paint! But I'm making progress.'

As we stand there, the first drops of rain start to fall.

He holds out his hands. 'Perfect timing.'

I glance at the sky. 'Or imperfect.'

He shakes his head. 'Definitely perfect. So, a walk in the rain or a cup of coffee somewhere? What's it to be?'

* * *

At the pub along the canal, this time we sit inside. As I sip my coffee, with Yippy lying on my feet, Will gives me a puzzled look.

'You're very quiet.'

'Am I? I suppose I am.' I don't know where to start with this sea change I'm feeling. 'Things have started happening, or rather, I'm making them happen. Yesterday was a really good day.'

'Oh?'

I smile. 'I gave in my notice and it feels incredible!'

'I can imagine!' He grins broadly. 'I can't tell you how much I would like to do that.'

'I know I'm lucky that I can,' I said more seriously. 'It's just that when I think of the years I've worked in that place, I see all this time I've wasted.'

'What does James think?'

'He never understood why I worked there in the first place. But when I told him what I'd done, it led to one of those conversations. An awkward one.' When I don't elaborate, Will looks nonplussed.

'So what now? Will you write your book?'

'I hope so.' For no reason, I start to tell him about the messages that keep appearing. 'They're random, just now and then, about things most of us take for granted. OK, like this one: "*There are many ways to find happiness.*" Yesterday, when I got back from giving my resignation letter to Meredith, it was, *"Life is filled with possibilities."* They're both true, aren't they?'

'Yeah.' He nods. 'But we're so bogged down by mortgages and bills and the practicalities of life, we can't think about anything else.'

But I haven't stopped thinking about it. 'We get bogged down by a whole lot more than mortgages. We take on all these limitations, mostly dictated by other people. They hold us back. Get in the way of our dreams.' I pause for a moment. 'Classic example last night, when I told James I wanted to make a difference in some way – maybe volunteer somewhere – abroad, even. He was more concerned about what other people would think, rather than what I wanted.'

Will frowns slightly. 'It sounds like you're working things out.'

'I'm starting to,' I say cautiously. 'I've been so busy being the person other people expect me to be – like frigging Carol Madison who wants me to help with the festival, for instance – I've stopped listening to myself. When I think about the last few years, it's like they've chipped away at the person I used to be.' Suddenly, my voice wavers. 'When I think back to how I used to feel, I used to be happy.' I look at him. 'I don't mean a euphoric, giddy kind of happiness. It's that feeling, deep inside, of knowing that life is good and you're where you want to be. I can't remember when I last felt like that.'

'It's what happens to us, isn't it?' he says quietly. 'Losing my mum, the way my dad treated me, losing Simon... My dreams literally fell apart around me. Life wasn't fun any more. It was about doing what other people expected of me.'

I shake my head. 'It's what happens, I think. But does it need to?' I think of what James said. 'We worry too much about what other people think.'

Will sighs. 'I'm guilty of that, for sure. But also I think the older we get, the less brave we feel. It's harder to make changes. It's easier to stick with what we know.'

I'm uncomfortable, because that's exactly what I've done. 'It's hardly a recipe for happiness, though, is it?' But it's why there are so many unhappy relationships. Safety and familiarity are not easy things to give up; which is why I've stayed with James, trading happiness for security. 'Who would have thought when we were teenagers, years later we'd end up having a conversation like this?'

'We were uncompromising.' Will looks rueful. 'No way were we going to get old like other people. We were going to travel and see the world, remember?'

'I know.' I remember how we'd felt unstoppable. 'So what happened to us?' As I look at Will, a sense of sadness fills me.

'The same that happens to most people,' Will says quietly. 'Things happen that make us lose faith – in ourselves, or in life.'

'Lucy once asked me if I was happy.' Unexpected emotion wells up inside me. 'It was a while ago. I think what I said was, *happy enough*.' There are tears in my eyes as I turn to look at Will. 'Only now? I'm not so sure.'

* * *

Back at home, I stand in the house, gazing around at the four walls, the carefully chosen furniture, expensive decorative items we've collected over the years. But as I look at them, I realise they're meaningless. Instead, what I'm yearning for is the sun on my skin, the wind in my hair; the feeling that comes from being at peace inside; a life lived fully.

Myriad vivid memories fill my head, of running with Yippy beneath wide skies; the scent of the earliest spring flowers. Millie – my heart bursts with love just thinking of her; days of wine, laughter and sunshine spent with Lucy. A wild sea crashing against rocks; the quiet hills of Ibiza. Times I've felt free and unencumbered – all of them joyful moments, transient maybe, but no less for being so.

Suddenly I'm uncomfortable, because James doesn't figure in any of them. On the surface, with our lovely old townhouse and a comfortable income, my life looks enviable; but it hides the growing chasm that's underneath as a question burns inside me.

Is it enough?

I think of the times mine and Will's paths have crossed over the years, catching the briefest, most intense moments together before life has carried us apart in different directions again. So many times, I've told myself that's all we were ever meant to be to each other; passing through each other's lives. But what if I was wrong? What if we're more? What if everything that's gone before has been leading to this?

PART II

11

WILL

Still in Bath, Will was aware of his time here running out. But it was extraordinary the difference a couple of weeks had made. And it was true what he'd said to Anna. When you were used to the way your life was, change felt daunting. But meeting her again had sparked his mind off in different directions, in a way he couldn't turn his back on.

'It's kind of weird. In my head, it's like I know you. But we were teenagers… A whole lot of stuff has happened to us since then.' They'd walked to a wilder, more isolated part of the park, a small herd of deer was watching them. 'I don't know the food you like, the music you listen to. Your friends. Your favourite colour.'

'Ha! That's easy. Lucy. And orange,' she answered the last two first.

'Green,' he said instantly. 'And Beatrice – one of the sheep,' he added.

'I love music,' Anna said wistfully. 'Right now, I keep listening to "The Luckiest" by Ben Folds.'

Will was bemused. 'OK. So I listen to all kinds of music, but I've never heard of him.'

'You call yourself a musician?' Anna looked at him with mock horror. 'You have to listen to it. Loudly – with headphones on. Seriously... It will carry you away somewhere.'

'I could do with being carried away,' he said wistfully, making a mental note to look it up. 'Will you come with me?'

Anna smiled. 'Listen to the song! Anyway, where were we? Vegetarian.'

'Carnivore,' he said apologetically.

She pretended to be outraged. 'How can you when you keep sheep?'

Carnivore or not, he had his boundaries. 'I will never eat lamb. And I have human friends, too, in case you're wondering. A couple of guys at work, but otherwise, mostly my old bandmates.'

The more they talked, the more the lid was coming off a lifetime of memories Will had never talked about before. He'd never believed talking would help in any way, but having someone listen had changed everything.

'I'm sorry,' he said suddenly. 'So sorry for the way I ended us.'

'It's OK.' Anna's voice was husky. 'I mean, it wasn't at the time. But I knew you were in a terrible place. I kept imagining how I would have felt if it was me.' Beside him, she shrugged. 'I just wished I could have been there for you.'

'I wish I'd let you.' His vision blurred as he looked at her. 'Thank you,' he mumbled. 'For listening. You've no idea how much difference it makes.'

'So much grief, Will,' she said softly. 'It isn't good to lock it away. Maybe it's time to let it go.'

If only it was that easy. As Will glanced at her, Anna went on.

'Seriously. You should stop giving yourself a hard time,' she said. 'You've had so much happen in your life.'

He shrugged. Stuff happened to everyone. 'No more than anyone else. And no one wants to hear *poor me* stories.' He pulled a comical face. 'Do you know how many years it's taken to perfect this?'

Anna shook her head. 'We're not talking about other people. We're talking about you and the people you've lost. Your mother, your brother and now your father... It leaves scars, Will.'

Will couldn't speak. Even now, his emotions had the capacity to hit him when he was least expecting them to.

Anna went on. 'OK. What you need is a big dustbin in your head.'

He frowned. 'What – like a virtual one, you mean?'

'Exactly, a virtual one. Trust me. When you have some time on your hands, take all these things you've stacked up over the years – your regrets, the things that went wrong... etcetera.' Anna was warming to her subject. 'But the other things, bring them into your mind, one at a time. Then ask yourself. Is this true? Then, does this serve me? You want a gut feeling answer. And if it's a no, it goes in the bin.'

A smile briefly crossed his face. 'You do realise, this isn't going to leave me with much.'

'That's the point! You don't need much! And definitely not all that stuff from the past.'

However nuts it sounded, maybe Anna had a point. 'So what happens when the bin's full?'

'It's a big bin.' Anna shrugged. 'But picture it in your mind, then blow it up. Or set fire to it. Basically, any means of destruction you can think of!'

As she took his hand, he felt his close around hers. Suddenly compelled to hold her, he moved closer, then his arms were around her. Feeling her heart beat close to his, for a brief moment Will was reminded of when they were teenagers. But it was more than that. Being with Anna was like coming home.

12

ANNA

Against the backdrop of spring, my restlessness takes root, as I have a new desire to learn. To experience the world differently, to question what I've always taken for granted, searching for wisdom anywhere I can find it, as book titles and random posts pop up on social media.

If you listen, the universe has messages for you, in music, the spoken word, the sound of the wind. Be still and listen. Everything you need is already inside you.

To start with, I don't know what to do with it all. But as it slowly starts to make sense, my thoughts are shifting direction until they're unstoppable.

As I sift between past and present, I try to work out what I want, suddenly remembering a list I once made in one of the diaries I used to keep.

In the sitting room, I search the oak chest that belonged to my parents, finding the diaries at the bottom, tied with ribbon. Pink and bigger than the rest, one stands out. It was the first time I'd had space to write more than the briefest of entries. Sitting on the floor, I untie the ribbon and open it.

Turning the pages, I reread the scribbled notes about homework and my gran coming for Sunday lunch. Lucy's name is there, with other friends' names, lists of music and bands I loved. Near the back, I find what I'm looking for.

Ten things to do before I die.

The idea had come from a teen magazine – probably *Jackie*, the bible of all teenage girls at that time. I carry on reading.

Kiss a rock star on a beach
Jump out of a plane
Go to Australia

When it came to travelling, Australia had always seemed the pinnacle.

Dye my hair blonde
Fall in love with a rich man
Learn a language – French or Italian
Live in a country where orange and lemon trees grow

I'd been fascinated by other countries and cultures. But it's the last two that get me.

Have lots of children
Be happy

It was a time when anything had seemed possible; when I could never have imagined losing the sense of freedom, the optimism I'd felt. Even in my twenties, I'd imagined I'd fall in love with a man with whom I'd live happily ever after.

But there's a lump in my throat as I remember how I'd taken for granted that I'd have children. *Even though I have Millie, precious beyond words,* I remind myself.

Thinking of the babies I've lost, tears blur my vision, a yearning filling me for those two little souls who are no less real to me for never having made it into this life. In the twelve weeks I'd carried them, loving them, imagining holding them, kissing each of their little fingers and toes; I'd dreamed up names, pictured the future; wanted to show them this world, the same world I'd fiercely protect them from.

Instead, I'd lost them. As I think back, grief wells up inside me, grief I've kept buried because it was easier than facing the pain. But now, as I sit here, instead of fighting it, I let it take me over.

Emotionally spent, it isn't until later that I pick up my diary again. Reading through the list pinpoints just how much I've changed; how my dreams have remained just dreams, when other than the first on the list, none of them should have been beyond me.

I didn't feel compelled to jump out of a plane but I'd had the chance to go to Australia – a chance I should have jumped at, but I'd talked myself out of it.

But it isn't too late. There's still time, enough to see the world, discover new dreams; to chase them wildly, passionately.

As I trace backwards through the years, it's as though I'm peeling away layers of the past. From James's affair; then before that, to the gradually expanding distance between us; my mother's death after losing my babies; my father dying a year after my cancer treatment; each and every one of which has taken something from me.

But things happen to all of us – it's up to us how we adapt to them. I think of the conversation with Will, then the message from the universe – *there are many ways to find happiness*, as closing my eyes, I visualise a rainbow-coloured box. Drawing to mind my grief for the people I've lost, the sense of time I've wasted, my frustration with James, the betrayal his affair left me with, I place them inside. Firmly closed and attached to pink balloons, it rises into the air and floats away.

As I open my eyes again, my phone buzzes with a text from Lucy. Opening it, photo after photo appears of the villa in the south of France – opulent and white, set amongst pine woods, the short path through the trees leading to pale sand and a sparkling sea. The interior is airy, Lucy's stylish touch evident throughout. It's a whole other world, of possibilities, of adventure, of sunshine, as a raw ache fills me for something I can't put my finger on.

Glancing back at my diary, I notice there are only nine items on my list. But it wasn't because I'd run out of ideas. I'd left a space for something I didn't yet know about.

* * *

That evening, when James comes in, instead of turning a blind eye to everything that's wrong, or telling myself trite phrases about long marriages going through phases, I search for a hint of the man I married, who had been so caring after my illness and supportive after my father died. But there's no trace of him.

If James notices I'm preoccupied, he doesn't say. But my diary has reminded me who I used to be, before life started to diminish me. Leaving what? Who is Anna? Apart from the wife, step-mother, would-be-writer, *who am I?*

MAY 2003

ANNA

In every sense it was a beautiful wedding, the ancient church decked out with flowers, the sun high in a cloudless sky. Having gone there with Sam for the wedding of his friend, Jim, with our relationship more off than on these days, already I was wondering what I was doing here.

It was a picture-perfect scene as we stood outside the church watching the last of the stylishly dressed guests drift out. Sam nudged me. 'Those are Jim's kids.' He nodded towards the two cherubic flower girls posing for the camera under a voluminous arch of flowers.

When we reached the reception, it was no less lavish. It was clear no expense had been spared in the marquee set up in the grounds of a stunning castle. The most perfect of days – the only problem was apart from Sam, I didn't know a single soul here.

But that was about to change as I took a glass of champagne from a passing waiter and a voice came from behind me.

'Anna?'

Recognising his voice instantly, I turned around. 'Will?'

A smile crossed his face. 'What are the chances?' In a dark suit, he looked as gorgeous as I remembered. A little older, his hair a little shorter, untypically smart, but as I met his eyes, he was the same Will.

Leaning over, as he kissed my cheek, the proximity of him was dizzying.

'What are you doing here? You look beautiful, by the way.' Without waiting for an answer, he went on. 'Who do you know? The bride or groom?'

'Neither!' As my unreliable heart started to race, I reminded myself what happened last time I saw him. 'I'm with a friend who's a friend of the groom.'

'A friend of mine is a friend of the bride.' He grinned broadly. 'I can't believe you're here! It's so good to see you again.'

Distracted, he turned as someone called out his name. But as I walked away to find Sam, a funny feeling came over me. The last time I'd seen Will, he'd suggested we meet at Covent Garden. I'd waited for him for over an hour, but when he hadn't turned up, I'd been forced to conclude he'd changed his mind.

As the most sublime of wedding breakfasts was served at tables decorated with roses, the wine was free flowing. Every now and then I caught a glimpse of Will. On form, playing life and soul of the party, his table erupted into uproarious laughter every so often.

I turned my attention back to Sam. He was a nice guy – considerate and thoughtful – and we'd been seeing each other for a few months – long enough to know that whatever there was between us, something was missing.

Today, seeing Will again, had highlighted what that was. It was the spark, the flicker of excitement; the way that, looking into his eyes, I could completely lose myself. But a wedding was not the place to break up with someone and after the speeches, leaving Sam deep in conversation with the girl sitting on the other side of him, I picked my moment and went outside.

It was later than I'd realised and gloriously romantic, the birdsong vibrant, the sun sinking lower, painting the sky in pastel shades. Away from the marquee, I breathed in the warm air, listening to the sound of voices drifting across the garden; amongst the happy wedding guests, suddenly aware of how alone I felt.

'Anna?'

Hearing Will call out, I turned to see him coming after me.

'I saw you go out. I thought...' His eyes met mine as he faltered. 'Are you with that guy?'

'Kind of. It isn't a big deal, though.' As I held his gaze, my heart started to race. 'What about you?'

'I'm a convenient date. But that's all. Look.' He hesitated. 'Why don't I grab a bottle and a couple of glasses? Don't go away. I'll be right back.'

Without waiting for a reply, he hotfooted it back towards the bar set up next to the marquee, where he exchanged a few words with the barman before turning and coming back.

'I think we should hide.' Will glanced around the garden. 'I want to hear all about your life,' he said quietly.

We walked across the grass and found a hidden corner away from everyone else that was bathed in evening sunlight. Will passed me the glasses. 'I hope white is OK?'

I nodded. 'It's great. Beautiful wedding, isn't it?'

'Bloody expensive wedding...' He poured the wine, before raising his glass and chinking it against mine. 'Cheers.' Sipping his wine, a slightly guilty look crossed his face. 'I owe you an apology.'

'You do?' Giving nothing away, I couldn't wait to hear this.

'Shall we sit down?' Will flopped onto the grass. As I sat down, he went on. 'Last time I saw you... that stag do in the bar in London?' He shook his head. 'I was so pissed, I wouldn't have blamed you if you hadn't turned up. But on the Sunday, as I left the house to meet you, the phone rang.' He shook his head. 'I wasn't going to answer it, but it rang and rang... It was as well I did because Simon had been in an accident.'

'God.' I was shocked. At the time, I'd imagined every scenario other than this one.

'I know. I went straight to the hospital. He was OK, luckily. Bruised, but nothing broken. Once I knew, I got over to Covent Garden as soon as I could. But by the time I got there, you'd gone.' He frowned. 'Assuming you were there in the first place. Maybe you weren't. The state I was in when I saw you, I wouldn't have blamed you,' he repeated.

'I was there.' I could still remember how disappointed I'd felt; how Lucy had been infuriated on my behalf. 'But when you didn't turn up...' I shrugged.

'I'm so sorry. Really I am,' he said earnestly. 'But I couldn't leave Simon, and I had no way of getting in touch with you.'

I was partly filled with relief that he hadn't changed his mind. But there was regret, too. I couldn't help wondering if Simon hadn't been hurt, if Will had come to meet me as planned, would anything have come of it? While here we are, brought together again. 'You did what you had to. Simon needed you.' But as the sun flickered through the leaves above us, I was aware of the same connection between us there'd always been; that I'd yet to find with anyone else. 'So tell me, what have you been doing – since you moved to Yorkshire?'

'Quite a long time ago, isn't it?' he said quietly. 'Believe it or not, I went to uni. Got a very average degree in advertising and media, which has so far proved utterly useless. I still play with the band now and then. And I've been living with Simon on and off – in London.' He paused. 'But I've just been offered a job in Australia.'

I was astonished. 'Wow. When do you leave?'

Will hesitated. 'Next week.' His eyes gazed into mine. 'I thought it would be good to see somewhere far away from here – for a while, though. Not forever.'

A feeling of regret washed over me that, yet again, it seemed our timing was out. 'You might not want to come back.'

'Immigration might decide that for me,' he said wryly. 'But I should be good for a year.'

My heart felt heavy as I smiled at him. 'It's like we used to talk about, isn't it? Seeing a bit of the world? I think it's great you're going.'

He topped up my glass. 'We're only here once. Might as well make the most of it... But anyway, I don't want to talk about me. Tell me about you.' Sitting there, his eyes didn't leave my face.

'Lucy and I lived in London for a while – she still does. But unlike you, I moved back to Bath. I got offered a job – I'm writing for a magazine based in Bath and Bristol. I know it's not adventurous, but there are certain advantages to being back there.'

He was silent for a moment. 'So you and the guy you're with?'

'Sam? We met when I lived in London – he still lives there. We see each other much less these days. In fact...' I broke off.

'What?' Will looked quizzical.

I shrugged. 'I think our days are numbered.'

As the sun sank below the horizon, the garden started to flicker with fairy lights. Will glanced in the direction of the marquee. 'Do you think anyone will be missing us?' he said quietly.

'Well, Sam seemed perfectly happy chatting up this girl... As for your date, I'd say she's probably wondering where you've got to.'

'Oh well.' Will looked unfussed. 'She and I... It really isn't anything.'

Emboldened by the wine, I looked at him. 'So is there someone?'

For a moment he was silent. 'There isn't.' He sounded hesitant, as though there was more he wasn't saying. 'Could I see you again? After tonight?'

'Is this like last time?' I arched an eyebrow at him. 'An idea that under the influence of too much wine seems a perfectly good one?'

'It wasn't like that.' Will moved closer. 'Give me another chance. It could be the best decision of your life.'

'Hah!' My smile faded. 'You're about to go to Australia.'

'I know the timing is terrible,' he said quietly. 'But I have this overwhelming desire to kiss you.'

I was helpless; powerless to resist as he lowered his lips to mine, losing myself in his kiss until suddenly I pulled back. 'This is nuts, Will – starting something when you're about to move to the other side of the world.'

'What if I didn't go?' He was suddenly serious. 'If I stayed, Anna?' He took one of my hands. 'I've tried to put you out of my mind, but wherever I go, you're always there. I'm putting my heart on the line here.' He paused. 'Say something.'

My heart twisted as I gazed at him, but it wasn't for me to ask him not to go. 'You have to go, Will. Life is for living, and all that...'

'Life is for loving,' he whispered seductively. 'Give me your number. I'll call you. Or better still, come with me.'

Startled, for a moment my mind wandered, imagining us on a flight, exploring Australia together, envisaging white sand and the ocean, the most far-reaching skies, before I shook my head. 'I can't.' I looked at him sadly, stopping myself from telling him why; that right now, I wasn't going anywhere.

'Think how great it would be,' he said softly.

'I know.' Tears glistened in my eyes. In that moment, I'd have given anything to be going with him. 'I know it would. It just isn't the right time.'

I could see the questions in his eyes as Will looked at me. But we didn't need words as the sound of music reached us. Getting up, he pulled me to my feet, holding me close as we started to dance.

* * *

The following day, when I told Sam it was over between us, he didn't try to persuade me otherwise. After the wedding, I think he, too, had realised that whatever there was between us, it wasn't enough.

I felt released. I also felt a sense of events evolving that were in some way out of my control when Will and I met just once more before he went away.

I'd wondered if, yet again, fate would intervene to keep us apart, but as I reached Covent Garden and walked out of the tube, Will was standing directly in front of me.

'I got here early – just in case.' Leaning towards me, he kissed me. 'You look beautiful.'

Breathing in the woody aftershave he was wearing, I felt my cheeks flush. 'Thank you.'

We stood there for a moment before Will took my hand. 'We could go somewhere for dinner if you like, or we could just walk for a while.'

'Let's walk.' The feel of my hand in his was achingly familiar.

As we made our way along the street, Will told me about his trip. 'The flight is tomorrow evening. I'm breaking the journey in Hong Kong for a couple of days before flying on to Sydney.'

I was envious. 'It sounds amazing, Will. I mean, so many people talk about travelling, but you're actually doing it.'

'I am excited.' As we came to a bar with tables outside, he stopped. 'How about we have a drink here?'

After a waiter brought us glasses of cold wine, Will raised his. 'To seeing each other again.'

'To Australia,' I said quietly.

Will's smile faded. 'You know, after last time we were supposed to meet – after Simon's accident – I tried to get in touch with your parents. But I couldn't get through to them.'

It's the first time he'd told me he'd actually looked for me. 'They moved. And they're ex-directory.' Small, insignificant details that, put together, had kept us apart from each other.

'It's a bugger,' he said unexpectedly. 'Seeing you again when I'm just about to go away.'

'It kind of is.' Reaching across the table, I touched his hand. 'But it's nice, too.'

Will looked hopeful. 'Couldn't we stay in touch? A year isn't that long.'

I shook my head. 'You never know, you might meet someone there and stay forever.'

Will looked perplexed. 'Right now, I'm already thinking about when I come back.'

'You can't do that.' I stared at him. 'You're going to have the time of your life out there.'

He looked at me uncertainly. 'You know, having seen you again, I'm not so sure.'

As he spoke, I felt my heart twist. I wanted so much to tell him how I was really feeling; that I felt the same as I always had; that I would have gone to the ends of the earth with him. But as I thought about the hospital appointment that lay ahead, I swallowed the lump in my throat.

Watching me, he frowned slightly. 'Is there something I don't know?'

'There's a lot you don't know,' I teased, forcing a smile. When he was about to go away, I couldn't tell him what was really going on. I changed the subject. 'Shall we get some food?'

'I have an idea.' Will's eyes sparkled. 'How about takeaway fish and chips in this secret place I know.'

I was intrigued. 'OK. So show me!'

After buying fish and chips, Will led me to a narrow alleyway, where halfway along there was a wooden door. Will opened it and, as we went through, it was as though we'd stepped into another world.

'Wow,' I breathed. Gazing around the garden, it was like an oasis as I took in tall trees, tumbling roses in every colour, lavender bushes alive with bees.

'Cool, isn't it?' Will looked pleased. 'This way.' He led me across the grass to a bench still bathed in the evening sunlight.

It was like a fairy tale. But, as I looked around, it became even more so as I felt Will's arms go around me, before he kissed me.

* * *

As I lay in his arms that night, my mind was all over the place, sleep impossible. It seemed surreal that just as I was facing the worst scenario of my life, I'd been granted this magical interlude.

But it was what I needed – a timely reminder of all that was good in life; of love. Something to carry with me in the days that lay ahead; a beautiful memory to lose myself in if times got tough. I didn't want us to say goodbye, but I had to let him go. If we were meant to be, I had to believe it would happen when the time was right.

13

WILL

The following day brought another glorious morning, a few fair weather clouds scattered in a wide blue sky as he and Anna sat outside the pub.

'Yesterday I found one of my old diaries.' It was warm enough that Anna had pushed her sleeves up to her elbows.

He watched her sip her coffee. 'And?'

She seemed on edge. 'It was typical teenage stuff. Live somewhere hot. Kiss a rock star on a tropical beach, that kind of thing.' Anna glanced towards the canal. 'I wanted to jump out of a plane.'

Will was impressed. 'So have you?'

'No. Not once.' Putting her cup down, Anna was oddly abrupt. 'To be honest, if you really want to know, it upset me. It's reminded me of how I used to feel; about the dreams you and I used to talk about. I wanted to go to Australia, too. Dye my hair blonde. Live somewhere orange and lemon trees grow. There were all these possibilities I've completely forgotten about. I've never been blonde and I haven't done any of the things on my list. I really wanted to have children...' Her voice was shaking. 'I was pregnant twice...' She swallowed. 'I carried them for twelve weeks. Then I lost them both.' Tears filled her eyes.

Will started. He had no idea she'd miscarried. 'I'm so sorry,' he said quietly.

'Over time, you get used to it, but most people don't understand how it makes you feel.' Wiping her eyes, Anna's voice wobbled. 'At the heart of it all, I wanted to be happy. It's like you and I used to say – about making the most of every day. But all this time is passing, and I'm not, and it isn't enough.' As tears spilled down her face, she reached in her pocket for a tissue.

Seeing her distress, Will felt his heart twist. 'Blonde hair wouldn't suit you.'

Reaching out a hand, very gently he stroked her tears away.

'It probably wouldn't. It isn't just that, though. I know I sound ungrateful for what I have, and I'm really not, but I want to travel. Catch up with the friends I've lost touch with. Go on an adventure... Stop living such a safe, predictable life... But it's like my head is exploding. There's you and me, whatever this is... while at home, James barely talks to me...' Her voice was unsteady. 'You know how everyone has their limit? Well, somewhere between yesterday and today, I've reached mine.'

He could feel her tension. 'He should at least talk to you, Anna. Not to, is completely unreasonable.'

'I know.' She sounded upset. 'But when I try to start a conversation about what's wrong, he just gets angry. I don't think I can take much more of it.'

'It's wrong.' Will could feel her frustration. 'You don't deserve to be treated like this.' He could see how she felt; that everything was stacking up around her. 'Look, I know you have a lot on your mind.'

'Too much,' she said tearfully.

Will nodded. 'I'm guessing it feels like there's a mountain in front of you, but it isn't always going to be like this.'

'It's frigging Everest, Will.' Wiping her eyes, words poured out of her. 'It's like I've woken up to myself. I'm seeing things in a way I haven't before. My mind can't settle. I feel uncomfortable all the time, and sad – and just terrible, because everything is changing and it's so frigging hard... But it's like a door has closed and I can't go back.'

'It's because you never expected it to go wrong with James,' Will says quietly.

'It's gone really wrong.' She hesitated. 'I haven't told you, but he had an affair.'

Will was shocked. 'When?'

'I found out two years ago.' She gazed at Will. 'I wanted to leave. But he begged me to stay. At the time, it felt like the right thing to do. *Right...* Can you believe I thought that? I suppose it was all that shared history between us. But this isn't just about his affair. It goes back further than that – on a subconscious level I think he knows that – it's probably why he met someone else.' Her voice was filled with angst. 'I loved him once, but we just don't work any more.'

And the next step felt insurmountable – Will could understand that. 'Have you talked to Lucy?'

Anna shook her head. 'Not for a while, but she knows we're having problems. She's been working in the south of France – interior designing a villa near the sea. She sent me all these photos yesterday. It made things worse.' She started telling him about Lucy's home in Ibiza. 'It's really old with wooden beams and thick walls, so it's always cool, even in summer. It's set on a hill covered in pine trees, with a terrace where you can sit and watch the sun set.'

It sounded like paradise. 'Could you go and stay with her for a while?' It would at least give Anna a chance to get her head straight.

'I can go any time.' Anna was silent for a moment. 'You know, I've always envied Lucy her life. I thought she was brave to move there, but it's the best thing she's ever done.' There was angst in her eyes. 'I've been thinking about doing the same.'

'Moving to Ibiza?' Will was taken aback. 'Could you?'

'Maybe.' Anna shrugged. 'I can't stay where I am. And nothing's impossible, is it? Not if you want it enough.'

'I guess not.' It just seemed like a world away, but as he'd been watching her, it was as though she was being carried along by some invisible momentum. Will felt his mind start to race. If she were actually to leave James, this time, nothing was out of the question. It changed everything.

There was anguish in her eyes as she looked at him. 'There's something I've never told you. Remember when you were moving to Australia?' Her eyes searched his. 'You asked me to go with you. I thought about it – but what I didn't tell you was I'd just found a lump in one of my breasts. The day after you left, I went for a biopsy.'

A wave of shock hit Will. 'Why didn't you tell me?'

Tears glinted in her eyes. 'How could I? You were going on the trip of a lifetime – and after what happened to your mother, I couldn't have put you through the worry. Anyway, what could you have done?'

'Stayed, obviously.' Just thinking about it, his mind was spinning.

'It wouldn't have been right.' She paused. 'The lump turned out to be malignant. It was a horrible year, but my parents were amazing – that's the real reason I moved back to Bath. Knowing I had cancer was the most frightening time. But you know what? However heartbroken I was to find you again and lose you, those two days before you left gave me something to hold on to. When I was waiting to go to surgery, I used to take myself back to the wedding, or to meeting you in Covent Garden, retracing our footsteps; even to the night we spent together.' Her eyes remained fixed on his. 'The same when I had chemo…' Her voice shook. 'When I felt ill and scared, I conjured you.'

He breathed in sharply. The thought of him gadding off to Australia while Anna was going through this alone was agonising. 'I wish you'd told me.' His mind was racing. 'That's why you stopped replying to my emails.'

Anna nodded. 'Yes,' she said quietly.

He realised he hadn't asked her. 'Are you OK now?'

To his relief, she nodded. 'But in a way, it makes it worse. When you have cancer, you become aware of all the time you might not have. You have no idea what the future holds. I made myself a promise, that if I got well, I wouldn't waste a single moment of a single day. That I wouldn't put things off, I'd do them now, while I still could.' Her eyes shone with tears. 'But somewhere along the way, I've lost sight of that.'

Will was silent; still reeling at this latest revelation. She was right, on every level. There was this human tendency to leave everything until tomorrow, when life was about now. Suddenly his mind was crystal clear, the strangest recklessness coursing through him.

Facing a life-threatening illness such as cancer was the starkest reminder of how fragile life was; that it was about love, too. A sense of urgency gripped him. 'You and me…' He looked into eyes he wanted to lose himself in, at skin he desperately wanted to touch, long hair he wanted to run his fingers through. 'Don't you ever wonder about all those missed chances? How we keep finding our way back to each other?' Fumbling for words, as he took Anna's hands, he felt electric-shocked. 'I felt it when we were teenagers. There was something about us – I think there always has been – and I haven't felt anything like it with anyone else.'

Her hands tightened around his. 'Me neither,' she whispered. As their eyes locked, neither of them moved, yet he could feel them being drawn closer, stranding them on the edge of something he had no reference for.

14

ANNA

Will's words only add to the sense of unrest I'm feeling. I want to believe him, that we are something, but right now there are too many complications in the way.

Feeling my life veering out of control, when I call Lucy, she answers immediately.

'Hold on, babe... You're breaking up. I'm just going up on the roof...' There's a clatter of footsteps, as I imagine Lucy climbing the rickety stepladder onto her roof terrace, barefoot, her toenails painted silver or turquoise, sparkling against skin that even at this time of year will be tanned. There's a muttered, 'Shit.' Then, 'Sorry. Right. Can you hear me now?'

'Perfectly. How are you, Luce? How was France?'

'Incredible, babe. Perfect for me – big budget and minimal brief, but they love what I do. I've come home for a party one of Gianluca's friends is hosting – I'm going back in a couple of days.'

Gianluca's the much younger Italian she's having a fling with. But Lucy's known me longer than James has. We've shared each other's joys and heartbreaks, know each other's silences. She can hear it in my voice. 'Something's happened, hasn't it? Are you OK?'

'Just more rows with James.'

'What is it this time?' Lucy sounds annoyed.

'Nothing specific. He refuses to talk about anything important. All he's interested in is test-driving a new Merc because Duncan's buying one and this fucking golfing holiday. He doesn't care about anything else.'

'He's a dick, Anna, I don't blame you for being so angry.'

I take a deep breath. 'Luce? I need to tell you something.' I hesitate. 'I've met someone.'

Lucy doesn't miss a beat. 'Good for you, darling. Everyone should do it, in my opinion. Anyone I know?'

As relief floods through me, I'm half laughing, half shaking my head. 'It's more than a flirtation! I'm serious.' It's the moment there's no turning back from as I tell my best friend. 'It's not just anyone. It's Will.'

'Fuck.' It doesn't happen often but Lucy's silent. 'Will? The same Will you were crazy about when we were teenagers?' She pauses. 'I don't believe it. When? How?'

'We met walking in Dyrham Park. We walk and talk – for hours, the way we always used to.' I'd wondered if once I told someone, the magic would be gone, but it hasn't.

'Has he kissed you?'

'Yes.' My voice is quiet, as I remember.

Lucy's uncharacteristically lost for words. 'I can't get my head around this. I mean, Will, of all people... Are you sure he isn't spinning you a line?'

'We both know he isn't like that.'

Lucy sounds worried. 'How can you possibly know? The Will you knew was a teenager who dumped you and broke your heart. What you should do is book a hotel, shag him senseless and move on. Then you can go back to James and your life, and no one will be any the wiser.'

For as long as I can remember, Lucy's been anti-James. This pro-James Lucy is unfamiliar. 'Honestly, Luce? It's far more than that. I know we're both older, but underneath, it's like nothing's changed.'

Lucy's silent for a moment. 'I still can't believe I didn't know this. When did you meet?'

'The same day you told me about your job in France.' I remember that morning vividly – Lucy's call that left me craving adventure; how I'd broken the bracelet that had been an anniversary present from James. Had it been a sign?

'That's nothing.' Lucy's matter of fact. 'I mean, it's one thing to have a fling, but you can't possibly know someone in that length of time.' Before, I might have agreed, but I've discovered you can know someone instantly, instinctively. 'Luce. I don't know where it's headed, but everything's changed.'

'Oh, Anna...' She sounds anxious but there's excitement in her voice, too. 'You and James have been through so much shit, but you deserve far more than he could ever give you, I've always thought that.' She pauses. 'What will you do?'

'I think James and I are over.' I can't believe how calm I feel. 'When he had his affair, I should never have stayed. I just wasn't brave enough to walk away.' As I imagine disentangling life with James, there's defiance in my voice. 'I don't know if Will and I have a future, but it's shown me how much is wrong with my marriage.'

'No marriages are perfect.' Lucy's voice is sober.

'No. But it's a really long time since I've been happy, Luce.' I pause before going on. 'I've never told you this, but I really envy you your life. It's filled with people – and interesting places. I know you work hard, but you have fun too, while mine... It's passing me by. Remember when I was ill, I promised myself that wouldn't happen? I've let it slip. And I've realised I can't go on like this.'

'I really get that.' She sounds thoughtful. 'So what will you do?'

'After I've left? Write, maybe? Travel…'

'Then come here! *Please…*' she begs. 'At least, to start with.'

'I'd really love that.' I glance at the time. 'I should probably go. James will be home soon. I'm trying to keep the peace until I find the courage to tell him.'

'OK, you go, babe, but don't take any crap.' Sounding anxious, she adds, 'Anna, keep me posted… And look after yourself…'

'I will, Luce! Love you…' As the call ends, I'm not sure she gets it. But if it had been the other way round, I'm not sure I would. Remembering I haven't told her I've left my job, I text her.

Quit my job too. Told you everything had changed! Xx

A few minutes later, she texts me back.

About bloody time too. Bloody Meredith.

It's followed by angry face and heart emojis.

I know we can choose love. But sometimes, love seeks us out in a way that changes the way the entire world looks. And change, it seems, is my only constant as the universe sends me another message:

People come and go in our lives
Not all of them are meant to stay

15

WILL

When he reached the pub, hidden away in the middle of beautiful nowhere, Anna had arrived ahead of him. Since he'd last seen her, Will hadn't been able to shake off the intensity of their conversation. Everything she'd said had struck a chord, shaken him out of the feeling of lethargy that it was all too easy to sink back into, while knowing he was leaving soon, time seemed tangible in a way it never had been before.

As he saw Anna sitting outside, it was there again – that jolt, the reminder of how alive he felt, before he remembered what he had to tell her. Taking his drink over, he sat down opposite her.

'Hi.' His head was full of things he wanted to say as he took a deep breath. 'I'm so glad you're here.' He wanted to hold on to this moment, for as long as he could, but he could almost feel time slipping away from them.

'Hello.' Sitting opposite him, Anna frowned slightly. 'Has something happened?'

He sighed. 'Real life, I think you'd call it. I have to go home.'

'It was always going to happen, wasn't it?' she said sadly. 'So what happens now, Will Anderson?'

'Well...' Putting off the moment they had to face the starkness of reality, he took in the swirly printed top she was wearing, the way her hair was caught back over one shoulder, as he pretended to think. 'If things were different... I'd take you to a very cool restaurant I know. We'd sit at a little table in the window, watching the world go by, eating the best pasta in London and drinking Italian red wine. Then, after, we'd go for a romantic walk under the stars – and I'd kiss you.'

He could picture them, Anna in a sexy dress, him in a shirt and jeans. A romantic restaurant; her hand in his as they walked through London's brightly lit streets.

Anna looked wistful. 'And after that?'

He played along. 'The next time, we'll drive to somewhere near the sea. You'll have to wear that big red jumper of yours and a woolly scarf, because we'll buy fish and chips, then eat them on the beach – fending off thieving seagulls. After, you'd come back to mine, and I'd light the fire and play some music – maybe even some of my music...'

Again, he could picture them there, imagining the breeze whipping up Anna's hair, his arm around her shoulders as they huddled together to keep warm.

'So after that...' Anna was talking fast, cramming their last moments with memories, albeit made-up ones. 'We could jump on a plane together and spend a romantic weekend in Amsterdam, where you'd fall madly in love with me...'

His heart missed a beat. 'What if I already am? Madly in love with you, I mean?' he said softly. Watching Anna's eyes widen, he went on. 'Maybe we'll go there – one day. Who knows?' But as reality closed in, one day seemed so very far away. In another lifetime, even. 'Darcey called me last night.' His heart felt heavy. 'She says Flo's really missing me. I miss her too. Plus Darcey has all these plans coming up – which is great because I get to spend the time with Flo.' *But*, he wanted to say; to tell Anna how conflicted he felt; how, if he was honest, he didn't want to leave her.

'When are you leaving?' Anna's voice was husky.

'Tomorrow.' Thinking of his daughter, he was silent for a moment.

'I can't think of you not being here,' she said.

Sitting there, Will couldn't speak. Apart from seeing Flo, he wanted to stay, to be with Anna, but the weight of responsibility was back. 'The house isn't sorted yet. I'll have to come back at some point.' There was a lump in his throat as suddenly he felt defeated by it all. 'You do know, don't you, these days together have been the happiest I've felt in such a long time?' He couldn't let her go. Not this time. Will felt his mind start to race. 'I realise you need to sort things out with James – and I'm entangled in this hideous divorce. But I meant what I said to you, about how there's always been something between us. It's like we've shown each other what's been missing in our lives. I want to hold on to that.'

'So do I.' Anna's eyes held his. 'Do you know when you're coming back?'

'Not yet. I'll call you,' he said softly.

* * *

After packing the last of his clothes, as Will stood in his father's house looking around to see if he'd missed anything, the strangest mixture of emotions was surging through him.

Watching Anna walk away had cut him to the core. He'd stopped short of telling her how over the last couple of days, he'd had Darcey calling him, giving him chapter and verse about how much she had to do and how demanding Flo was. After the freedom of the time he'd spent with Anna, the familiar weight of responsibility had clamped down on him. But Flo was his world and she needed him.

You couldn't always have everything you want – didn't he, more than anyone, know that? It wasn't how life worked. He had to believe that if it was meant to be, they'd find a way to be together. But maybe for now, this was for the best. Space from each other. A chance to find out how they really felt; once he was back in Glasgow.

He went upstairs and did a final check in the bedroom to see if he'd left anything, then, coming back down, glanced at his watch. He needed to get a move on – he had a flight to catch. After switching off the lights and picking up his bag, he went out to his car.

But as he drove away from the house, it was as though powerful elastic was pulling him back. Mentally wielding a large pair of scissors, he flinched as he sliced through it, knowing he was kidding himself. He'd been lying when he'd told himself he wasn't leaving something behind, because he was. Something precious. Anna.

16

ANNA

With Will gone, I cling to a life that's growing less familiar by the day, in the home where the ghosts of Millie's childhood play; in a marriage I can feel tightening its tentacles around me.

With James increasingly absent working in London, it's a measure of our relationship that I don't care more, but the realisations are stacking up. When James is away, I don't miss him.

Getting out our wedding photos, I gaze at the two of us, trying to remember how I felt. My relief and disbelief; the brief flashes of euphoria that never lasted; the vulnerability – because when you've had cancer, nothing feels certain any more. There was fear, too, that it would return. With my body still ravaged by the treatment, my dreams had long been put on the back-burner. But I hadn't craved excitement any more. It was enough simply to be alive.

But it had given me an appreciation for the simple things in life, too. The warmth of sunlight, the people in my life; the start of another brand-new day. And James had been there when I needed him; our quieter, ordered life together one without demands; offering me a safe place where I could heal.

After... A new determination to fully live life had taken me over. I'm not sure James ever really understood. But however unlikely we may have seemed, he'd cared. And I'd loved him for it. The realisation brings a lump to my throat. Since then, so much has changed.

Sitting there, I imagine starting again in another house. Leaving and never coming back, a thought that contravenes everything I've always believed in, but the questions keep coming. *Who decides what's right or not? When you're not happy, how can you stay?*

* * *

'It's dry,' James says critically, prodding at the chicken in front of him. 'I thought you were going to try that fish recipe of Carol's.'

Fighting the urge to hurl my plate at his head, I try to stay calm. 'For God's sake, you like chicken, James. It was simpler, that's all.'

But my appetite has gone. Putting down my fork, I stare at the unwanted food; the ornate plate, part of a dinner service that had been a wedding present. It's just a chicken breast cooked in olive oil and herbs, but suddenly representative of so much more.

'Carol and Duncan have invited us for dinner,' he says shortly. 'Next weekend.'

'I think I'm busy,' I say quickly. Duncan is like most of James's friends – overbearing; only interested in talking endlessly about their fancy villa on the Costa del Sol.

'Surely you can change your plans?' He frowns at me. 'Why aren't you eating?'

'For some reason, I've lost my appetite.' My voice is icy.

He doesn't ask why and I say nothing, watching James push

the remains of the chicken to the side of his plate, then go on eating what's left, as unexpected sadness fills me.

* * *

After clearing away supper, I pour myself another glass of wine, glancing at James, now engrossed in his paper; no longer able to stay silent.

I stare at my husband. 'Are you happy, James?'

Looking up from his paper, he frowns. 'What?'

'I asked you if you were happy.' Needing to break this deadlock, my desire to know is genuine.

'What are you talking about?' A flash of realisation crosses his face. 'Oh, I get it... You've been talking to Lucy, haven't you?' His voice is sarcastic. 'She has very strange ideas. I wish you wouldn't take any notice of her.'

Rattled, I bite my tongue. But he still hasn't answered my question. 'You don't seem it, that's all.' I hold my breath, waiting for James's response, but he shuts me down.

'For God's sake, this is real life. I've got a lot on at work and I'm tired.' He sounds annoyed. 'If you don't mind, I'm in the middle of reading something.'

In a few sentences, there it is. Safely ensconced in middle-aged complacency, an example of what happiness isn't. But I can see it for what it is – yet another example of how different we've become; how sad it is that what I once thought was love has come to this.

2004

WILL

Australia had been incredible, mind-blowing, inspiring. But being the other side of the world from Anna had wreaked havoc on his head. It hadn't helped that his emails had elicited only the briefest of replies from her. For six months he'd kept sending them – along with photos of what he'd seen, amusing anecdotes of things that had happened, until the first email she didn't reply to. When it happened again, Will had put it down to him being thousands of miles away. But he was back, now, and with only one thought on his mind. He wanted to see her.

After a concerted effort, he'd managed to find where she worked and he'd even got the number of her office – which left him torn. Should he call her? Or go there, and wait for her outside? At least that way, she wouldn't be able to hang up on him.

Plucking up the courage, he'd got on the train from London, and as it sped through the countryside, he rehearsed what he wanted to say.

'Can I buy you a drink – or maybe dinner? I've missed you, Anna... I haven't stopped thinking about you.'

He couldn't wait to see her, to tell her all about Australia; to find out what she'd been doing since he'd left.

As the train pulled into Bristol Temple Meads, it felt like a moment of gargantuan proportions. Will took a deep breath. This was it – and if things went according to plan, who knew. It could be the beginning of the rest of his life.

Walking along streets he'd memorised in his head, he headed towards the block where he knew Anna worked. It was cold for March, the sun shining, his breath freezing as he walked, but even that had its advantages. It would make the pub he'd take Anna to all the more welcoming.

Outside her office, he stood away from the entrance, rubbing his hands together to keep them warm, his heart jumping as he thought he saw her come out, before he realised it was someone else.

Half an hour later, chilled to the bone, he was about to give up when he saw her. In a black calf-length coat with a hat pulled over her eyes, she looked serene – and beautiful. As he started walking towards her, her face lit up. But Will stopped suddenly, his heart sinking as he realised it wasn't him she was looking at.

He turned to study the man coming towards her. In a navy coat and polished shoes, his hair neatly cut, he looked everything Will wasn't.

Rooted to the ground, he watched the man reach Anna, kissing her on the cheek. It was clear from Anna's face that he'd said something amusing to her. Her eyes were sparkling in that way he knew so well; a smile playing on her lips.

He felt his heart sink. All the way here, on the interminably long flight, then on the train, he'd been so sure Anna would be pleased to see him. What a fool he'd been not to imagine that in the year he'd been away, she'd meet someone else. Hope fleetingly came to him, that maybe this man wasn't important to her. Hope that was destroyed as the man pulled Anna close. This time, as he kissed her on the lips, Will looked away.

* * *

In the pub, an air of despondency hung over Will. As he started on his third pint, he was still struggling to take it in. He'd come here tonight prepared to persuade, plead, beg even – out of every scenario he'd imagined, this hadn't been one of them.

Presumably this man was the reason she'd stopped replying to his emails. Perhaps he should call her. Make out that he hadn't seen her today. Ask her out – see what she said. But having seen her with the man, he knew he'd be setting himself up for rejection. He wasn't sure his heart could take that.

All this time, he'd been so convinced there was something special between them. It had been there when they last met, just before he went away. As he thought back to that night, he knew he hadn't imagined it – the feeling had stayed with him the whole time he'd been in Australia.

Feeling yet another of his dreams shatter, he knew he had to resign himself to the fact that clearly in the year he'd been gone, things had changed. Anna had moved on. It left him no choice but to do the same.

17

ANNA

Now that I'm no longer working for Meredith, I dedicate my days to writing my book. But unable to focus, I to and fro with conflicting emotions. I oscillate between my feelings for Will and misplaced loyalty to James, while in bed, I roll away from him, not wanting to touch him. The restlessness I feel refusing to still.

But the next step has epic proportions, even though I'm young enough, that if I'm lucky, there are good years ahead.

Not for just settling. No one should just settle. It's about living your best life.

The voice comes from nowhere, unnerving me.

When you have so much, don't you think it ought to be enough?

But as I think about sharing the rest of my life with James, I answer my own question.

Inside, I would be screaming.

True to form, one morning, the universe hits me with a new message, which like the others, seems right on:

Let go of what no longer works for you.

As usual, I stare at it. It's almost exactly what I said to Will. No question, the universe is ramping up the pressure. But, for once, I'm ahead of the game, because I know what needs to happen. All I have to do is find the courage.

* * *

While a new transparency enters my thoughts, Lucy's calls keep me sane. 'Come over for a few days. It's getting hotter by the day and the bars are starting to open. It would do you good to get away.'

I'm torn, imagining the quiet peacefulness of Can Mimosa, the spring sunshine, a few days of the island's magic. 'I can't, Luce. I need to get things moving.'

'Have you heard from Will?'

'Not yet. He said he'd let me know when he's coming back. But right now, maybe it's for the best he isn't here. I need to focus on sorting my life out.'

'Well, if it gets too much, just come here, OK?' Lucy sounds anxious. 'Any time. Even if I'm away.' She pauses. 'Whatever happens, Anna, things will work out.'

'Thanks, Luce.' It's what I need to hear. 'I'm not mad, am I?'

'Don't get me started. You've been unhappy – for far too long. You and James are very different people.' Then she says something that surprises me. 'Maybe that's the reason you met Will again – to open your eyes to that.'

* * *

While I'm still in limbo, around me the landscape bursts into life as spring takes a hold, blossom festooning the trees, the roadsides adorned with a froth of cow parsley. At my laptop, I glean gems from other writers' stories to publication, taking an afternoon off to meander through Bath's stone streets, where a familiar voice calls out.

'Hey! Anna!'

Turning around, I see Hannah coming towards me, her lilac hair gathered into an unruly updo. 'Not working today?'

'Tea break.' She rolls her eyes. 'I had to get away from Meredith. I swear she's getting worse. This morning, she walked in and snapped my head off – for no reason.'

'Don't stand for it. Don't you think you need to...'

Hannah sighs. 'Look for another job? I know I do.'

Just then, Carol Madison waves at me from across the road. Crossing over, she completely ignores Hannah. 'Now, Anna. I'm rather glad I've caught you.' Flipping her hair back, as usual there are no social niceties. 'We're having a meeting – this Friday. I think it would be a good idea if you came.'

'Hannah, this is Carol. She's involved in organising the Festival.' I turn to Carol. 'Carol, I'm so glad I've seen you. Only I'm afraid I'm not going to be able to help with the Festival after all. You're going to have to find someone else.'

Carol stands there like a goldfish, opening and closing her mouth. 'You can't do this,' she says at last. 'People are relying on you.'

'I've always helped, Carol. You've given me the most tedious tasks and I've always got on with them. But not this year. Now, if you don't mind, Hannah and I were in the middle of something.'

Glancing at Hannah, I take in her look of admiration. For a split second, Carol stands there, a look of disbelief on her face, before she turns around and walks away, her heels clicking. A feeling of relief fills me. 'Don't ask,' I say to Hannah. 'Something I agreed to when I should have said no. Seriously, never do that.'

'You were awesome.' She looks slightly shocked.

'Believe me, I should have done that a long time ago.' But it feels really good, this small step forward in standing up for myself suddenly representative of so much more.

18

WILL

'Will, I've emailed you the information from the sales meeting. Could you populate the spreadsheet and fire it back when it's done? We'll need to circle back on the other points later.'

Sitting at his desk back in Glasgow, Will scarcely had time to look up and nod his approval before his boss closed himself into his shiny, glass-fronted office. Why he couldn't just fill in the spreadsheet and catch up instead of circling back, was beyond him. The joy others seemed to get from office life, particularly the current desire to replace perfectly adequate words with florid alternatives, was utterly lost on Will.

But for the most part, being thrown back into work felt good. For sure, he was struggling to share the same intensity of reactions some of his colleagues were displaying for mission critical events. But during the time he and Anna had spent together, something had happened to him. Something there was no going back from, that felt like a magical beginning.

As he thought of Anna, he felt his heart warm. Letting his mind wander, he allowed himself to imagine a different life, one with her in it, a smile crossing his face.

'You won the lottery or something, Will? Can't remember you ever smiling so much!' The passing comment came from Hacker in accounts, aptly named for the less than salubrious activities he was allegedly engaged in before he started working here. As Hacker's eyebrow rose mischievously, Will felt his face grow hot.

'I think I probably have, mate. All I have to do is claim the prize!'

Hacker laughed instinctively, giving Will a friendly slap on the back. But as he walked back to his desk, Will was already miles away, his head filled with memories of him and Anna together.

The feeling stayed with him as he left the office that evening. His day had been largely uneventful, but he was realising more and more, that sitting behind a desk was not a recipe for long-term contentment. At least he'd been able to discuss taking more time off to sort out his father's affairs. And there was no question the office had provided a benign sanctuary for Will's emotions. Even far away from Anna, his imagination danced relentlessly with the fantasy of a life with her.

The thirty-minute drive home took him from the centre of Glasgow to the quiet isolation of the Campsie Fells and the converted crofter's cottage he'd moved into when he and Darcey split up. After locking his car, Will stood there for a few minutes. It was a beautiful night, the luminous moon picking out the high hills, their silhouettes stark against the open countryside, the still, crisp air that held echoes of restless sheep.

Inside, he was changing into jeans and an old sweater when he heard a car screech to a halt on the road, followed by the sound of doors slamming. Hearing heels on the path, Will braced himself.

Opening the door, he stood back as Darcey walked in, followed by Flo.

Darcey's hair had been swept up in some elaborate updo, her cheeks flushed – from the cold or alcohol? Will hoped it was the former.

There was no hello. Just, 'Eric's expecting me to go to this dinner tonight and Flo has to be in school early tomorrow. I can't possibly take her, so you'll have to.'

'Fine with me.' Will winked at Flo. 'You should have called. I could have saved you a journey.'

Darcey ignored him. 'Is your father's house on the market yet?'

Will shook his head. 'It's going to take longer than I thought.'

'Please get it sorted, Will.' Darcey fixed her dark eyes on him. 'I need this divorce finalised. Eric wants us to start planning our wedding.'

'OK.' Will hid his shock. It was the first he'd heard of any wedding.

'I have to go.' Darcey headed for the door. 'Flo has homework. Don't let her go to bed late.' She turned to her daughter. 'I'll pick you up after school tomorrow.'

It was about as much of a goodbye as you could expect from Darcey. Closing the door behind her, as her footsteps faded, Will exhaled slowly. 'Hey.' He looked at Flo. 'I haven't fed the sheep yet. Do you fancy helping me? Then after, how about some fish and chips?'

'Cool.'

The tightness in his daughter's face tugged at Will's heart-strings. 'Come on, then.'

He pulled on a jacket and boots and Flo did the same. Closing the back door behind them, side by side they crossed the garden to the acre of paddock and outbuildings that housed half a dozen Jacob sheep.

In the moonlight, Flo's face was pale.

'You warm enough?' Will asked.

'Yeah.' She paused. 'Dad, I wish Mum wouldn't be like this. She gets so stressy about everything.'

'I know she does.' Will couldn't bear it either when Darcey was like this. As they got closer to the barn, the sheep called out. 'I think they're hungry.' They went in and the sheep jostled around, barging against his legs. It was the part of the day he loved best, out here in the dark with them – a complete antithesis to another day in the office with a load of stuffed shirts. He knew whose company he liked most.

'Look at Effie, Dad.' The smallest and tamest, Effie had her nose in Flo's pocket.

Watching Flo stroke her, he could imagine Anna here, too. Flo would like her, he was sure of it. 'Cute, isn't she? Let's get them some hay.'

After checking each of the sheep in turn, they fed them, then headed back towards the house. Inside, he took off his jacket. He looked at Flo. 'Coke?'

She nodded. 'Mum hadn't told you about the wedding, had she?' The anxious look was back.

Will sighed. 'She hadn't. But it's OK, Flo. Your mum... She's with Eric and it's fine. You know she doesn't mean half of what she says. And she deserves to be happy.'

'So do you, Dad.' Flo's worried eyes stared into his.

The anxious look made Will's heart twist. 'Don't you worry about me. Anyway, I am happy! I love being here with the sheep. Now, I'm going to put some food on, then while it cooks, maybe we should look at your homework. I'll help you if you like.'

'You won't want to. It's maths. So gross.' Flo looked disgusted.

After some maths equations that tied Will's brain in knots and Flo whizzed through, followed by fish and chips, the colour had come back to her cheeks.

'I wish I could live here. I could see Mum at weekends…' She looked at him with those big eyes Will could never resist.

'I do, too, sweetheart.' Will's heart was heavy. Darcey would never agree but he couldn't bear to see Flo so torn. 'I'll talk to your mum again – see what she says.'

* * *

As more days passed, Will was finding it increasingly hard to concentrate. He couldn't get into the rhythm of things at work. The first week, he'd held on to the belief that somehow, he and Anna would be reunited. After all, when he went back to finish clearing his dad's house, there was no reason not to see her. But as more time was passing, he felt himself torn between an uncontrollable longing to see her and an equally powerful need to be with Flo that seemed insoluble.

'You spent it all?' Hacker flopped a report on Will's desk.

'Sorry, mate. You've lost me.' Will picked up the report with two fingers as if a cat had peed on it.

'A few days ago, you looked like you'd won the lottery. Now, you look like shit.' Picking up pace again, Hacker disappeared to the other side of the office.

Will returned his gaze to his computer. Opening Google, he typed into the search bar, 'Anna Fitzpatrick Bath'. Having done it before, he knew what to expect. When the results returned 0.046 seconds later, he clicked on 'Images'. Down a few lines, he clicked on the photo of a group of women, zooming in, far left. There it was again. Just as it had been the two dozen times before, when he'd done the same thing. Anna's calm face looking straight back at him. He could have kissed the screen. In fact, he might have done just that, but Hacker was back.

'For fuck's sake, Hacker.' It was out before Will could stop himself. 'Are you an accountant, or a bloody private detective?'

'Touchy, aren't we? Anyway, you don't need to be much of a detective to work out what's eating you.' As Hacker skewed his upper body and neck sideways to get a closer look at the screen, Will lurched left to avoid the accountant's buffeting shoulder, his irritation hidden behind a smile that was forced. But his secret was safe.

'The accounts office is that way.' Will nodded towards Hacker's desk. 'Why don't you go and screw a few spreadsheets. Leave the women to me.'

Stunned by the bluntness of Will's retort, Hacker froze like a statue, no doubt trying to eradicate the image conjured by the suggestion, as he responded, 'I'll let you know how it goes.' The customary slap on Will's back was gentler than normal.

* * *

The conversation with Darcey didn't go well.

'Flo can't possibly move in with you. Her life's in Glasgow.'

'I live half an hour away, Darcey.' His patience was wearing thin. 'I can pick her up when I finish work.'

'What is she supposed to do until six? She finishes school at four.' Pointing out the bleeding obvious.

'Three days she has swimming and the other days, she could do her homework at school. A lot of her friends do.' Will was obstinate.

'It's ridiculous.' Darcey was uncompromising. 'She needs stability and routine, neither of which, frankly, you're able to offer her.'

'What about what Flo wants?' Will could feel his anger rising.

'It's one of life's lessons, isn't it?' She sounded dismissive. 'You can't always have what you want, can you?'

The conversation left Will with a sinking feeling. The fact was, with Flo's life in Glasgow, there was no way he could move to Bath. He wondered if Anna would consider moving here. When he saw her next, maybe he'd run it past her.

But it only played on his heartstrings further when that evening Will had a call from a tearful Flo.

'Dad, she told me. It isn't fair. It's not like she's even here half the time.'

Will gritted his teeth. 'I haven't given up, sweetheart.'

'I can stay late at school and do my homework there.' Flo was distraught. 'Loads of people do. And you could pick me up on your way home.'

'That's exactly what I said to her.' It was perfectly workable – if only Darcey wasn't so hot-headed. Coming in, she'd snatched Flo's phone from her.

'Will, this isn't helpful. All you're doing is making it harder for everyone.'

'We're not done with this, Darcey. And I'm quite sure when you and Eric want to go away next, you won't think twice about Flo's whereabouts.' Not for the first time, Will wondered how on earth he'd got embroiled in this. But this difficult, controlling Darcey bore no resemblance to the woman he'd fallen in love with.

'My mother's coming to stay.' Darcey spoke coolly. 'In fact, we're thinking about asking her to live with us.'

Will felt the breath knocked out of him. While the presence of Darcey's mother was good where Flo was concerned, it would only strengthen Darcey's case. If he wanted Flo to live with him, it was time he sought legal advice. 'This isn't over, Darcey. I'm going to speak to a lawyer. I'll be in touch.' Angry, Will hung up.

* * *

The following morning, far from diminishing, his turmoil was escalating. He'd already made an appointment to see a lawyer. Meanwhile, knowing he'd be going back to Bath at some point, the thought of Anna was ever-present.

At work, Will was one of six people sitting around the oval table in his boss's glass-fronted office that looked out across the open layout of desks.

'And if we drill down further into the data, we can see exactly where we need to monetise the eyeballs.' Will studied his boss's back, watching him rhapsodise over his projected wallcharts with passionate efficiency. He had no idea how anyone could be so interested in this mind-numbing shit. He nodded dutifully towards his boss with practised sincerity, his eyes scanning the technicolour graphs, his mind filled with Anna.

As the meeting ground interminably on, Will's eyelids began to feel impossibly heavy. The increasingly sleepless nights were catching up with him. Trying his best to show proportionate reactions to subjects like Trojan horse sales approaches and cross-silo verticals, he was losing the battle as his phone, on silent, buzzed in his pocket. Jolted into life, he took the phone and placed it in his lap, out of view of the others. On the screen, he could see the first line of a message.

Hey, Will, I miss you...

His heart skipped a beat as instantly he was wide awake again. Looking up, as his boss's eyes rested on him, Will assumed an expression of focus, as suddenly cross-silo verticals had never looked so interesting.

* * *

With Darcey back from her latest set of outings, Will had flown from Glasgow to Bristol that morning, picking up a hire car and reaching Dyrham twenty minutes early. As he re-read Anna's message for the hundredth time, in spite of his concerns about Flo, he couldn't stop smiling.

Hey, Will, I miss you! Anna xx

Compared to the nonsensical mumbo-jumbo he faced at work, it struck him just how powerful words could truly be, like these words that had brought him back to a lane on the edge of Dyrham Park.

While he waited, Will was warm with unstoppable butterflies as he distracted himself by playing with all the toys that came with a brand-new car. Panoramic sunroof, open fully, shut, half open. Music on and loud. Air con, fan up full, blowing cold air into his face and forcing his hair back. He angled the rear-view mirror to check his look, before turning his attention to the impressive panel of dashboard buttons, pressing randomly to see what came to life. He played with the satnav but gave up when it failed to display his current location. But he was off the beaten track in more ways than one, nervous and excited, all at once.

As Flo came into his head, guilt struck him as he thought of those eyes that were so like his. Her determination, thwarted by her mother at every turn, when Flo was old enough to know her own mind. With every battle, Darcey was damaging her relationship with her daughter. Before he left, he'd tried to talk to her again about Flo moving to his, but it had triggered yet another completely irrational outburst, the strength and passion that he used to find attractive now nothing but a nightmare.

Returning the dashboard controls to their original settings, Will summoned the contrived dignity a pilot might display shutting down cockpit systems at the end of a long-haul flight. He felt a thrill of excitement as he read Anna's message again. Then he checked his watch. Checked the mirror. Took a deep breath and got out.

In the warmth of the spring sunshine, the cable knit jumper he was wearing wasn't going to need a jacket. After the crowded airport and heavy traffic on the drive here, he felt the peacefulness soak into him. Leaning against a tree, he waited, longing to see Anna – he didn't question that. But beyond today, tomorrow... Right now, Will didn't know what the future held, just that he wanted her in it.

As her car came into sight, he felt his heart lift. By the time she'd parked and let her dog out, he was already walking to meet her. Then he was holding her, completely motionless as the magic was back. Will didn't want to let her go. Not ever.

19

ANNA

'I'm so happy to see you.' As we stand there, our arms wrapped around each other, Will speaks quietly into my hair.

Closing my eyes, I lean into the warmth of him, surrendering to a sense of peacefulness that's been missing since he left. 'It's been so long. I was starting to wonder if I'd see you again.'

'I was always coming back.'

Pulling away, as Will takes my hand the atmosphere around us is heightened somehow. Then as we start walking, the last time we were together feels like yesterday. 'How long are you staying?'

'Two weeks – hopefully more than enough time to do what I need to.'

I feel a weight lift, a sense of freedom. Two weeks sounds like forever.

'I've missed all this. I've missed you!' He sounds happy.

'I missed you, too!' I'd worried it would be awkward between us, but it isn't. It's gloriously easy.

Will's hand tightens around mine. 'I've thought so much about you – about us. With everything else that's going on, I thought maybe some space would be good for both of us.' A shadow crosses his face. 'And it hasn't been easy with Darcey and Flo.'

I frown slightly. 'Oh? Tell me.'

He sighs. 'It's hard to know where to start. In a nutshell, Flo wants to live with me, but Darcey isn't having any of it.'

'Why not? Shouldn't Flo be able to spend equal time with both of you?'

But Will shakes his head. 'That's exactly how it should be – especially given how often Darcey's away. But there's nothing rational about any of this. It's about control.'

It's obvious he's worried about it. 'Sounds like you need a lawyer.'

'I have one. But in the middle of it all, there's Flo.' Will looks wretched. 'She's thirteen and I'm trying to protect her, but here I am, hundreds of miles away.'

'You were always going to have to finish with the house.' Seeing how torn he is, I try to be objective, but as I know too well, it isn't always that simple. 'If you ask me, Darcey sounds incredibly selfish. You'd think she'd care more about what Flo wants.'

'You would, wouldn't you? But Darcey wants what Darcey wants. It's always been the same.' Will adds more gently, 'So that's me. I'm guessing things probably aren't easy for you, either.'

I feel myself tighten. 'It's been pretty stressful.' Will leaving, the spiralling decay of my marriage, all adding to the strain I'm under.

'I can imagine,' he says quietly. 'How are things with James?'

I'm quiet for a moment. 'Falling apart, if I'm honest. I just have to find the courage to talk to him.'

Will looks stunned. 'So nothing's changed.'

'Not really. When I've found somewhere to live, I'll move out.' My voice wavers as I think about what lies ahead. 'I feel terrible – most of the time. I just have to believe I'll get through this.'

'It isn't easy.' Will's voice is sober. 'When I moved out and left Flo with her mother, it felt like ripping my heart out.'

It's exactly how it feels. 'I've really tried,' I tell him. 'I was going through old photos, trying to remember how I used to feel about James. But it isn't just me who's changed. He has, too.'

'I know how that one goes,' Will says wryly. 'Since Darcey met Eric, I've seen a whole different, ruthless side of her.'

'It's hard to describe what it is about James.' I'm quiet for a moment. 'He just seems completely closed off from me.'

As we emerge from under the trees, the daylight's starting to fade. As Will gazes around, an expression of joy crosses his face, before he makes a pretence of bowing then grabs my hands. 'We have about half an hour before the sun goes down. May I have this dance?'

In spite of everything, it's impossible not to laugh at him. I pretend to curtsey. 'But of course.'

Letting go of one my hands, he twirls me around, faster, as the sun sinks lower, shades of rich ochre intensifying, fanning out against the ice blue sky. I start laughing again and he joins in, before pulling me close, humming in my ear as we start to waltz.

As we make our way back, any remaining barriers between us melt away. 'I don't know how we're going to make this work, but I want to see you tomorrow, and the next day, and the one after,' Will murmurs. 'Are you free in the morning?'

I imagine walking under the trees watching the sun rise beside him; knowing there's nowhere else I'd rather be.

'Yes,' I whisper, before reaching up to kiss him.

MAY 2005

ANNA

Extending my fingers, I gazed at the ring on my left hand. A solitaire diamond set in platinum, it was bigger than anything I would have chosen for myself, but I was growing used to it surprisingly quickly.

'Bloody stunning ring, I'll give him that much.' Lucy stared at my hand.

'James chose it.' There was pride in my voice as I turned it slightly, catching the light. I couldn't think of anyone else I'd been out with who would have chosen something that was both ostentatious yet so utterly conventional, but then marriage was a convention, wasn't it? A convention set amongst many others that kept relationships and society running smoothly.

Never lost for words, Lucy's silence was out of character, taking me aback as she took hold of my hands, clasping them in hers. 'Anna? You are sure about this, aren't you?'

I pulled my hands away. 'Of course I am.' I couldn't believe my best friend was questioning the biggest decision I'd ever made. But it was out of love, I did know that. My voice softened as I reassured her. 'Life's changed, Luce, since being ill. James gives me what I need. I am sure.'

'Well, that's all I wanted to know.' But she didn't sound convinced.

Suddenly I realised, Lucy had doubts. I'd been intending to ask her something important, but now, I wasn't so sure. Summoning my courage, I took a deep breath, needing to know. 'Luce...' I paused. 'Would you be my bridesmaid?'

Before this conversation, I'd imagined her reacting with delight, but her expression was wistful. 'Oh, Anna... I'd be honoured.'

I was waiting for the but. Only when I was sure it wasn't coming, did relief flow over me, as at last, her face lit up. 'It's wonderful, hun. Just don't make me wear pink, for fuck's sake.'

'Deal.' Jumping up, I hugged her. 'I'm getting us a drink! Same again?'

'No way are you paying! Stay there. I'm getting these.' Sounding more like the old Lucy, I watched her make her way towards the bar where she looked through the wine list before coming back a few minutes later with a bottle of champagne and two flutes. After pouring the champagne, she offered me one, then raised her glass. 'To you and James! I'm thrilled for you both – I really am!'

As the champagne's nutty taste and dry fizz danced in my mouth, I started to believe her.

But with my wedding just months away, I was shocked to feel goosebumps when I glanced through the window just as Will walked past the pub, guilt flooding over me as silently I berated myself, before forcing myself to rationalise it. Marrying James didn't mean I'd never be attracted to anyone else. And as I'd said to Lucy, everything was different since my illness.

'Anna? Are you all right? You're miles away.' Lucy's words broke into my thoughts.

Blinking, her face came into focus. 'Sorry. I'm fine! I was just thinking about something.'

The furrow on Lucy's forehead deepened. 'You are sure, aren't you? I mean, you and James? It's the biggest decision of your life. If you're having second thoughts, far better to say so now.'

I shook my head. 'I'm really not.' Looking up, I met her eyes. 'Honestly! It's what I want.' But there was a tiny part of me that wasn't sure. Not 100 per cent, except I could hardly tell Lucy that. Nor could I tell her I still thought about Will.

'I love James. And I absolutely know it's going to work.' There was all the conviction I could muster in my words, but my smile was half-wattage.

'As long as you're sure...' Lucy scrutinised my face, but then her expression changed. 'Look, we should go away together before you tie the knot.' Her voice filled with excitement. 'It could be your hen weekend! I can easily get some time off. Somewhere near the sea – and hot. Why ever shouldn't we? It's been a crap summer. I swear, one day, I'm moving away for good.' Unlike mine, Lucy's adventurous streak had stayed strong. 'Do you ever think about it?' When I didn't reply, she reached across the table towards me, clasping my hands again. 'Just answer me this. When you could live anywhere in the world, why would you choose to stay here?'

'Family?' I offered. 'My life's here, Luce. James's too.' Remembering the dream I used to have of living somewhere the sun shines, as I brought it to mind, I felt it fade.

'It's a tiny part of a very big, lovely world,' Lucy reminded me, as in a day that seemed full of them, I ignored another flicker of discomfort.

'We should finish this.' Lucy picked up the bottle to top up our glasses.

Thinking of James's views on drinking, I hesitated. But then James wasn't here. 'Why not?'

Lucy got up. 'I'm starving. Shall we order pizza?'

I watched her go over to the bar. When she came back, I changed the subject. 'So, if we're going away, do you have any idea where?'

'I have the best idea.' Lucy's eyes twinkled. 'My aunt's finca – in Ibiza.'

Before Lucy had told me about her aunt's house in the countryside, all I knew about Ibiza were the bars and clubs and hordes of drunk British tourists, which might have been my scene once, but not now. Lucy went on. 'There's a small bar up the road and it's a five-minute walk to the beach. My aunt's rarely there and she's always trying to persuade me to use it. Seriously, Anna. It's heaven there! And it's free! You can't say no!'

I imagined myself and Lucy sitting on white sand, the sun on our skin as we gazed out across the sea. A rush of excitement filled me. 'When can we go?'

20

ANNA

I slip out early before James stirs, hoping that by the time he's back from a day of golf, he'll have forgotten I wasn't there when he woke up. As I drive away from the house, the city is quiet, my mind anything but.

When I reach Dyrham Park, Will is already there, his car parked with the door slightly open. Pulling up and letting Yippy out, as I walk towards him, his face lights up.

'I brought breakfast!' Getting out of his car, he looks pleased with himself and I notice the rucksack slung over his shoulder.

As we walk towards the footpath, around us the air is still, the dawn chorus a full-on orchestra. Will stops, turning to watch the first rays of sun as it rises behind the trees, reaching into a pocket for his phone.

But as he takes a photograph, I don't need a camera to capture the moment. The warmth of his eyes, the silhouetted branches, the peacefulness, are imprinted indelibly in my mind.

Putting his phone away, he turns to look at me. 'It's crazy how much I've missed you.'

Wanting to tell him I feel the same, I thread my arm through his. 'Come on. Let's walk.'

As we carry on up the path, I breathe in more perfect moments – the low sunlight, the sound of the birds, the coolness of the air; the layer of mist that lingers. Walking further, we find the same fallen tree we've sat on before.

Will gets a flask of coffee out of his rucksack. 'Not exactly the Italian place I told you about, but our first meal together!' He looks proud for a moment. 'I made Marmite sandwiches. Not my idea... I met this elderly couple up here once, when I was a teenager. They said they came here every Saturday morning with coffee and marmalade sandwiches.' He hesitates. 'Um, I don't even know if you like Marmite. I didn't have any marmalade...' Suddenly apologetic, he looks around. 'It's fine if you don't. Maybe the sheep will eat them?'

Laughing, I take the coffee he passes me, then one of the sandwiches. 'Marmite's good!'

He beams happily. 'A few weeks ago, I never could have imagined this.'

'Me neither.' I sip my coffee. 'But I can't help thinking that if there's some grand plan to our lives, whatever there is between us is unfinished in some way.'

Will sounds surprised. 'You really think that?'

I meet his eyes. 'Honestly? I don't know anything any more. Remember those messages from the universe I used to tell you about? I had another last night. *This is my time.* What if it is?'

Will gives me a look of amazement. 'So you think being up here eating Marmite sandwiches with me is where you're meant to be?'

'Maybe it's part of it!' In spite of myself, I laugh. 'I mean, since I found you trying to catch that lamb, my entire life has been shaken up. I used to think I had a rough idea of how it would work out – I'd get married, have children, live happily ever after...' Suddenly my eyes are filled with tears. 'James seems to have everything he needs. The big house, his impressive job and snobby friends... It was my life too – but it hasn't made me happy.' A tear rolls down my cheek.

'Don't cry.' He gently wipes it away. 'I know what you mean. I spend my days surrounded by corporate bullshitters who'd say anything to anyone to get what they want. And you might think I'm exaggerating, but I'm not.'

'It's not your world,' I tell him. 'You're not like that. There's more for you.'

He's quiet for a moment. 'I like to think so.' He pauses again. 'Maybe one day, I'll do something I can feel proud of. But for now...' He shrugs. 'My job pays the bills and I have Flo to think of.'

'Do you have much left to do at your dad's house?'

A look of uncertainty crosses his face. 'I need to finish the painting and there's furniture to get rid of.'

My heart sinks slightly. Even though he's just arrived, it isn't going to keep him here for long.

* * *

Back home, my day takes another turn when that afternoon, there's a knock on the door. When I open it, Grace, my neighbour is standing there. In a thin dress and slippers, her usually neatly pinned-back hair is untidy, her face is distraught. When she clutches at my arm, I'm worried.

'Come inside, Grace.' I help her inside, noticing her shiver. 'You'll freeze, dressed that like that. Where's Ron?'

But her eyes are terrified. 'You have to come.'

I grab my jacket and drape it over her shoulders, before

hurrying next door as fast as I dare with Grace holding on to my arm. Their front door is open and she takes me through to their sitting room.

Lying on the carpet, Ron's body is twisted at an awkward angle. Seeing me, he tries to move. 'Anna... I'll be all right in a minute.' But his voice is faint, his colour terrible. Unfolding the blanket left neatly on one of the armchairs, I place it over him before getting up.

'Don't move, Ron. I'm calling an ambulance.' Cursing that I haven't brought my mobile with me, I glance around the room and see their phone. After dialling 999 and telling them about Ron, I search for their daughter's number in the address book on the side, then call her. When she doesn't pick up, I leave a message, then sit with them until the ambulance arrives.

After checking Ron over, the paramedics lift him onto a stretcher and take him to hospital. Knowing Grace can't be left alone, after we watch them drive away, I help her back inside, following her upstairs where I suggest we pack a few things to take to the hospital for Ron. Their bedroom smells of lavender and talcum powder and she's remarkably calm as she goes to their wardrobe. Looking around, it's as though I've been transported to another era, of dated flock wallpaper and faded velvet curtains framing the sash windows, a collection of old photos in silver frames charting their story from their earliest meeting to present day, happiness never far from their eyes.

Seeing Grace struggle to fold some pyjamas for Ron, I go to help her. 'I hope you don't mind. I was just looking at your photos. How old were you when you met Ron?'

As I fold the shirt of Ron's she passes me, a ghost of a smile lights her lined face. 'He wasn't my first husband,' she says in hushed tones, conspiratorial as she turns the wedding band on her finger. 'He was a cruel man. I met Ron after we were married.

Kept seeing him everywhere. He said it was happenstance, but I don't believe in that for one minute. It was destiny.' The light in her eyes briefly dims, before she goes on. 'Ron and I have been so happy.'

Tears prick my eyes. Then she surprises me. 'Don't settle, Anna.' She's oddly focused as she looks at me. 'Lots of people will tell you marriage is for keeps, but it doesn't always work out like that. When you find the kind of love Ron and I have, it isn't right to turn your back on it.'

Her face blurs in front of me as she takes my hands in both of hers. 'Take me to be with Ron.'

* * *

An hour later, while I'm waiting with Grace and Ron in a small cubicle in A & E, a nurse pulls the curtain back and shows their daughter in. After giving her my number and asking her to let me know what happens, I slip away, still thinking about what Grace said earlier. When she left her first husband, divorce would have been unheard of. That she did it is a measure not just of how brave she was, but of her love for Ron.

I'm still preoccupied that evening when James comes in. He barely looks at me.

'Hi. Dinner's in the oven. How was golf?'

He's silent for a moment. 'Not bad.'

'I've been at the hospital... Ron had a fall. An ambulance took him to A & E.'

'Best place for him. I assume their daughter turned up,' James says dismissively. 'Where were you this morning?'

That he can be so uncaring flabbergasts me. 'I couldn't sleep. I got up early and went for a walk.'

'For a few hours?' He stares at me.

Silent, I wonder if this is it – the moment I tell him. But I hold back, because I don't have anywhere to go. 'Yes, James. I knew you weren't going to be here because every Saturday without exception, you play golf.' Even though it's the truth, I can't look at him. 'I didn't know you were keeping tabs on me.' Hot all of a sudden, as I get up and walk through to the kitchen, I know I can't go on like this.

21

WILL

The following morning, after making a pot of coffee, Will checked his phone and read the predictable text from Darcey, nagging him about this and that, none of which was important. Ignoring it, he texted Flo.

You OK? How was swimming practice? Xx

She got straight back to him.

Hey, Dad, really good. We're competing next month. Are you coming?

Typically Flo, she followed it with a row of hearts alternating with sheep emojis.

Count on it x

No way was Will missing it.

Whistling as he started painting the house, the radio turned up loud, his head was filled with daydreams of another life, one with Anna in it.

The thing was they were becoming less like dreams, more real. He wanted Flo to meet her – Anna would be such a positive presence in her life. He wanted to travel the world with her. Take her to Baltimore; go on a fishing trip with old Mad Mac O'Riley, who could make even the fish laugh. He imagined gigging again, with Anna sitting at the front listening; to be sharing a home with her, where she sat writing her book in one of her oversized jumpers, while he'd play music with the same freedom he used to have.

As he thought about asking her if she'd move to Glasgow, he wondered if it was too soon. How would he tell Flo? *There's someone I want you to meet... Flo, this is Anna...We knew each other when we were teenagers...* OK. So it might be awkward at first, but they'd soon get over that. Smiling to himself, he imagined a whole new future opening up.

* * *

At the park, as he watched Anna walk towards him, Will felt his heart sing.

'Hello,' he said softly.

'Hi.' Her eyes turned to follow the flurry of her mad dog doing his usual bonkers racing between the trees.

He took her hand. 'You look lovely.' He meant it. Her hair clipped back, she was wearing faded jeans and one of her shapeless sweaters – a dark blue one. But it wasn't about her clothes. It was about the brightness of her eyes, the sense of calm she radiated.

'Thank you...' An anxious look appeared on her face. 'One of my neighbours had a fall yesterday. He's still in hospital. If he's broken a hip, I've no idea what will happen to them.'

'What about his wife?' He remembered Anna talking about them before.

'She can't manage on her own. Their daughter's staying for a while, but I don't know what happens after that.' She shook her head. 'While I was helping pack a few things for Ron, Grace said something to me. She said that she knew marriage was for keeps, but it didn't always work out that way – I hadn't realised before, but this is her second marriage. It was like she knew something was wrong between me and James. Then she told me not to settle.' Anna frowned slightly. 'She's never said anything like that before.'

'Maybe she's seen you together.' Will frowned.

'I don't know, but it made me think.' She was quiet for a moment. 'It's like everywhere I look, there are signs. What Grace said about settling was another.' Her eyes were wide as she looked at him. 'I have to talk to James. Things are changing.'

Will could feel it, too – change, as a tangible entity. As they turned onto the path across the fields, there was the sudden whistle of a slipstream as a glider flew past.

'It's a sign.' Glancing at the glider, Anna was teasing him. 'The universe is going to keep reminding you until you fulfil that childhood dream of yours.'

'You think?' Will watched uncertainly as the glider pulled up steeply, before banking right and fading into the layer of haze. 'Anyway, I've ditched the dream. They look a whole lot flimsier than I remember.' But there was something else on his mind – something he still hadn't told her.

'There's something you don't know.' He hesitated. 'When I came back from Australia, I found out where you were working and came to find you. I stood outside your office, waiting for you to come out. When I saw you, you smiled. It was the moment I'd been imagining… But then I realised it wasn't at me. I'm guessing it was James.' All these years later, he could still remember how he'd felt.

Anna turned shocked eyes to his. 'But I didn't see you.'

Will froze. 'Would it have made a difference?'

Anna's eyes were fixed on his. 'Maybe.'

Pulling her close, he put his arms around her. 'I love you, Anna. I want to go to sleep with you, wake up with you, go on dates with you, get old with you… I want to be with you.'

She held a finger to his lips. 'Will. I know…'

Will felt his heart start to hammer. 'I'm going to be divorced before long. And when you leave James… Is there anything to stop us being together?'

She raised an eyebrow. 'You mean, proper out-there actually being together?'

'Actual dating – going out.' He was getting into his stride. 'We can go to that Italian restaurant… Or eat fish and chips by the sea. We'll have to work around Flo's life, but we can do that, can't we?' Feeling himself getting carried away; stopping short of asking her about moving to Glasgow.

'*Yes.*' Anna's eyes glowed.

A warm feeling came over him as he imagined them having time, rather than snatching moments here and there. But everything about this felt so right.

As they reached the lane, Anna turned to him. 'Are you doing anything tomorrow?'

'Other than painting and meeting this gorgeous woman I've fallen in love with…' Will hesitated. 'Not much.'

Anna pushed her hair out of her eyes. 'You know, I'm really quite good with a paintbrush…'

A smile plastered itself across his face. 'I'll let you use the best one.' He paused. 'Call me in the morning?'

* * *

Back home, Will had pulled on old clothes and carried on painting, excitement filling him as he thought about tomorrow. Whistling to himself, he finished another wall. But as he put his paint brush down, he was suddenly restless.

Changing again, Will got in his car and drove to Bath. Wandering the streets, he headed for the Stonemasons. Ordering a half, he sat at one of the tables, thinking how it wasn't the same in here any more; silently reminiscing about the old days, when his mum had been alive; when life had been simple. Before he and Simon had been uprooted, after which an aching loneliness had filled him. But it made no difference where in the world you were. It was all about sharing it with the people you love.

22

ANNA

As I drive home, I'm unsettled. It's finding out Will came to find me when he came back from Australia. If only I'd known; if I'd seen him and we'd spoken, maybe I would have ended it with James. Maybe my whole life could have been so different.

When our timing in the past has been so out, I feel a rush of excitement that after all these years, we have a chance together. But it's followed by a sense of trepidation because what I need to do first is to move out. I try to picture myself, one month from today, in a quiet little place, imagining somewhere that could feel like home; somewhere, maybe Will and I could be together.

Knowing what I have to do, a new sense of resolve fills me as I prepare myself to talk to James. When I've given us time, when I have no doubts about what I'm doing, there seems no point in dragging this out.

Back home, I get out my laptop and start searching for a house – a small one, with a spare room for Millie, firing off an email enquiry, before looking for another.

Sitting back, I think about what I'm going to say to James. Usually he's home sometime around seven. As I imagine how angry he'll be, my stomach churns nervously. But though this isn't going to be easy, it's no reason to put it off. Whatever he says, he must have noticed the distance between us. When we're not getting any younger, none of us have time to waste. Anyway, life isn't about the future. It's about now.

Glancing at the clock again, I get up and make a cup of tea. Then, sitting at the kitchen table, I wait.

JULY 2011

ANNA

The monotony of my daily routine was broken by the sparkle of Millie's presence for a couple of days. I held on to our hours together, feeling a happiness in her company that made the truth about my marriage all the more obvious. It's a happiness that ebbed away when her mother came to pick her up, leaving me to face the midsummer party Lucy wanted me to go to with her.

'Why don't you come?' I gazed at my husband.

'I've got better things to do than spend an evening in the pub.'

'But they're our friends, James,' I tried to persuade him. 'They'd love to see you.' Maybe 'love' was a bit strong, but it would have been nice to be doing this as a couple.

'They're not my friends, Anna. They're yours.' Settling onto the sofa, James picked up the newspaper. 'I have absolutely nothing in common with any of them.'

As the words sat there, I acknowledged this other side to my husband. His arrogance; the absence of empathy; the way he didn't consider anyone else, all of them traits I didn't like. Several times I'd found myself questioning whether we had a future together, but loyalty, habit and familiarity had always held me back; the wrong reasons, when I should be with him because of love.

After the exchange with James lowered my mood, a party was the last place I wanted to be – in a perfect world, I'd have met Lucy for a quick drink and she'd have gone on without me. Searching through my wardrobe, under a threadbare cardigan, I found an old dress I'd forgotten about. Pulling it out, I held it up. It was black, short and too tight, the kind of thing I stopped wearing when I married James. On impulse, I slid out of my clothes and tried it on.

To my astonishment, it wasn't tight at all. As I stood in front of the mirror looking at myself, a memory of a very different Anna came rushing back, one who lived and laughed, whose eyes were full of light – a light that went out a long time ago.

God. I looked so bloody old. Then I remembered the make-up Millie had left me. If I used enough, just maybe, it would help.

In the crowded pub, the dress felt shabby, the make-up too obvious.

'Anna, you look fucking stunning, babe!' Even the look on Lucy's face didn't make me feel any better. 'Come on... The others are over here. That dress! I can't believe how amazing you look! I wish I'd seen James's face...'

But James had barely looked at me.

Grabbing my arm, Lucy carried on talking. 'I told Charley we'd wait for her.'

Pinning on a smile, I tried to lighten up and enjoy the evening, but in spite of the wine I was drinking, my spirits were low. When Charley arrived a while later, on her own, they sank even lower. Her eyes glowing, she was a living, breathing reminder of what happiness looked like. Fuck it... I swallowed another glass of wine; behind my brightest smile and forced laughter, hid the fact that inside, I felt desolate.

A feeling I couldn't describe descended over me as we left the pub and walked through the town, then up the narrow lane that led to the entrance to the Fergusons' massive old farmhouse.

Distant music reached my ears. This walk on this starlit night would have been so romantic – if only things were different; if I was walking with someone I really loved, who loved me as much. In a flash, it came to me in stark black and white, as we turned up the drive towards the house. That person never was, never would be James.

As I admitted it to myself, the revelation shocked me. Then as we reached the front door, the music from inside grew louder. Going in, it was like stepping into a parallel universe, one filled with love, life and laughter, in which there was no place for the Jameses of the world. On a table, there was a huge arrangement of tumbling flowers, while ahead of me, the curved staircase was swathed in fairy lights.

Suddenly I recognised the music. Pulled towards it, my eyes scanned the faces of the band, my cheeks burning red as I saw him. Will. Shrinking back, I watched him play, taking in his blue guitar, how absorbed in the music he was, how happy he looked. A feeling of wistfulness came over me.

Transfixed, I didn't notice Lucy beside me. 'I didn't know Will would be here.' Lucy's voice was sober. 'You OK?'

I shrugged. 'Not really.' Seeing him had reminded me how happy I used to feel. Happiness that had been eroded by so many things. 'I don't think I can talk to him, Luce.' I was too scared of what it would do to me.

I lurked at the back, staying out of sight – or so I thought – as the band started up for one last song. It was poignant, with a guitar solo that made the hairs on the back of my neck prickle, as for a moment, I imagined Will playing it to me. Lost in the music, as he reached the end, he looked over at me and our eyes met.

Suddenly, I got a hold of myself. This was insane. Tearing myself away, I looked for Lucy, but as I went through to the kitchen, I walked straight into someone.

'Sorry.' Feeling the coldness of a drink soaking into me, I took in the embarrassed face of a young man I'd never seen before. While he apolo-

gised profusely and clumsily grabbed a cloth to mop up what he'd spilt, I stood there trying to dry my dress, before quickly I went to find Lucy.

'I have to go, Luce.'

Her face was troubled. 'I'll come with you.'

'No. You stay. I could do with the walk.' Turning, I walked towards the door, desperate to get away. I didn't belong in there. Right now, I didn't belong anywhere.

* * *

At home in bed, I closed my eyes, tuning out James's snores, conjuring Will's face. If I'd stayed... If we'd talked... I knew it would have triggered the same feelings I used to have. Far better to do what I did and walk away.

But as I stared at James's back, I was wide awake all of a sudden, the same restlessness I'd felt earlier back. I knew I shouldn't be having feelings like these, but I couldn't go on denying the truth. James wasn't the man who made my heart sing. If I was honest with myself, he never had been.

23

WILL

It was still early when Will awoke the next day. As he lay in bed, the house was silent and his mind filled with thoughts of Anna and the prospect of her coming here. Glorious, dizzying thoughts that swept everything else out of his head. Trying to distract himself, he focused on the thin strands of light behind the heavy curtains. But the diversion was momentary. Thoughts of Anna were dominating. Would she actually come here or would sanity prevail, keeping her away?

Feeling his doubts seep back like floodwater, Will sat up, running his fingers through his hair. 'For Christ's sake, I love her!' He said it out loud, trying to snap himself into action. '*I love her, I love her, I love her...*' As he started singing the words to a nondescript tune, Will was joyous, throwing the duvet back, singing anything that entered his head as the nervous uncertainty he'd woken up with evaporated, leaving him happier with every tuneless line.

Opening the curtains, he gazed outside, listening to the distant sound of horses' hooves trotting up the lane on an early morning hack in the spring sunshine. Waiting for Anna to call, by eight fifteen, Will had already showered and was downstairs straightening cushions he'd already straightened several times, before going outside and picking a handful of daffodils. As he put them in a jug on the dining room table, inspiration struck him. If he couldn't take her out on a date, he'd do his best to invent a make-believe one, right here.

After setting the table with the best knives and forks, he'd found the same crystal glasses he remembered from his childhood. As he added the finishing touches, his phone buzzed with a text.

With twenty minutes to kill before she arrived, Will straightened the cushions again, before hurrying upstairs to change his dark jeans to the lighter ones, before changing back again. Did the leather boots look better or his trainers? Suddenly the blue shirt he'd been happy with all morning made him look five months pregnant. The light pink one was kinder. *Oh shit.* He looked at the clothes strewn across the bed and settled on the dark jeans, light blue shirt and trainers he'd started with, before shoving the rest into the chest of drawers and heading back downstairs, halfway down glimpsing Anna's car pulling into the drive.

Trying to play it cool, Will waited in the kitchen for what seemed like forever, until he'd convinced himself that she'd had second thoughts and driven away. There was only one way to know. Opening the front door, he found himself face to face with her, her finger raised to press the doorbell.

'Impeccable timing!' Her face lit up in a smile.

Relief flooded through him as he pretended to shrug, holding his arms up. *What else could she expect from a genius?* 'Come in, come in.' Standing back, he held the door open. As she walked past him, Will noticed her dark grey top that skimmed her hips, skinny jeans the perfect shade of faded, with heart-shaped orange stitching on the back pockets, her dark hair glossy and loosely tied back so that strands escaped. All this and more, in less than a second.

'You look beautiful.' The words came out without him intending. But she did. So did everything suddenly, in this dusty old house with all its history, the shabby sofas, the sun streaming through the window. Everything looked different with Anna here.

'Thank you.' She was nervous, Will could tell. 'Nice shirt.'

'This?' Will tried to look nonchalant. 'It was the first thing I grabbed out of the wardrobe.'

In the kitchen, as he made a pot of coffee, already he was thinking how if they were together, it could be like this, every day.

Anna followed him into the kitchen. 'I've decided to tell James I'm leaving.'

Will froze. Given what she'd just told him, she looked remarkably calm.

She went on. 'I was going to do it last night. But he'd forgotten to tell me he was out all evening. I was asleep by the time he came in. Then this morning, he went out early – bloody golf. Hopefully I'll talk to him later.' She glanced towards the photos. 'Is this you?' She held up a photo of a chubby toddler.

''Fraid so.' Will hung his head. 'Coffee?'

'Please!' She picked up another photo. 'This is you with Simon?'

He looked more closely at it. He had a thing about old photos, couldn't bring himself to get rid of them. 'That's us. I'm the good-looking one,' he quipped.

Anna picked up another, studying it. 'Your father was lucky,' Anna said quietly. 'That you didn't disappear out of his life for good. And that you came back when he needed you.'

Will shrugged. 'Even sad old gits need someone.' He changed

the subject. 'Normally, I'd suggest going out for lunch. But I, er, improvised.' He nodded towards the dining room.

'Oh?' Anna looked pleased. 'Through there?'

'You can have a look, if you want to!' He followed her over to the door, slightly proud of himself. He'd even found a few candles and got the wood burner ready to light, not that it was dark. The spring sunshine was pouring in.

Standing in the doorway, she peered through. 'It's lovely, Will.'

Beside her, he was close enough to smell her perfume, see the curl of her eyelashes against her skin. Skin he suddenly wanted to touch. The coffee forgotten, Will took her hand, then silently led her upstairs.

24

ANNA

After. A memory of crumpled sheets, of skin on skin I can't unlearn, of limbs interwoven with mine, a body that's instantly familiar to me.

'That day... With the escaped lamb...' As we lie there, I trace the line of his cheekbone with one of my fingers. 'After all those times before, I couldn't believe it was you.'

Will rolls over. 'I couldn't, either.' His eyes don't leave mine. '*I love you, Anna.*'

'I love you, too.' *I've always loved you*, I want to add, as, unable to speak, I soak up every detail of this moment, adding it to all the others, knowing this is what I want. Always.

* * *

When we go downstairs, Will picks up the pot of coffee he made earlier that's gone cold. 'I'll make some more.' He says it quietly, kissing me again before heading for the kitchen. Through the doorway, I watch him move around, dishevelled, his hair ruffled, oblivious to his undone shirt buttons, a man happy in his own skin.

As he comes back in carrying a small tray, he's whistling. 'I'll start cooking lunch in a minute. When I say cook, I'm not the best chef but I have one signature dish.' Placing the tray on the coffee table, he grabs one of my hands, pulling me close to him. 'Do you have any idea how you make me feel?'

My heart's racing as I look into his eyes.

'Wind-blown. Like my whole life is being shaken. My roots pulled up. You, Anna Fitzpatrick, have changed everything.'

'Ditto,' I say softly. 'You and me, Will... I didn't know it was possible to feel like this.'

'Me neither.' He pauses. 'We need to talk, don't we, about what comes next?'

'I want this. Us,' I tell him. 'The talking, the loving, the dreams – the feeling of freedom.'

'I have to think of Flo.' His eyes flicker. 'I need to be around, at least while she's in school. Obviously, her life's in Glasgow.' He pauses. 'I had this thought...'

'Yes?'

He looks uncertain. 'I was thinking... I know you have a life here, but would you think about moving to Glasgow? Just until Flo's older? It might just be weekends, at first. Let Flo get used to us...' He watches me. 'If you're OK with that?'

My heart flips over. It's a moment I never thought would come. Clasping his hand in both of mine, I know we can work this out. 'Of course I am. It's important that Flo's OK with us.'

And we have time.

***

After lighting the wood burner and pouring us each a glass of wine, Will carries in a seafood pasta dish, which he serves with exaggerated panache.

It's garlicky and creamy, flecked with prawns. 'You have hidden talents. This...' I say through a mouthful of food, '... is seriously good.'

He looks pleased. 'It's not bad, is it?'

'I have another place for our list,' I tell him, winding more pasta onto my fork. 'Cornwall... Think craggy rocks and secret beaches and coast path walks. Rain, too – just like Ireland. And daffodils.' I glance at the jug on the table, amazed that he's thought about flowers. 'We could take Flo – and Millie! You'd love it!'

'I would.' He tops up our glasses. 'We must go to Italy, too.'

'I wanted to go to Venice last year, for my birthday. But James bought me a painting instead.' Shaking my head at the ridiculousness of it.

'Venice would be cool.' He shrugs nonchalantly. 'I better get this house sold to pay for it all. Or maybe you'll write a bestseller and I won't have to!'

'Ha! You're getting ahead of yourself!' But as we talk, I can envisage the future opening up.

'Ever thought you might be talking yourself down?' he teases.

I love that he believes in me, even if he hasn't a clue about writing. 'I'm realistic, that's all.'

'That idea I told you about. Teaching music.' A thoughtful look crosses his face. 'I was thinking about what you said, about this being your time. Maybe it's my time, too.'

As I look at him, I wonder if he's right; that these are moments we should both be seizing, because there are infinite possibilities out there, if you're brave enough.

It's a day I'll never forget. A window through which I glimpse a different future, of hopes and dreams; of fears shared without judgement; where love is an unstoppable force, never in question because it just is.

I leave in a state of bliss, imagining the years stretching ahead of us filled with laughter and adventures, until I get home. Looking around the house, I know the moment I leave, I'll be breaking something that can't be mended. *But it's already broken*, I remind myself.

Checking online to see if any other properties have become available, I tell myself I'll wait another day, as, cooking James a pork chop, I keep my silence. I'm putting it off, yet again. But there is no going back from where I am. There never could have been. Will was written into the song of my soul.

* * *

The next morning, I wait for James to go out, checking my emails before getting in my car to drive to Will's house, my radio turned up loud, my heart light as I think about the future. There's no hint of yesterday's spring sunshine. But even the heavy mist that lingers can't diminish how I'm feeling.

As Will opens the door, his face is haggard, the look in his eyes making my blood run cold.

'Hi.' My heart starts to hammer. Noticing the bags packed at the bottom of the stairs, I freeze. 'What's going on?'

He closes the door behind me. 'I have a flight in a couple of hours. I had a call half an hour ago from Darcey. Flo's run off. They had a row and Darcey thought she'd gone upstairs to her bedroom. But when she went to try and talk to her, she'd gone.'

Shock hits me, then I shiver as I imagine how I'd feel if Millie went missing. 'Has she called the police?'

He nods. 'I have to leave in a minute. I'm sorry. I know we

have things to talk about, but right now, I can't think about anything else.'

'Of course you can't. This is really important. You have to go.' Powerless to help, I watch him pull on his jacket.

'If anything's happened to her...' His face is ashen, his fingers fumbling with the buttons.

'Will, try not to worry.' But knowing your child is missing, it's impossible not to. 'She's probably at a friend's.' I don't know what else to say. 'Let me know when you find her?' I can't bear to think that they won't.

25

WILL

After the worst hours of his entire life culminated in finding an emotional Flo, Will was exhausted.

Back at Darcey's, a long afternoon had followed, meaning it was the evening by the time he called Anna.

'We found her at one of her friend's houses.'

'Thank God.' Anna sounded relieved.

'She walked ten miles.' He felt dead beat, guilt ridden. 'Anything could have happened.'

'But thank goodness it didn't.'

'I blame myself.' Will felt wretched. 'If I'd been here, it wouldn't have happened.'

'Did Flo say why she did it?' Anna sounded anxious.

'It was a cry for help.' There was desolation in his voice. 'She says she's unhappy. That ever since Darcey and I broke up, she can't think about anything else. She isn't sleeping – she worries about me and she feels pulled between us – all because of what Darcey and I have done.'

'Poor Flo.' Anna was silent for a moment. 'At least now you know, you can help her.'

'Yes.' He hesitated. But there was more he had to tell her. 'Anna... Darcey and I have been talking.' His voice was flat as he went on. 'This has really spooked both of us. If something had happened to Flo, we wouldn't have been able to live with ourselves. None of this is her fault. We've been so preoccupied, neither of us have been thinking about what she's been going through. While Flo's been feeling like this, I've been in Hinton... I feel terrible about it.' His voice broke. 'Darcey suggested... She wants us to try again, Anna. See if we can be a family – for Flo's sake.'

There was a silence. 'What about the divorce?'

'There isn't going to be one. Darcey's going to tell Eric it's over between them. She feels as bad as I do. Anna...' He desperately needed her to understand that this wasn't about her, it was about doing the right thing for his daughter. '*I'm so sorry*. But if Darcey and I can make this work, I'll be giving Flo what she needs. I have to put her first.'

'What about us?'

Hearing the shock in her voice was agonising, but Will had no choice. 'I'm sorry, Anna. I can't do this.' He broke off, before forcing himself to go on. 'I have to stop thinking about us.'

PART III

26

ANNA

I'm not prepared for the feeling that sweeps over me as I walk through Dyrham Park the next morning. Yesterday's mist has dissipated and the early light casts the sloping fields in a haze of purple. The temperature is cool, my breath forming small clouds, but I'm not cold. Nor am I reckless. I'm here deliberately, confronting the truth, retracing our footsteps.

After Will's decision, there's nothing I can say. All I can do is face the fact that Will's back in Glasgow trying to patch up his marriage; that just like that, this is the end of us. I'll never see him again and I have to be OK with that. I'm not, though. I'm torn apart.

But however devastated I feel, a part of me understands, because no one is more important than your child. Even if he can't be with me, though, it changes nothing between me and James. There is no future for us. As usual, the universe sends a message when I most need it, even if it isn't one I want to hear.

Sometimes life has to fall apart for change to happen.

Tears fill my eyes as I shout at the universe – why does it have to fall apart? Can't it just seamlessly move on to the next chapter? But when I most need answers, none are forthcoming.

I try to call Lucy to fill her in, but it goes to voicemail. It isn't until later that morning, she calls me back. 'How's it going, babe? I've been worried about you.'

'Not great.' I tell her what's happened with Will, tears filling my eyes.

'Oh, Anna... That's so sad.' She pauses. 'It must have been awful for them – and for you. Why don't you come out here for a bit? I'd love to see you.'

'I can't, Luce. There's too much going on.'

'You're still moving out?' She sounds uncertain.

'I have to. This is about more than me and Will. I've started looking for somewhere.' More tears stream down my cheeks. 'This wasn't a blip, Luce. I don't love James – I haven't for a long time. I owe it to myself to do this.'

* * *

I view a couple of rental cottages, as around me, change gathers speed. Gripped by an urgent need to clear my life of clutter, I go through my clothes, taking bags of them to charity shops.

Yet again, I try to talk to James. 'Have you called Millie recently?'

'No.' He frowns. 'Why?'

'No reason – except that she's your daughter, James. She's doing so well with her painting. I'm sure she'd love to share it with you.'

'We both know what I think about that.' Then he adds, slightly more kindly, 'But you're right. I should make more of an effort. I'm really proud of her.'

* * *

In my continued quest to declutter my life, I find some old photographs taken in my early twenties. As I peruse the faces, I wonder what's happened to everyone, but as often happens when life gets in the way, in the intervening years, they've drifted away.

One photograph in particular catches my eye – of me with one of my oldest friends, Charley. Taken about ten years ago, we're wearing matching faded denim and posing for the camera. As I take in the familiar gleam in her eyes, I can't believe how long it is since I've seen her.

I pick up my phone. After her marriage hit the rocks, she moved to France. Sure enough, when I call her number, there's a foreign ringtone before she answers.

'Anna?' She sounds breathless, happy. 'Oh my God! I can't believe it's you! How are you?'

'It's been too long, hasn't it? But you don't sound any different! How's life in France?'

'Wonderful! Hot! Come over and see for yourself.'

'Maybe I will!' The new is what I need more of in my life. 'Is this a good time? I was just looking at old photos of us from back in the day. I can't believe how long it is since we've seen each other.'

'It's been too long.' She pauses for a moment. 'So much has happened! But it's weird the way things work out. I wasn't sure when I first came here, but it's my home now and I really love it here.'

'And you and Rick?'

'A horrible episode of my past that I'm well and truly done with,' she says quietly. 'But if it hadn't happened, I wouldn't be here, would I? And I've met someone, Anna! The only English-speaking builder for miles. When you see the house, you'll realise how much I needed him. It was a wreck, but Jacques has made it beautiful again.'

It sounds as though he's been good for her, too. 'I'm so happy for you...' After the pain of her marriage ending, she deserves this.

'There's something else.' She pauses. 'Anna, I'm pregnant.'

I'm stunned. But I shouldn't be. Younger than me, Charley's always wanted children. 'That's amazing news. Congratulations,' I say softly. 'When is the baby due?'

'In two months.' She hesitates. 'I've thought so often how it must have been for you.'

I swallow the lump in my throat. Charley's one of the few people who knows about my miscarriages. 'It wasn't a good time. But I'm so pleased things are working out for you.'

'I know how lucky I am,' she says quietly. 'Not that long ago, I could never have imagined how much would change. But enough of me – I want to hear about you! How's James?'

I hesitate. 'A lot's been going on here, too. Things aren't good. I'm leaving him – I just haven't found the courage to tell him yet.' Then it all comes out. 'I met someone, Charley. I don't think we're ever going to be together, but he's shown me what's missing in my life. But I should have left a long time ago. James had an affair – and to be honest, we've never got over it.'

'Jeez.' Charley's uncharacteristically quiet. 'I didn't know. When?'

'I found out a couple of years ago.' I shake my head. 'He begged me to stay – though honestly, given how he is, I'm not sure why.'

'Maybe because divorce is so excruciating,' Charley says feelingly. 'So who's this guy? How did you meet?'

'His name's Will. I've known him for years. We used to go out when we were teenagers...' Going on, I tell her the story of how we met again.

Charley sounds stunned. 'It sounds like you're meant to be.'

'I used to think that. But I misread the signs.'

'Why? What happened?'

'Flo, his daughter, ran away – she was desperately unhappy about Will and his wife splitting up. So they've decided to give it another go – for her sake.'

'How does that even work?' Charley sounds exasperated. 'If he loves you?'

'He can't bear to hurt Flo,' I say simply. 'Everything else comes second to that.'

'Oh, Anna...' Her voice is sad. 'Has James any idea?'

I shake my head. 'I'm psyching myself up to tell him.'

'It isn't going to be easy.' She pauses. 'When Rick left me, it was hideous. But whatever happens, remember it will get better. You have to follow your heart,' she says earnestly. 'James will get over it.'

Hiding the sinking feeling I have when I think of telling James, I try to smile. 'I hope so.'

It's the measure of our friendship that years have passed and nothing's changed between us. As I think about everything we've shared, warmth fills me, as a tentative plan comes to mind. After leaving James, I'll go to see her.

It feels like another step forward along this uncertain road I'm walking. When I've been preoccupied with moving out, it's the first thing pencilled in for *after*.

27

WILL

As he tightened his boot laces into a double knot, Will was glad of his thick wool socks. The strong spring sunshine was having little effect on the temperature and it was bitingly cold. Parked in an isolated spot at the foothills of the Campsie mountains, he stood for a moment to stare across the sharply rising slopes; their rugged beauty enhanced in the crystal-clear sunlight. Since coming back from Hinton, it was the first chance he'd had to break free and walk, needing to be part of this dramatic landscape in a rapidly changing world, needing solid ground under his feet.

Flo running away had shocked him to the core. He still couldn't believe he hadn't seen any warning signs. But in the few hours she'd been missing, Will had known fear the like of which he'd never imagined; felt swamped in guilt that he hadn't known how she was feeling; that he'd been selfishly spending time with Anna, thinking of no one but himself. He didn't at all like how that made him feel.

The thought of Flo coming to harm had brought out a whole other side of him, altering his perspective about almost everything. And in a short time, so much was already different. After giving up his rented cottage, he'd moved back in with Darcey and Flo. True to her word, Darcey had spoken to Eric. Overnight, her behaviour had changed as she tried her best to put Flo's needs first and be a mother. Meanwhile, he'd rehomed the sheep at a friend's farm, burying the regret he felt.

Memories of Anna came into his head – her silence after he told her about him and Darcey; the sadness in her voice; how dead inside he'd felt – still felt. Will sighed. He'd never felt so conflicted about anything. He wasn't with Darcey because he loved her – it was purely about Flo. As her father, her happiness came first. But he had no idea if this could work when he and Darcey loved other people.

They hadn't even discussed living apart in a way that would work for their daughter. Will didn't even know if it was possible. United by fear, they'd simply settled for the most obvious solution. He sighed quietly. As long as Flo felt more secure, at least for now, it had to be enough to go through the motions.

After an hour and a half of steady climbing, Will reached the summit of his destination, his leg muscles burning from the last fifty or so footsteps. But when his efforts were rewarded with a 360-degree panorama of silent magic, it was worth it. Slopes carpeted with pine trees, silver rivers snaking through a jigsaw of emerald lowland speckled with isolated farm buildings that were huddled together against the wind. Snow-capped mountains, much higher than his, skirted the horizon, the whole scene electrified by the dazzling light cast by an uninhibited sun from its low point in the sky.

Protected against the wind, Will raised his face to the cold breeze and felt his senses taken over in the remote isolation, his mood meditative. Inhaling long slow breaths, he could feel the power of the elements reaching deep inside. Since coming back, his mind had been dominated by unsolvable problems, his emotions firmly buried. His job was also pushing for thinking space, his thoughts like clothes being flung around in a tumble dryer.

Away from everything, alone on a mountain top, nature was distancing the noise, granting him half an hour of serenity. But inevitably, the relief was temporary and as he arrived back at his car, the freedom of the wilderness felt a million miles away. After what he'd said to Anna, he knew it was well and truly over with her. From now on, he'd block out every thought of her, every dream they'd shared, the excitement of the future he'd imagined with her. She'd been a magical interlude in his life, but that was all. Dreams of happiness were for other people. He needed to remind himself of what Simon had been through, ground himself in reality; focus on Flo.

OCTOBER 2017

ANNA

Only as the aircraft door closed and the cabin crew began the safety demonstration, did the tension ebb from my shoulders. All the way to the airport, I'd been battling with myself, convinced I shouldn't be doing this – not now, just weeks after my mum's death, when things with James had blown up again, when Millie had just fallen out with her best friend. Going away with Lucy was pure selfishness.

There was a jolt as the aircraft pushed back and an involuntary sigh escaped me. Outside, raindrops traced their way down the small windows. As we taxied out, I barely heard the safety announcement.

After taking off, we climbed through the clouds, and already my life seemed a world away. I gazed out at the blue sky, letting my mind empty. Aware that I needed this time to sift through my thoughts, Lucy barely looked up from her book during the flight; the two hours passing in no time before the plane started its descent.

Lucy nudged my elbow. 'Look.'

Through the window, I made out sea the colour of ink lapping the rocky west coast of Ibiza, the land punctuated by white sugar-cube villas, a memory of the almost visceral sense of peace there coming to mind, before Dalt Villa came into view just before we touched down.

In what seemed like no time, we'd left the airport and were driving through a parched landscape that was crying out for rain. Even in October, the hot, dry summer showed in the faded green of the pine woods, the dried stalks of grass at the roadside, the fine layer of dust that covered everything.

As we turned into one of the dry, twisting roads with hairpin bends and silvery green olive trees, Lucy started to sound excited.

'The finca's lovely as it ever was, but it's changed a bit since we were last here.'

I thought back to last time – just before my wedding. Can Mimosa belonged to Lucy's aunt, as did the beaten-up Hyundai we'd picked up from the airport car park. The house I remembered was small but comfortable, attached to a ramshackle collection of old buildings, with uninterrupted views towards the sea.

Lucy went on. 'She finished converting it a few years ago. You won't recognise it.'

I wouldn't have cared if it was a shack in the woods. It had felt frivolous to be getting on a flight to Ibiza, of all places. But now that I was here, I found myself craving a peace that had long been missing from my life, the kind that was found in hills covered in pine woods, in the sound of the wind, the sun's heat as it soaked into you.

'Sounds wonderful, Luce.' But I wasn't really listening. Last time, we'd arrived late at night and I'd seen Cala d'Hort for the first time the following morning, washed pink as the sun rose behind the hills.

Reaching Can Mimosa, I was awestruck. The simple white-painted finca with two bedrooms had been seamlessly merged into the outbuildings without losing the patina that only age can give. Along the front, there was a terrace cast in shade by rough old timbers off which bougainvillea cascaded, while gravel paths were broken up with cacti and herbs.

After unlocking the house, Lucy walked around throwing windows and shutters open, then the huge doors that opened onto another terrace, while I followed her. The house was beautiful inside – simple and rustic, with stone floors and antique furniture, splashes of colour and soft lighting making it homely. As I looked around, I couldn't help thinking there was an irony in being here: having come here for the first time just before marrying James, I'd come back to get away from him.

'I'm pouring us a bloody humungous drink.' Lucy reappeared from one of the bedrooms. 'Thank God for my aunt's fridge – there's a ton of booze in there. Go outside and find a comfy place to watch the sunset, and I'll be right with you.'

I wandered outside, past the wooden table and chairs to the far end where I collapsed onto the huge day bed.

Gazing towards the sea, I heard Lucy come outside.

'It's been a hell of a year – and you were brilliant.' Passing me a glass, Lucy dropped onto the day bed next to me. 'Cheers, babe. It'll do you good being here.'

'Cheers.' I raised my glass automatically, clinking it against hers. It had been tough, but I'd only done what anyone else would have, when their mother was dying; staying with her, holding her hand as she left this life. 'Anyone else would have done the same.'

'Why do you always do this?' Lucy sat bolt upright. 'Bloody everyone doesn't, Anna, but you did. You were great.'

I sipped my drink in silence. None of what I'd done had been calculated. I remembered James's complaints when I missed a dinner with one of his work colleagues, because I wanted to be with my mother. He'd apologised, but what he'd said had stuck with me. I turned to Lucy. 'You won't believe what James said – when Mum was ill. I missed a work dinner he wanted me to go to. He actually said, what about me?'

I watched Lucy's mouth open to say something, but as our eyes met, she howled with laughter. Hearing myself snort, suddenly I couldn't contain myself.

'Finish your drink.' Lucy's voice was uncompromising. 'Down in one, then I'm getting you another.'

* * *

The following morning, we took our coffee out to the terrace. 'We need to talk about it, babe.'

It had been hanging over me since I found out, that James had been having an affair. 'He says it's over.'

'That's all very well, but it shouldn't have happened, should it?' Lucy made no attempt to hide her feelings. 'He's a cheating bastard, Anna. You should leave him.'

'Some days, I agree.' I sipped my coffee. 'Other days, it feels like giving up on a large chunk of my life. People do get over affairs. Maybe we can.' I shrugged. 'I'll figure it out.'

Over the days that followed, I soaked up the sun's heat as the island's magic seeped into me. It was easier to see things clearly here, to feel the rawness of losing my mother, then start to let it go. But loss had changed the way I saw things. Life was different now – always would be. More real. Less certain.

Anna and James... Other than two strangers who shared a name and a house, who were we? He would never sit out here on a Spanish hillside with me, listening to cicadas or lie under the stars pondering the meaning of life, the universe and everything. But then, who did that? In reality? I tried to, but I couldn't think of anyone.

* * *

By day two, I was thinking of Will.

'There's something I've never told you, Luce. But when Will went to Australia, he asked me to go with him.'

'How don't I know this?' she demanded. 'And why didn't you go?'

'I'd found my lump, remember? The day after he left, I was going for a biopsy.' I shook my head. 'It wasn't the time.'

'Did he know?'

'I never told him. I couldn't. He was excited about going away... For ages, he kept emailing me. But eventually, I stopped replying.' When my illness had taken over my life, I hadn't wanted Will to know.

'How does that make you feel now?' Lucy said gently.

'I don't know,' I said miserably. 'How do I know if marrying James was a mistake or not? How does anyone ever know?'

'Because the person you're with should make you happy.' Lucy sounded exasperated. 'At least, they should most of the time.' She hesitated. 'Has Will been in touch since?'

Thinking of the photo I found on his Facebook page, I shook my head. 'I think he's with someone.'

* * *

By day three, I was growing impatient with myself. It didn't help when James called. He didn't say much, just asked me how I was and said he hoped I'd soon feel better, his words showing how little he understood.

Meanwhile, the sun changed everything, wine an essential for dissolving stress in its icy sharpness, painting a veil over the truth. Friendship, however, was timeless, forgiving, understanding, unchanging. In short, everything a marriage should be. Except, mine was none of them.

Our last night, as Lucy came out with drinks, I was still undecided. 'We've been married for thirteen years, Luce. I'm more of a mother to Millie than her birth mother. What do I do?'

'Only you know the answer to that.' The mood between us was suddenly sober. 'I guess you have to ask yourself, babe. What do you want from the rest of your life?'

I took a swig of my drink. 'I want a safe place for Millie in case she needs it. And I want James and I to be happy.' There was stubbornness in my voice. 'But I can't go on feeling like this.' I looked at Lucy. 'Either I walk away, knowing I've tried my hardest to work it out with him, or I stop looking at what's wrong and build on what's good between us. Things may have changed but we loved each other once.' I paused for a moment. 'I suppose, the way I see it, I have a choice.'

I was expecting one of Lucy's outbursts, not for my friend to reach out and take my hand. 'I do get it. And whatever you decide, I'll always be here for you.'

Swallowing the lump in my throat, I nodded, knowing nothing was going to make this any easier.

28

ANNA

The decision I made in Ibiza meant James and I stayed together, clinging to what was left of us. If he'd been worried about losing me, when I came home he didn't show it. Everything had gone on, just the same. Maybe I'd expected too much. But if I'm honest with myself, I'd known at the time, it wasn't enough.

* * *

Will is etched into my every moment. I walk in Dyrham Park, ludicrously hoping to see him, knowing he's sitting at his desk back in Glasgow.

Back home, restless, I go to my laptop, checking to see if any more properties have come up. Frustrated when I find nothing in my price range, I think about moving further away, on impulse turning to look at properties in France.

It's unbelievable how much further my money would go – not just renting, but eventually buying somewhere. My teenage wish list comes to mind, as I imagine all these years later, finally finding somewhere to live where oranges and lemons grow.

Now and then, Charley or Lucy call me for updates. Then Charley goes quiet. I find out from Lucy that Charley went into labour a month early and her baby is fighting for her life.

'It's crap, Luce. Charley doesn't deserve this.'

'I know.' Lucy's quiet for a moment. 'We just have to hope they'll be OK.'

It feels like one of those times when nothing is going right. When it's taken this long for Charley to find happiness, when I know how much she wants this baby, it leaves me wondering what the point of it all is. Why so many people have to suffer... It fuels my restlessness, the world as I know it shifting irreversibly, my despair building to the point that I want to run, anywhere, far away from here.

The world shifts again when for the first time since leaving my job, I run into Liza Merrow. 'Liza! Hi! How are you?'

She almost doesn't stop. 'Anna?' Lifting her sunglasses, she reveals eyes red from crying.

A cold feeling comes over me. 'What's happened?'

'I can't stop now.'

I gently touch her arm. Liza and I have always got on. 'Can I buy you a coffee?'

She shakes her head. 'I'm sorry, Anna. It isn't you – Alison...' A sob erupts from her.

My blood runs cold. Alison's her teenaged daughter. 'What about Alison?'

As she looks at me, her eyes are filled with tears. 'There was an accident. The driver didn't stop... Alison... *She didn't make it.*' Standing there, she seems to crumple.

'God.' The worst kind of shock hits me. 'That's just so awful, Liza. I'm so sorry...'

'I have to go... I'm meeting David. There's the funeral to plan and the wake...'

I hug her gently. 'If there's anything I can do...'

The sadness in her eyes is devastating as she nods. 'Thank you.'

Though I never met Alison, like anyone else, I can't help but put myself in Liza's shoes, imagining how I'd feel if it had been Millie; how it's the worst kind of sorrow when it's your child.

But as one life ends, another is just starting as a text from Charley comes. Two words that mean the world.

We're OK x

* * *

I go to Alison's funeral, standing at the back of the packed church, unable to make sense of losing someone so young, as more and more, the bigger questions in life dominate my mind.

After, needing to hear a friendly voice, I find my phone. 'Hi, Luce.' She's the only person I can talk to about any of this.

'Anna! Are you OK?'

'Not really.' I swallow. 'I'm finding this really hard.'

'Oh, Anna...' My friend pauses. When she goes on, her voice is kind. 'You know what? You take each little bit at a time. And it's going to be bloody tough. But you know that. It may not seem like it right now, but you will come through. And it will be OK. I promise you.'

'But what about James? And Millie...' My voice cracks.

'Anna. James will play lots of golf and get drunk every night with the friends you can't stand and bitch about how badly he's been treated by you. Then he'll dust himself off and meet someone else. He'll be OK.' Lucy sounds unsympathetic, but then her voice softens. 'Millie will understand, hun. I think she'll admire you for making a difficult decision and being strong. I wouldn't be surprised if she knows things aren't right between the two of you. She isn't a child.'

'Even so...' I'm drowning in guilt. 'I've always been there for her. Always.'

'And you always will be.' Lucy's matter of fact. 'Get this clear, Anna. This isn't about Millie. It's about you and James. You've really tried. For years. There's no way Millie won't have seen that. You have to do what's right for you. No one's going to be surprised – apart from James, of course. And don't forget, he hasn't exactly done himself any favours. I mean, let's face it, babe, if he treated you like the beautiful, clever, gorgeous woman you are, none of this would ever have happened.'

Words that bounce off me, because I'm none of those things. I'm silent, duplicitous, fraught.

'Any time you want to get away, you know you can come here.'

It's what she says every time we speak. But right now, it isn't going to solve anything. I have to stay and face the music.

* * *

As I find the courage to tell James I'm leaving, the universe intervenes with another life-defining moment. While the stony silence between us has thawed to an awkward truce, when he marches in one evening looking triumphant, I'm nervous.

'You've splashed out...' Taking in the bottle of champagne he's holding, I'm racking my brains, imagining a missed anniversary or a birthday – something else to add fuel to the flames.

James hesitates, but only for a moment. 'I have news.'

Registering the excitement on his face, a feeling of foreboding comes over me. 'What's happened?'

'I've been headhunted for a job in the States.' As he speaks, he looks impossibly proud of himself. 'In New York. It comes with an apartment near Central Park. I've almost certainly got it. I'm going to open this.' He disappears into the kitchen while I sit there, unable to take it in.

Thoughts start racing through my head, then I hear the cork pop, before James comes back in clutching two flutes, giving them to me to hold while he pours the champagne. No ordinary champagne either, I notice, looking at the bottle. It's top-notch stuff. My feeling of foreboding grows stronger.

'Congratulations, James. I'm really pleased for you.' My hand shakes as I raise my glass, clinking it against his.

'Great, isn't it?' He doesn't wait for me to answer. 'I suppose I ought to get an estate agent round to see what our options are.'

That he can brush aside the last months as if nothing has been wrong astonishes me. 'You haven't actually been offered the job yet?'

He frowns at me. 'You don't sound very enthusiastic.'

I'm dumbfounded. 'What about Millie? And Yippy?'

'Dear God, Anna. It's New York. Millie will love to come and stay with us. As for the dog… Surely you can find a home for it?'

Fleetingly it comes to me that if I loved him enough, I'd go to the ends of the earth for him. *But if he loved me, wouldn't he want to know what I think?* James carries on talking, his words blurring until I can't listen any more. It's the moment I've been putting off, that's suddenly here in front of me.

'James? Stop. I'm not coming.'

'What?' He looks at me as though he doesn't understand.

'Can't you see that everything's wrong?' There's sadness in my voice. 'We barely speak, James. We don't share anything. And you never listen to me.'

He looks furious. 'I always listen. Bloody hell, Anna. It isn't my fault you're not happy. It sounds to me like you're having a midlife crisis.'

'Like yours, you mean?' It's a cheap jibe that brings him up short – he knows I'm talking about the affair he had. 'It isn't that.' Here in front of me is my chance, the perfect opportunity for us to go our separate ways. 'Maybe this is for the best.' I shrug. 'I never wanted this to happen, but something has to change.' I wipe away the tears suddenly filling my eyes. 'You should go to New York. I'll move out. We can sell the house or rent it out.'

I watch his face freeze, before a look of comprehension dawns. 'I know exactly what's happened.' His eyes narrow. 'I can't believe I haven't seen it before. You've met someone, haven't you?'

When I don't deny it, there's an explosion he can't contain. Angry, venomous words that can never be taken back. My guilt, the shock as James hurls his glass at the wall, followed by the bottle.

'I'm so sorry, James.' Watching the glass shatter, the champagne soak into the carpet, the blood drains from my face. 'I'm not seeing him any more. But this isn't about him. It's about our marriage.'

'Who is it?' he demands angrily.

'No one you know.' He can't force it out of me. 'I haven't been happy for a long time. Neither of us have. Not really.'

'Tit for tat, eh?' His eyes are narrow slits. 'You never had any intention of trying, did you?'

'You had the fucking affair, James.' My teeth are gritted, my fists clenched in anger that he has the nerve to stand there and say that. 'Maybe we should have called it quits then. We're long past working it out.' And even if we could, I wouldn't want to.

'You're not having the house.' Arms folded, he glares at me. 'Or that painting.'

I tell him it's over between us and all he can do is tell me I can't take the painting he gave me, the one of St Mark's Square that in all honesty he bought for himself. 'I don't want the house.

And you know what, James? That just about says it all. I never wanted that fricking painting in the first place. I wanted to go to Venice, if you remember, for us to spend some time together, to try to breathe life into our dying marriage.'

Grasping the magnitude of what I'm saying, he tries to gather himself; clutches at straws. 'Look, we need to talk about this. Please, Anna...'

'You know what?' I gaze at him sadly. 'I've wanted to talk – so many times. But every time without fail, you've refused.'

'You can't just walk away.' For the first time, I see tears in his eyes, too. 'Marriages come through the worst of times. Please...'

It cuts me to the core to see him like this. 'We don't work any more, James. We haven't for a long time. Surely, if you're honest, you can see that?'

He doesn't answer. But we are not one of those relationships that can be fixed; James and I are not salvageable. Through my tears, I try to explain, but he picks up his phone and walks out. An hour later, when he comes back, neither of us speaks. Instead, sitting there, we stare at the floor in silence.

29

WILL

The next day back at work, Will was staring out of the office window, his mind anywhere but focused on work when his thoughts were interrupted.

'You fancy getting out for a bite to eat at lunchtime?' Hacker's voice was strangely welcome. 'I mean, unless staring at the car park looks like a more interesting option,' he added.

'Cool.' Will had no plans. 'I'll come and find you in an hour or so.'

'I'll be in my cubbyhole polishing turds before the auditors get here.' Hacker gestured with his hand as if growing a Pinocchio nose, before sweeping away across the office.

Later, outside the building, they headed for a large old pub a few streets away, where the food was not likely to be featured on *MasterChef* anytime soon, according to Hacker. Will hadn't eaten there before and couldn't decide if Hacker's additional comment, that what it lacked in style and flavour it certainly made up for in volume, made it any more appealing. But he was happy to take his chances.

After sitting down with their drinks, Hacker glanced over his shoulder before looking at Will. 'This is off the record, but I thought you should know, mate. There are problems in the pipeline. In fact... things are looking pretty bleak.'

Will was taken by surprise. He already knew that after two big account losses, the company was having cash-flow difficulties. Was Hacker telling him that his job was in jeopardy? 'Surely they can't be that bad... Or do you know something I don't?' He was trying not to sound overly concerned but alarm bells were ringing.

'I don't know anything officially, but if the weekly figures I prepare for the directors are anything to go by, I'd say they're going to need to make big changes. Very soon.' His bumbling manner had gone as Hacker looked Will in the eye. 'They either need to win some new business, or start cost cutting. And we're talking quite massive cuts.'

He didn't need to elaborate further. Will knew the significance of what Hacker was saying. He couldn't tell him that his job was on the line, but he was being a mate and giving him the heads-up. Feeling his head start to race as this latest development shot to the top of his list of problems, Will tried to keep his external cool. 'If you were a betting man, what would you say my chances are?' He was expecting Hacker to either reveal his hand or laugh it off.

He did neither. 'Let's just say... your future probably isn't with that lot.' Taking a large sip of his drink, Hacker pointed in the direction of the office.

'And if you were going for the accumulator bet, how long before they dust off the gallows?' Will was keeping his reaction breezy, trying to hide the rising sense of panic he felt. He had a mortgage to pay and while he and Darcey had some savings, unless he found another job, they'd soon be gone.

Hacker looked troubled. 'I really don't know. But I'd say they're going to be moving quickly on this. You're not the only one, but I haven't said anything to anyone else. I'd probably be fired if they knew I was talking to you. It's just that you're a mate, and I thought a little notice might help you to get prepared. Of course, I may be wrong, or they might get a major new account win. But as things are, I've seen the figures and it isn't pretty.'

'I won't tell anyone we've had this conversation.' It was shit, but would at least help him get his head ready for the inevitable. Will raised his glass. It couldn't have been easy to tell him. 'Cheers, mate. Thanks for the inside track.'

* * *

At home that evening, Will sat motionless on the sofa, eyes locked on the ceiling, as Darcey's voice came from the kitchen.

'Dinner will be about ten minutes.'

While spiralling thoughts had become the norm, his conversation with Hacker had added to the pressure as he thought about mentioning his likely redundancy to Darcey. What would he do about a new job? Or was the universe sending him a sign?

He wondered if Anna had left James yet. Right now he'd give anything to talk to her. More than once, he'd debated telling Darcey about her, in the end deciding against it. When they were trying to make their marriage work, it was hardly going to help.

'Hey, Dad. I've sent you the email about the swimming competition.' After coming downstairs in baggy tracksuit bottoms, Flo perched on the edge of the sofa.

'I saw it. Exciting, eh? Does Mum know about it?'

'Yes.' Flo rolled her eyes. 'She's coming.'

'I'll be there, too, sweetheart. I wouldn't miss it for the world.'

For the first time in ages, Flo would have both parents, sitting side by side, watching her compete. They were doing OK – so far. An atmosphere of calm in the house, a united family – in appearance, at least; doing ordinary things together, like tonight, for instance, sitting at the table eating Darcey's lasagne. Normal, like tens of thousands of other families. That had to be good.

* * *

Until he got official notification that his job was at risk, Will had decided to keep his worries to himself. It came three days later, in a meeting with his boss. After reading up on redundancy procedure, he already knew what the first stage was. A meeting, to 'let you know your job may be under review'. Somewhere among his boss's waffle and office babble-speak, Will did discern those exact words, confirmed the next day in a letter removing any uncertainty, despite it stating, 'a full evaluation process will be carried out before anything is decided'. Having read the letter, Will remembered an old phrase Simon had occasionally used. 'Give them a fair trial and hang them.'

That evening, after Flo had gone to bed, Will showed Darcey the letter.

'What are we going to do?' Darcey looked shocked. She went to the kitchen and topped up her drink. 'Have you started looking for another job?'

'I've had a word with a couple of people. But there's nothing as yet.'

Coming over, she sat on the sofa next to him. 'Selling your father's house would buy us some time. Unless...'

Will could see her brain ticking. 'Unless what?'

'Could we move there?' She shrugged. 'It would be easier to sell this house, wouldn't it? Flo could go to school in Bath. And it's an easy commute if I need to go to London.'

'Flo might not want to.' Plus it was too close to Anna. 'Her life and her friends... they're all here.'

'Children move schools all the time, Will.' Darcey paused. 'As long as she can join another swimming club there, we should at least consider it.'

'Don't you think she's had enough turmoil in her life?'

'We're together now. The turmoil has gone. Anyway, it's another good reason. A new start – for all of us.' Moving closer, Darcey placed a perfectly manicured hand on his arm, her voice dropping. 'Will, you don't have to go on sleeping in the spare room.'

Will was silent. He was grateful for the effort she was making for Flo's sake, but beyond that, he felt nothing. 'It's going to take time.'

She got and stood in front of him. 'I hope we can try. Marriages do get over these things. It would be good if ours could be one of them.' She paused. 'Think about what I said – about moving?'

'You never know, they may decide to keep me.' Throwing his stinger across the road, to stop her getting too far ahead with her plans. The thought of her and Anna bumping into each other was somewhere he couldn't go. 'I should know for sure in a couple of weeks.'

* * *

It was almost exactly two more weeks before the predictable second meeting and the inevitable announcement with all appropriate sympathies, that his job had indeed become redundant. Even though it came as no surprise, as his boss talked, Will's mind fell into a removed state of numbness, with only occasional words and statements, all meaningless, cutting through his thickening mental fog. *It's nothing personal... if there was another way...*

painful decision... essential part of the team... All of it complete and utter bollocks.

Leaving the office that evening, the pressure was building. Will's future had never felt so uncertain. Right now, he wished he was standing on top of the mountain again, feeling the power of the elements raging around him, emptying his mind of questions he had no answers for.

30

ANNA

It feels like my life is imploding around me when after a long silence, at last, I speak to Charley. 'How are you? And Freya?' Freya's her baby, named after Charley's mother.

'We're good! She's doing well.' Charley pauses. 'Can you hold on a moment, Anna? I'll just get her.' In the background I hear a shrill, high-pitched cry that comes from Freya, then Charley's murmured response, before she comes back.

'I've been so worried about you both,' I tell her. 'You're sure you're OK?'

'We're really good.' Charley's voice is filled with happiness. 'It was touch and go for a while, but this little girl is a fighter.'

'I'd love to come and see you.'

'Come any time! How are things?' Charley sounds anxious. 'I'm so out of touch.' In the background, there's the sound of more crying. 'Oh, Anna... I'm sorry, she's hungry. Can we talk another time? I have to go.'

'Everything's fine. I'm fine...' I lie. 'You go.' It isn't the time to fill her in. But hearing her voice again, even the shortest of conversations somehow reminds that I'm doing the right thing.

* * *

On impulse, I take a detour and drive past Will's father's house, but it's closed up, empty, the *For Sale* board no longer outside. A sense of finality washes over me as I imagine Will never coming back here, then someone else moving in.

I endure the hardest conversations, the toughest days of my life. It's like a death, but then it is a death. The death of a marriage, one James clings to, symptomatic of his belief that he can forcibly, obstinately mould me.

I can't stay here. Words that have remained silent, lodged at the back of my throat, become nuclear bombs, exploding their way into the world.

We have to talk, Anna... The prison-cage of James's desperation, as he steps closer.

I have to go. Suffocate or leave, Anna.

I choose air.

* * *

Having failed to find somewhere to live, I move my possessions into the spare room, doubling my house-hunting efforts, avoiding James as best I can. But when estate agents arrive to value the house, it feels like my life is unravelling.

Ignoring their attempts to engage me in conversation, I leave them to it, repeatedly telling myself, it's just a house. This has to happen. Unless it does, nothing will change.

31

WILL

The pressure of preserving the image of happy family life was mounting and, underneath, Will was feeling the strain, stressed about money, the tension amplified by the need to watch his every word; living with the fear that if he didn't, Flo would pick up on something.

If she saw him now, Anna would barely recognise this dry, parched shell he'd become. With his emotions numbed, Will had parked any dreams he had of him and Anna being together, resigning himself to being what was expected of him; to a life of obligation and responsibility.

Only when he was walking did he allow the mask to slip and his frustrations to surface. Out there, he replayed his conversations with Anna, reminded himself of the sense of freedom he'd found; the happiness he'd felt. All those hours of talking had tapped into something deep inside him. He'd never had that with Darcey. Conversation with her was about food, a new sofa, the latest films, new clothes; anything but the nuts and bolts of what really mattered.

In short, he was stuck, while losing his job had only

compounded the feeling. Meanwhile, it felt as though the universe was conspiring against him. After failing to find another job, along with the fact that his father's house hadn't sold, Darcey's questionable logic won the day, as she made the case for moving to Hinton with the focus of a barrister, flattening any objections he had.

'I'm not going.' Flo's outrage made Will's heart ache. 'My friends are here. My whole life is here,' she said theatrically, for a moment reminding him of Darcey.

Knowing they were only moving because he couldn't find another job, he felt terrible. 'Listen, Flo. I've been looking for jobs around here and there aren't any. If we move, there's Bath and Bristol. There are really good schools and we'll find another place for you to swim.'

Flo's eyes had flashed. 'I've worked for years to be in this team, Dad. Do you really think it's that simple?'

Knowing she had a point, he'd tried to persuade Darcey that they should wait a little longer. But Darcey wasn't having any of it.

'It would be fine if you were working. But you're not.'

'At the moment,' Will said firmly.

'I don't understand why you're so against the idea.' Darcey's eyes had been fixed on him.

Feeling uncomfortable, Will had mumbled something about how it felt like a step backwards. But right now, his whole life felt like a bloody step backwards. Not sure how he'd cope with living so close to Anna, he'd doubled his efforts to find a job – but to no avail.

With Darcey heaping on the pressure, eventually, after a weekend in Bath and a trial session at the swimming club proved Flo's talent, she caved in. Back in Glasgow again, they started to pack. The move was on.

32

ANNA

As I disentangle myself from the ties of my old life, out of the blue, Liza Merrow calls me. 'Anna? Are you free to meet me in Bath? I have a favour to ask you.'

I park near the centre of Bath and walk to the end of the street where I've arranged to meet Liza. When I reach her, seeing the sadness in her eyes, my heart twists. Around the corner, she shows me a run-down corner of land.

'David and I have bought it. We want to turn it into a memorial for Alison – she died not far from here.' Liza swallows. 'We thought it would be a good way to remember her.'

I blink away the tears that fill my eyes. 'It's a lovely idea.'

She hesitates. 'Neither David nor I know anything about gardens. But you've told me about yours. We wondered if there's any way you could help us?'

Gardening used to be a passion of mine – something else I seem to have lost sight of. After sitting down with Liza and coming up with a plan, I start straight away, loving that I can do something that will make a difference to her.

Now and then, we meet to decide on plants, while because I'm in the middle of Bath, the garden draws all manner of unwanted comments.

'This has to stop,' a strange woman tells me. 'It's like having a grave under your nose that you're forced to walk past every day.'

'Excuse me?' I stare at her. 'It's no such thing. It's going to be a garden. This has been neglected for years.' How dare she speak to me like that? 'You honestly have no idea what you're talking about.' Months ago, I would have let it go. But I have as much right as she does to speak my mind. As she glares back at me, I completely ignore her.

Another time, Meredith stops. 'Anna?'

'Meredith.' I shake the worst of the soil off my hands.

Her eyes narrowing, she looks down her nose at me. 'Is this what you do now? Work for the council?'

'For your information, I'm helping a friend, Meredith. And by the way, the council employs excellent gardeners.' I pause, looking at her. 'How is business these days? I wondered if it might take a hit, what with the new farm shop opening...'

Giving me a look, she doesn't answer, just turns and stalks off. But word clearly gets around and during her lunch break, Hannah comes over.

'This is so cool, Anna. I mean it's sad, obviously, but it's a lovely way to remember someone.'

'I think so, too. Meredith doesn't, though.'

Hannah rolls her eyes. 'She's a mean old bag to pretty much everyone at the moment. Between you and me, the shop's in trouble. Customers are realising the new shop is better.' She glances over her shoulder. 'I've just applied for a job there!'

'I hope you get it. Honestly, leaving Meredith was the best thing I could have done. Let me know what happens, won't you?'

When James comes in that evening, there's an air of determination about him.

'I've been thinking, Anna.'

Imagining another attempt at conciliation, I stiffen. 'What about?'

'You don't need to say it like that,' he says abruptly, before pulling himself up. 'Sorry.' He sighs. 'Look, I was hoping we could talk.'

'There's nothing to talk about,' I say sadly. 'You're going to New York. I'm staying here. Some agents came over this morning. One of them seems to think the house should sell quite quickly.'

'How can you be so cold?' His eyes bore into me. 'After all these years, don't you think you owe me?'

'Me owe you?' I stare at him, incredulous that he can even say that. 'I don't think so.'

Sighing, he rests his head in his hands. 'I fucked up – I realise that. I suppose I'm asking you to give us another chance.'

'It's what we've been doing, James,' I say sadly. 'For two years. Don't you understand, it hasn't worked?'

For the rest of the evening, he stonewalls me, but instead of beating me down, it strengthens my resolve. In the end, needing to get out, I put on my coat, then whistle to the dog and clip on his lead. Halfway along the street, my phone pings with a text from Lucy.

How goes it? x

I'm going mad, Luce xx

She replies straight away.

What's happened babe?

The weather's crap – and I can't find a fucking house. xx

Her reply is predictable.

Easy, bring the dog and come to live with me.

The breeze picks up, swirling around me, the intensity of the rain picking up too. I turn around and, passing Grace and Ron's house, I notice the lights on, imagine the cosiness inside. I think about knocking on their door, under the pretext of checking up on them, but when the light in the downstairs window goes out, I keep walking.

I'm craving change, change that, despite my best efforts, I'm unable to set in motion. I even think about going to see Lucy, but a few days or weeks in the sun won't solve anything. What I seek is longer lasting, further reaching.

When I get back, James barely acknowledges me, pointedly talking loudly on his mobile to a couple of his golfing friends.

I've yet to tell Mille what I'm doing – it's her I worry most about, but Lucy's right. She's a grown-up. When she has her own life, is it wrong to think about myself? I know what Lucy would say – that it isn't; that each of us owes it to ourselves to live our fullest, best life.

Unable to sleep that night, I toss and turn, realising I've been drifting through most of my life, never questioning what I've been doing. But in the darkness, I'm awake; questioning everything.

* * *

The next morning, I check my emails before calling Liza. 'Good news,' I tell her quietly when she answers. 'The last of your plants will be in tomorrow. The garden will be finished in a few days.'

Knowing it's going to be exactly as Liza wanted, I feel slightly proud of myself.

'That's such great news, Anna.' From the way Liza speaks, it's impossible to gauge her ocean of grief. 'David and I want to gather a few people there when it's ready. Nothing formal, but we'd both love it if you could come. Your husband, too, if he'd like to.'

I deliberately haven't told her that I'm leaving James – but even if I wasn't, there's no way he'd want to go, and I wouldn't want him to. He doesn't have the sensitivity to understand why the Merrows are doing this; how the garden means everything to Liza. Planning it has given her a focus, bringing people into her life as well as being somewhere to channel her pain, as she does the only thing a grieving parent can do – take each step forward one at a time.

* * *

It's as though karmic scales are being balanced as while my relationship with James deteriorates further, I receive a call from a rental agent about a property that sounds perfect for me. I view it the same day – a small cottage with a spare room under the eaves that would be perfect for Millie. The deposit is eye-watering.

As I finish packing what is mine, James insists I leave the house exactly as it is. I don't fight him. I have chosen this, I tell myself, stricken with guilt.

When I turn on my laptop, the first post in my Facebook feed is a picture of the sun rising behind the trees, the following words imposed on it:

The calm after the storm.

I stare at it, suddenly angry, before clicking on 'hide post'. The last thing I need is fucking patronising messages about calm after fucking storms. Not when I'm surrounded by hurricane force bloody winds that show no sign of abating.

After another row about money, James begrudgingly pays a sum into my bank account. In time, there will be our house and our savings to split, but that can wait.

Having decided to take the cottage I viewed, there's a further twist when I call the estate agent to find someone's got there before me. That my impending freedom has been taken away is devastating.

Just when I think it isn't possible, it gets worse.

'I'm not taking the job,' James says when he comes in.

'What?' I look at him warily. 'Not because of me, I hope.'

'It might have something to do with it,' he says quietly. 'Can you blame me for trying?'

'There's no point, James,' I say, frustrated that he can't see the futility of what he's doing. 'Haven't you listened to anything I've said?'

* * *

The next morning, as I come back from walking Yippy, Ron catches me getting out of my car.

'How are you, Anna?' He's frowning slightly. 'We were just saying, we haven't seen you in a while.'

I force a smile. 'I'm fine. I'm so sorry, I've been meaning to come round but I've been so busy lately. I don't know where the time has gone…' Feeling his hand lightly on my arm, I break off.

'How about now?' he says quietly. 'A quick cup of tea? Only if you have time, of course.'

Suddenly desperate for a few minutes away from my own life,

with people who care, there's a lump in my throat. 'Thank you. I... I'd love to.'

But even in the peacefulness of their home, I'm agitated. I tell them about Alison's garden. I don't mention James, yet it's as though they know. But my suffering is visible, in the weight that's fallen off me, in the dark circles drawn under my eyes.

'Come and see us again soon,' Ron says, a frown wrinkling his brow as he shows me out, pausing as he opens the door. 'Look after yourself, Anna.'

It isn't something he normally says, but nothing's normal any more. 'You too.' Then in an unfamiliar gesture, I kiss his cheek.

* * *

Through all the turmoil, there's a voice I can't ignore inside my head.

You can't go back, only forwards.

Lucy calls me daily. 'You've got to get out of there.' Her voice is kind, but no-nonsense. 'You need time away from him to let the dust settle.'

'It isn't so simple,' I tell her. 'I've been looking for somewhere, but the rental market is dead and the smallest place costs the earth around here.'

'The right place will come up.' Lucy pauses. 'It always does.'

'I hope so.'

* * *

While James and I reach an impasse, the universe sends me a reality check when I meet Jessica. A good friend of Liza's, she invites us over for coffee, except at the last minute, Liza cancels.

'Not surprising, is it.' Jessica's voice is full of sympathy. 'She's been through so much. I think some days, she needs to hide herself away. Would you like me to show you around?'

Her house is old – and untidy – the garden planted with medicinal herbs and flowers, organically grown; while beyond, the few acres of grazing are home to the collection of animals she's rescued. Abandoned dogs and cats, a couple of ill-treated ponies, unwanted goats and sheep, all of them grateful for the smallest of kindnesses.

As she introduces me to them, my phone buzzes with a call from one of the rental agents. Hoping it's about a property I've just emailed them about, I glance at Jessica. 'I'm sorry, this is important. It won't take a minute.'

Walking away, as the agent tells me the property has been taken, a feeling of despair comes over me. Ending the call, as I walk back to Jessica, I'm barely holding it together.

Seeing my face, she frowns. 'Anna? Are you OK?'

'Just one of those days.' I try to smile, but it's a step too far as tears fill my eyes and the floodgates open. Trying to pull myself together, I feel Jessica's hand on my arm.

'Why don't we have a cup of tea?'

In her farmhouse kitchen, I tell her about leaving James and losing the cottage. 'This morning, it all got on top of me.'

'I'm not surprised. It's bad luck about the house. But actually, it might not be...' She breaks off, her face thoughtful. 'A friend of mine has a cottage she rents out – in Marshfield. Shall I call her to see if it's available?'

* * *

Later that afternoon, Jessica drives me to see her friend's cottage a few miles out of Bath in the village of Marshfield. Up a quiet lane, it's affordable, with two bedrooms and a private garden. I walk around it, effortlessly picturing myself living here, as a sense of relief comes over me.

* * *

On Friday afternoon, I knock on my neighbours' door. When Ron opens it, he looks pleased. 'Anna! We were just talking about you. Come on in.'

'Just for a minute.' I hesitate. 'I can't stay long.'

In the warmth of their kitchen, when I tell them I'm leaving James, neither of them says anything, only the tick of the grandfather clock breaking the silence.

Sitting at their table, it's Grace who speaks first. 'I don't blame you.' When Ron glances at her, she goes on, untypically lucid. 'Ron, I wasn't going to say, but I have to.' Her eyes are alight as she looks at me. 'He doesn't deserve you. You're a jewel, Anna. That husband of yours has never known your worth.'

* * *

Then that weekend, while James is playing golf, with the help of the man and van I've booked, I move out.

33

WILL

Will had wondered how it would feel, coming back to Hinton and indefinitely moving into what had been his father's house. But calm, with their stuff unpacked, in no time he'd felt at home. He'd also met up with an old school friend who owned a farm a couple of miles away, who'd agreed to rent Will a small paddock to keep a few sheep.

Meanwhile, instead of buzzing up and down to London, Darcey had started working at the theatre in Bristol. There was a peacefulness, but a tentative one, while Will was baffled. She appeared resigned to them being friends rather than lovers, which knowing Darcey as well as he did, made no sense.

Two weeks after moving to Hinton, with Flo starting school and Darcey on her way to Bristol, Will was alone in the house. His plan had been to get his laptop out and start seriously looking for a job, but as the sound of Darcey's car faded, almost immediately he began pacing around the house, straightening cushions. Within the hour, he'd left home for Dyrham Park.

The truth was he couldn't close the door on the dream of a life with Anna. In Glasgow, with five hundred miles between them, that had been one thing. Moving to Hinton had the potential to expose everything.

Logically, he knew he shouldn't have come here, but he hadn't been able to stop himself. As he walked, surrounded by memories, he was on edge. It had been six months ago that they'd last met up here. Being here was bringing it all back.

He'd considered getting in touch with her – if only to tell her he'd come back. What if they just bumped into each other and he was with Darcey or Flo? Or maybe she'd moved on, meaning Will was no more than part of her past.

Sitting on a sawn off tree trunk, in the cool breeze, he thought of the song Anna had told him to listen to, months ago. Until now, he'd resisted the temptation, but getting out his phone, he found it. As it started to play, Will was transfixed. The music was emotional, the surrounding landscape his backdrop and as it reached somewhere deep inside him, the feelings he'd buried began to surface. Anguish, then emptiness, followed by an aching, visceral kind of grief – for the love he'd lost, for the life he wasn't fully living.

Feeling his vision blur, he wiped away his tears with the back of his hand. God, what a mess his life was. He knew it would be sensible, easier for everyone, if he were to write Anna off as an amazing fantasy in his mind. More tears filled his eyes. It was impossible to write her off when he loved her.

As he sat there looking over the autumnal fields, Will noticed a figure in the distance, coming through the gate that led onto the path across the open pastureland. Wiping his eyes with his sleeve again, he studied the figure as it moved closer, frowning slightly. Something about it reminded him of Anna.

34

ANNA

As Jessica's friend's cottage becomes my home, I fill it with an eclectic mix of furniture gifted by friends and Lucy's mother, while Lucy calls me daily and friends rally round. But alone, without the routine of my life with James, my life feels emptier than I'd have thought possible.

Lucy is no-nonsense about it. 'You're not telling me you miss doing his washing and cooking meals you don't want to eat?'

'Something like that,' I sob pitifully.

'Listen. There are much more worthwhile things to spend your time on than looking after that fricking man.' Her tone softens. 'It isn't surprising you feel uprooted. It's early days, babe.'

At the end of my first week, when Millie comes to stay, I buy bunches of flowers and cook enough for ten people. But it's clear from her face it's difficult for her. 'Mills? I know it's strange. It's strange for me, too. But I really want you to think of this as home.'

Her face is conflicted. Millie already has two homes. Now that James and I are not together, she has to spread herself even more thinly.

Bracing myself, I tell her about Will. 'We met months ago,

Mills. Neither of us was happy – otherwise I don't believe we would have found each other. He isn't the reason I left, but he showed me everything that was wrong between your dad and me. Even though it didn't last, in a strange way, I needed to meet him.'

Her eyes are full of hurt. 'I didn't know you weren't happy.'

I shake my head sadly. 'To be honest, I'm not sure I did. But when I met Will, I woke up to a lot of things. Your dad and I were good together once. But over time, we've grown apart.' I leave out the part about her father's affair. It's up to James if he wants to tell her.

There are tears in Millie's eyes. 'You should have told me.'

Stroking her long hair over her shoulder, I shake my head. 'You're probably right.'

'What happened with him?' she asks.

'For all kinds of reasons, he's stuck,' I tell her. 'He and his wife were getting divorced. But then their thirteen-year-old daughter went missing.' My voice wavers. 'She'd been desperately unhappy since her parents broke up. Will said if he'd been there, it wouldn't have happened. They're giving it another go. I think they feel they're the reason she ran away.' I pause. 'And he knows how it is to lose a parent.'

There are tears in Millie's eyes. 'That's so sad – that she feels like that.'

'It's really sad. But there's nothing I can do.' I pause, looking at her. 'You know, sometimes it's easier to be the person people expect us to be. But we have one life, Mills. We have to do what is right for us.'

Millie's presence brings life into my cottage. That evening, we eat more of the food I've cooked and drink a couple of bottles of wine. Then the next afternoon, she takes Yippy and her sketchbook and disappears for a couple of hours exploring the countryside, while I unpack a few more boxes. When she comes back, her eyes are bright, her face flushed from the cold.

'It's gorgeous round here.' She looks more at peace than when she went out. 'I've been thinking, Anna... About you and Dad.' A shadow crosses her face. 'I do get it. You are such different people. He didn't treat you well, but I don't think he knows any different...' A tear rolls down her cheek. 'I just want you to know I understand. I don't want anything to change between us.'

My own eyes fill with tears. 'Oh Millie...' I go over to her and hug her tightly. 'Nor do I. You're my daughter.' For a moment, as she slumps against me, I realise she's been worried she'd lose me. 'It's your home too,' I whisper ferociously, my fingers tangled in her hair. 'Wherever I am... it will always be your home, too.'

* * *

As Jessica and I become friends, now and then I help her with her farm and her ever-increasing collection of animals. Meanwhile, alone in my cottage, as I settle into a new way of living here, I think about what I really want from my life.

Outside, in the privacy of my garden, as a much-needed sense of peace returns, I realise how depleted I've become. But I have everything I need here: nature, quiet, the sound of the wind through the apple tree, so that as time passes I can recharge myself. But beyond that, it's as I said to Will. I want to write my book. When it's done, maybe I'll go and see Charley, then Lucy; maybe after that, go somewhere new.

Meanwhile, I load the last of the plants for Alison's garden into my car. As I reach the garden, pale shafts of sunlight break through the clouds. Already there are buds on the camellia that will turn into soft, pink flowers, while behind them, in time, honeysuckle and a rambling rose will cover the wall. Today, I dig in clumps that will become tall daisies and vivid marigolds, forget-me-nots that will colonise, covering the ground with blue. Then standing back, I take a photo and send it to Liza. By next summer, this small corner will be a mass of flowers, which will later die back and self-seed, Alison remembered forever by nature's circle of life, as Liza intended.

But at home, the nights are too long, as I go through a grieving process, for the past, for the future I'd imagined. Even the universe goes quiet on me, only now and then sending me ambivalent messages which don't really help.

Embrace the uncertainty

How can I embrace the uncertainty when my entire life is uncertain?

In an act of self-preservation, I avoid everywhere that reminds me of Will, but after fruitless days at my laptop, trying and failing to write my book, one cold morning I'm drawn by an invisible force back to Dyrham Park. And it's as it was in March when we met. As I reach the slope where he and I used to walk, as the trees thin out, I see someone across the fields.

As I watch him walk towards me, disbelief fills me. Even at a distance, I recognise his jacket and the way he moves. Then as he gets closer, I remind myself, he hasn't been in touch. It tells me all I need to know.

'Hello.' Will's eyes are red, as if he's been crying.

'Hi.' My faithless heart is jumping all over the place, but I'm wary. 'How come you're here?'

'We moved back.' He looks closed off, as though a light inside has been switched off. 'I lost my job, and as the house hadn't sold, Darcey thought it made sense.'

'You're in Hinton?' I'm stunned. It seems unbelievable after everything that's happened. But as it sinks in he's still with Darcey, I realise nothing's changed. 'How's Flo?'

'She's so much better. She didn't want to move, but she's settled really well.' He pauses. 'I've thought about calling you.'

'There isn't really anything to say, is there?' There's no point going there. 'I'm sorry about your job. What will you do?'

'I'm waiting on a couple of interviews. Nothing particularly exciting, but at least it would pay the bills.'

'Maybe it's a sign. That it's your time,' I can't help saying. 'To follow your heart. Start teaching music, maybe – or do something else you feel passionate about.'

'Maybe.' Something flickers through his eyes. 'So how are you?'

'OK. It hasn't been great, if I'm honest.' There's so much he doesn't know, I start with the best. 'I'm halfway through writing my book.'

This time, the smile reaches his eyes. 'That's brilliant – you must be so pleased.'

'I'm loving it.' I hold his gaze. 'But while that was happening, I moved out.'

'You've left James?' His expression is guarded.

'I couldn't stay,' I say quietly.

He frowns. 'Are you OK?'

'I'm getting there.' My voice wavers. 'I'm keeping myself busy, but it takes time.'

'Of course... So where are you living?'

'Marshfield.' Then suddenly I'm filled with anguish, because if this is the universe having a laugh, it isn't funny. 'You know, this is the first time in weeks and weeks that I've come here – and you happen to be here. What are the chances?'

A look of disbelief crosses his face. 'It's the first time I've come here, too.' As we stand there, he takes a tentative step closer.

In that moment, it would be so easy to be pulled in – again. But if he and Darcey are together, there's no room for me in his life. I step back. 'Please, Will. Don't.'

He flinches. 'I'm sorry. I thought...'

'You thought what?' I stare at him. 'That you could waltz back into my life and hurt me again?' I shake my head. 'I've been through enough. Half of you... it isn't enough.'

'Anna. Listen, please...'

The anger goes out of me. 'So that you can tell me you love me – again, but you can't be with me?'

'What I want, in here...' He rests his hand on top of his heart 'is to be with you.'

'The tangled webs we all weave,' I say sadly, wanting so much to believe him. 'I know, you're thinking of Flo. What about Darcey? Is she happy the ways things are? You could still be united parents even if you weren't living together.'

'Please, Anna.' Will's eyes are sad. 'You know why Darcey and I are doing this.'

I do know. But he clearly isn't happy. 'You could have me and Flo, if you were brave enough.' I look at him sadly, because it isn't his relationship with Darcey that's holding him back. It's his ability to deny his own happiness.

When Will mumbles something indecipherable, I'm frustrated. 'Maybe we have to face it – this isn't our time.'

'Oh no.' He shakes his head. 'You're not telling me to give up.'

I hold up my hands. 'I don't know what else to say.'

He looks stricken. 'In another lifetime I can imagine us together – doing everything we've talked about. But when I think of Flo, I worry what it will do to her if I leave.' His voice is desperate, riddled with angst. 'I'd give anything for things to be different, but they're not.' His eyes gaze into mine. 'I'm so sorry, Anna.'

I push my hands into my pockets. 'It is so sad.' My voice trembles. 'But if this is how it is... there's nothing to say.'

Turning around, I'm numb as I start walking away; half wanting him to come after me, telling me he's made a mistake. There would be no point, though. I've already wasted too much time. But no more. It ends here.

* * *

One week later, I go for a run. It's early, the sun bursting through the trees, the air around me vibrant with the sound of birdsong. Reaching the top of the hill, I stand there for a moment, as suddenly everything starts falling into place, answers coming to me, answers that have evaded me for weeks, if not forever.

Life isn't about standing still. It's time to move forward; to leave behind what I can't change, to embark on a brand new chapter. But there's one thing I have to do. Reaching into my pocket for my phone, I text Will.

I have an idea for another book.

It doesn't take long for him to reply.

But you're not going to tell me.

He knows that thing I have, about not telling anyone about an idea until it's fully formed – and hopefully, mostly written. But this time's different.

I'm giving our story an ending! But you'll have to wait.

I hesitate, knowing it's as much his story as mine.

I've got to write it first. But one day, when it's written, I'll send it to you.

Not wanting to encourage more communication from him, I switch off my phone. I know what his fears are; that after all the people he's lost, he's used to feeling alone. But he's made his decision to stay where he is and there's nothing I can do, except go wherever this is taking me.

There's a basic need in all of us to be the master of our own ship, to command our destiny. But it doesn't always work like that. Things happen that are beyond our control, so that at times we feel as powerless as a tiny boat on ocean waves, carried along, only going one way. Resisting only means it takes longer.

SEPTEMBER 2012

WILL

It was the day he'd been dreading and as Will sat in the church, his heart was pounding, his face hot and flushed, his head bowed, the organ's slow mournful tones taking him back to his mother's funeral.

Simon John Harrison. Through his tears, they were the only words Will could focus on, the Order of Service shaking in his hands. His body was rigid, his nerves taut so that he could hardly move, while beside him his father remained poised, his gaze fixed firmly on the ground.

Even today, there was no connection between them. Before leaving the house, Will had tried to reach out to him, hoping for a word of warmth, a shared memory of his brother. But his efforts had been futile.

In the pew behind him, he was aware of Darcey and a couple of Simon's closest friends, but crippled with an onslaught of emotions, he couldn't turn around. As the murmur of voices reached his ears, dizziness overcame him as he thought about all the familiar faces who'd want to meet him afterwards.

'Let us all stand and sing the first hymn. "Guide Me O Thou Great Redeemer".' The vicar's solemn tone held the compassion befitting the moment, as the church filled with the noise of the congregation stand-

ing, puncturing the intensity of the atmosphere so that Will was suddenly able to breathe more easily.

Throughout the service, Will stared between the blurred photograph of his brother on the Order of Service and the coffin, just a few feet away, his eyes permanently filled with tears. It was a photo of Simon smiling as he leaned against a signpost in Land's End. Will remembered how Simon had joked that one day he'd do the walk to John O'Groats but for now, 'a photograph implying I've done it is just as good!'

As the service came to an end and the stone-faced undertakers hefted the coffin to their shoulders, Will could barely bring himself to watch. Then as they headed for the door, he felt a sense of history repeating itself.

He didn't remember the walk to the corner of the churchyard, only watching as Simon's coffin was lowered to its final resting place a few feet from their mother's grave, feeling a sudden rush of guilt. Simon was the one who had lived life responsibly, looking after himself, carving out a successful career, finding contentment in life. In comparison, going through the motions, Will felt a failure.

It had been hard enough losing his mother. But when he'd taken for granted his brother would be around forever, it was like a light had gone out. For the first time in his life, Will felt utterly alone.

35

ANNA

With Alison's garden finally planted, I take up Liza's invitation to join them. It's a chilly October night, the air damp with drizzle, but in this tiny corner of Bath, Alison's parents have created their own little corner of magic.

Tiny white fairy lights have been threaded through the shrubs, with candles pushed between the plants into the soil. Since I was last here, a wooden bench has been placed against the wall. Amongst the small group gathered, I notice a couple of teenagers who I guess are Alison's friends.

Liza comes towards me.

'Anna.' She kisses me on both cheeks. 'I'm so pleased you could make it.'

'I love what you've done. It's beautiful.'

'It's you who's done the work. I wanted it to be special – and it really is.' Liza's voice catches. 'What do you think of the bench?'

'It fits perfectly.' Just above it, David fixes a simple plaque to the wall, on which *Alison's Garden* has been engraved, while Liza watches, her eyes filled with tears.

'We were hoping people might come here, just to sit.' For a

moment she's quiet, as if she's somewhere far away, but I know she's thinking of her daughter. But she'll always be thinking of her. When David comes and stands beside her, I slip away, leaving them alone together.

* * *

With the shortening daylight hours, I work on my book. Meanwhile, the mellow warmth of autumn gives way to strong winds and heavy rain. Overnight, the year's leaves are deposited, then the river at the end of the lane floods, the fields morphing into a surreal waterscape.

Staying inside, I write, uninhibitedly, cathartically, not for anyone else to read, but for myself; still going round in circles when Lucy calls me.

'Babe? How are you?'

'I'm writing it all down,' I tell her. 'I saw Will again. He lost his job, and they've moved back to Hinton.'

'Shit. He's still with his wife?' She sounds wary.

'Very much so. It's crazy, but there it is.'

'Anna, you need to keep away from him.'

'I am, believe me.' My words are hollow. 'I've been avoiding him.'

'Book a flight, for fuck's sake. You need to get away.'

This time, I do what my friend says, because she loves me and because she's right. After looking at flights, for the first time in my life, I buy a one-way ticket. The next morning, I lock the house and leave Yippy with Jessica. Then I drive to Bristol and by ten o'clock, I'm on a plane.

* * *

Arriving in Ibiza feels like coming home, even more so when I walk out of the terminal and Lucy's waiting for me.

'Anna!' As she hugs me, I blink away tears I hadn't known were there. 'I'm so glad you're here.'

Beyond getting myself here and meeting Lucy, I haven't thought any further. All I know is how achingly tired I am.

Gazing out of the car window, it's still late summer here, with no evidence of the autumn I left behind. 'I can't believe how different it is.'

'It's cool at night, babe, but we've had some glorious days! I have all these places I want to take you to. You are staying for a while, aren't you?' Lucy suddenly sounds anxious.

'I have a one-way ticket,' I tell her proudly, loving how that feels. 'Don't make me too at home. You'll never get rid of me!'

Arriving at Can Mimosa, as I get out into warm sunshine, at last I feel I can breathe. From Lucy's terrace as I gaze across the hills, life in England already feels light years away.

'Here.' Lucy passes me a large glass of gin and tonic with ice and slices of lime. 'Salud.'

'Salud.' I clink my glass against hers. 'Thanks so much, Luce.'

'Nonsense.' Lucy shakes her head. 'I want to talk to you, though. I want to know what your plans are.'

'When the house is sold, I'll probably try and buy somewhere. I have my cottage for now – and I'm writing. I'm doing OK, Luce. It was tough for a while, but it's getting easier.'

'You think?' As Lucy pauses, the volume of the cicadas picks up. 'How can it, when you live so close to Will?'

'I've been thinking of moving away, Luce. For good. I'm even thinking about France. Charley's really happy there – and property is cheap, the weather's warmer...'

Lucy leans forward. 'I'm so glad you've said that, because...

I've had a much better idea.' Her voice is suddenly serious. 'I think you should move here. To my casita.'

Startled, I shake my head. 'I can't do that. You rent it out. Coming to stay is one thing, but you have an income from it.'

She has that look on her face she always has when she's made her mind up about something. 'I'd already decided I was going to offer it to you. I've been thinking about it for a while, now. I'm sick to death of drunk tourists – I don't make nearly enough money out of them and they come and go all hours. I'd much rather you had it. Think about it.' As she goes on, it's clear Lucy's thought this through. 'You can store or sell your furniture. Actually, my mother gave you some of it, didn't she? She'll take it back and I'll ask her if you can store the rest of your stuff in her barn.' Lucy's mother lives in a farmhouse with numerous redundant outbuildings. 'At least that way, it'll be there if you go back – not that I think for a minute you will. Then you pile everything else into your car – along with the dog – and drive here.'

The casita is in the grounds of Lucy's finca. And she makes it sound so simple. As I contemplate doing what she's described, quiet excitement fills me. 'Are you sure?'

'Of course I am!' Lucy raises her glass again, chinking it against mine. 'It would be brilliant, babe.'

It could be. But the thought of Millie tugs at my heartstrings. 'I have to think about Millie.'

'Anna.' Lucy speaks firmly. 'Millie has her own life. She'll visit! She'd love it here.'

And I can't argue with that, because I know she would. I can imagine her here, inspired to paint. 'I still need to think about it.'

'Come for six months,' Lucy says quietly. 'It's long enough to see if it's right for you. If it isn't, you can always go back. But if it is, which it will be, you can stay.'

'OK.' A broad smile spreads across my face. It's the moment

I've been waiting for; when at last I know I've found it. The beginning of the rest of my life.

* * *

When Lucy goes to London, I stay here, by day, seeking out the empty beach at the end of the road, where the water is clear and the cicadas louder. Then, in the evenings, I sit outside, watching the changing hues of peach and lilac as the sun sets. Back at Lucy's, as the temperature drops, I light the fire pit, my excitement building as I imagine the road trip, knowing the old me would be so proud of what I'm doing. *If only Will was free to come with me...* I think about sending him one of his spreadsheets populated with reasons to live, laugh, fall in love, follow your heart, versus reasons to be miserable, but there's no point. He'd read it, smiling sadly, listing just as many reasons why it's impossible.

Maybe that's what triggers my restlessness that night. Unable to sleep, as I think of leaving James and losing Will, it's as though my heart has been ripped open, everything I've been through catching up with me. Overwhelmed by an ocean of sorrow, I tell myself I had choices. I could have kept my head down and stayed where I was. Life could have gone on, just as it was. When I think of Millie, my heart shatters into a million pieces, because I've failed her, just as I've failed James. I wasn't enough. And though I've laid myself bare, given him everything, nor am I enough for Will.

Alone in the darkness, my emotions engulf me, as from what feels like far away, I survey the ruins of my past, questioning what the point is, of love, of suffering; of life itself.

But you're suffering too. My inner voice startles me, triggering another deluge of grief, spiralling me downwards, until in the blackest place I've known, it stops.

There, as I face the reality of everything that's happened to me, through the darkness it finds its way to me. A quiet voice, telling me there are things we have no control over. Times you have to stop fighting. When you have to let life happen in its own time, trusting that it's the way it's meant to.

As a feeling of warmth cocoons me, I'm not sure if it's the universe that whispers. *Surrender,* as the storm stops raging and there is calm.

The following morning, the calm stays with me. While life can be every shade of darkness and light, not all great love stories end in the happiness we believe they should.

But on this beautiful island, there is much to be grateful for, and later that morning, as I drive to one of the beaches, I pull over and stop the car. It's silent around me as I get out, the air pine-scented; soft with the hint of a breeze. But it's the view I can't take my eyes off – the one from my list, as I take in the fields of orange and lemon trees.

36

WILL

Starting a new job had provided a much needed distraction. OK, so it wasn't the most exciting, but it had given his self-esteem a boost, while having sold their house in Glasgow, financially things were looking up. All in all, Will should have been feeling pretty good about things. After all, for a while it had looked so much worse.

But all the money in the world couldn't change the emptiness inside him. Like Anna had said, once you'd realised the material niceties of life didn't make you happy, it left you searching for something deeper. A sense of purpose; a life lived now, in this moment. The one thing that mattered more than any of them. Love.

Having glimpsed all those things and walked away, Will knew how it felt to miss them. More than once, he'd thought how much easier it would have been if he and Anna hadn't met again; if his life could have continued as it was, unchanged. Maybe he and Darcey would have had a chance. But in his heart, Will knew that he'd changed; that the transformative power of love had reached into his frozen heart, awakening it.

In the garden, Will pulled his jacket around him as he sat on one of the chairs. The scent of winter honeysuckle reached him, as for a moment he was reminded of that day Anna came here. It would have been inconceivable then that he and Darcey and Flo would end up living here.

In the apple tree, a robin watched him with beady eyes before flying away, as suddenly Will envied it its freedom. His eyes turned to the holly tree laden with berries, a reminder that Christmas would soon be here. He imagined them decorating the house, Flo's excitement, the rich food, trying to find Darcey a present when in reality, she had everything she needed; when the only reason he would be doing it was for Flo.

After that, it would be the start of another year. It wasn't a prospect that filled him with excitement. However positive a spin he put on his new job, already the gloss had worn off. Leaving Flo out of the equation for the minute, settling, drifting, wasn't how he wanted to spend the rest of his days.

Will gazed up at the sky. Grey, it threatened rain, as frustration filled him. He was stuck; had a feeling that what he wanted was permanently out of his reach. Far from this being a fun chapter of his life, he felt like he was suffocating.

Out of the corner of his eye, he noticed a light switched on in the house, before the back door opened and Flo came outside.

'Hi, Dad.' She sounded bright, Will thought. Happy.

'Hello, sweetheart.' His heart warmed as he smiled at his daughter. 'How was swimming?'

'Really cool. Mum said to tell you she's gone to pick up some dry cleaning. I'm going to change,' she announced, turning and going back inside.

Getting up to follow her, Will sighed. This, right here, was what mattered, he reminded himself. The three of them being a united family – and not his own selfish needs, but his daughter's happiness.

37

ANNA

After flying home to an England that's gearing up for the Christmas thrash, in spite of my best efforts to avoid Will, inevitably we're brought together again.

As I stop to fill my car with petrol, he walks towards me, the look in his eyes desperate. 'I miss you.'

'You can't do this, Will,' I tell him. 'I need to get on with my life. Without you.' Getting back in my car, I forget about the petrol and drive away.

I take it as a sign of healing that it doesn't get to me the way it used to. And it's taken time, but one morning I find myself driving through Bath, my heart lifting at the sight of windows lined with Christmas lights, quietly proud as I realise I'm moving on.

* * *

With her mother away and James staying with friends, on Christmas Eve, Millie arrives for a couple of days. Determined to make an occasion of it, we cook a roast and all the trimmings, then eat the traditional cake I always make. There are poignant moments, where we're both thinking of Christmases past. But there's hilarity over the sloe gin I've made, followed by unspoken relief when it's over. The house is quieter than ever when she goes.

I see the New Year in alone. Outside in the darkness, I gaze at the stars, thinking how everything I've been through this year has brought me to where I am now. It's how it works, though. Life slowly changing us; guiding us to where we're meant to be.

But I'm not dwelling on the past. As midnight arrives, I raise a glass of champagne to the universe, excitement rippling through me as I think of what lies ahead, because this is the year everything changes.

38

WILL

Stepping outside, Will glanced up at the sky. It had been cloudy earlier, a hint of drizzle in the air, but it had cleared and in the darkness he could see millions of stars twinkling. As the muffled sound of Big Ben came to him from the television inside, heralding the start of another year, he wondered what the next twelve months would bring; if something would magically happen to break the deadlock in his mind.

At least what he'd always called the *fucking dire bit* was over – the bit between Christmas and New Year that was like seven Sundays in a row as you waited impatiently for the next party to start. But that was back in his partying days and tonight, he'd wanted to spend the evening alone, so that he could stand under the stars as he was right now, hoping something etheric would reach out to him.

Will sighed. The start of another year and where was he? Watching joyous television presenters conducting mindless three-second interviews with street revellers, only underlined his feeling of 'them and us'; the whole world happy – apart from him.

Maybe the beginning of another year was the time for a New Year's resolution. Since moving back to Hinton, he'd felt his life close in around him, but he could change that. He was going to call up some of his old band mates, suggest they get together and do something with their music – he wasn't sure what exactly. Maybe just play some of their old stuff. Or maybe he'd actually start on that idea he'd had and mentor teenagers, the kind who lived for music, like he used to. Perhaps he'd talk to Flo, get her involved, too. He could already feel the plan gathering momentum.

As he stood there, suddenly his mind was racing. Instead of this charade with Darcey, this living separate lives under one roof that left him so hideously empty, there had to be another way. They could make it work around Flo, surely, now that he and Darcey were at least amicable again. He couldn't go on simply going through the motions.

He wanted more. Chasing hopes and dreams; loving, were what life was about, while instead, here he was, chalking up an ever-growing list of regrets.

39

JANUARY 2020

Anna

Having settled on a date to leave the UK, I get on a train to London and spend a wonderful day with Millie. We go shopping, then for lunch in a new vegan restaurant. After, she takes me back to her studio and shows me the latest commission she's working on. Art is subjective and I'm no expert, but her brushstrokes convey energy and light, with a brilliance that takes my breath away.

More than ever, I'm determined she has to fulfil her dream of being an artist. 'These are incredible, Mills.' I'm transfixed. 'I mean it. Never let anyone tell you otherwise.' Having held back over Christmas, I tell her about Lucy's offer.

'In Ibiza?' Her eyes are wide. 'You mean, you're actually moving there?'

I'm nodding. 'Well, for six months to start with. It isn't far away... only a couple of hours on a plane... You can come over any time, as often as possible. It's beautiful. And peaceful, Mills. You'll love it there, I know you will... And in between, I could fly back to see you...' I can't bear her to think I'm deserting her.

Her eyes glitter with tears as she hugs me. 'It's a brilliant idea! I don't know why I'm crying really. I suppose it's just that it seems a long way away.'

Suddenly, I'm anxious. 'Will you promise to visit? Often?'

Millie smiles. 'Try stopping me.'

* * *

The next day, back at home, I immerse myself in writing. Fired up, I manage ten thousand words, which is the fastest I've ever written. I'm being swept along by a wave I don't want to get off, so that, five days later, when Will's number flashes up on my phone, I ignore it.

In my mind, it's like a light has been turned on. We could have worked things out around Flo's life, but he's spurned the universe, destiny, fate, pushing him in a new direction, using all his strength to resist them. Whatever he might have thought when we met, he isn't ready for anything new. He's chosen a life where he's missing out on happiness, where he'll never take risks, while what he'll gain, a thousand fold, is regret.

But I know where it all started. My mind conjures an image of the teenaged Will who'd lost his mother. His eyes are blank, his face closed off, but deep inside, he's broken. With no one to talk to, his pain is unresolved. He doesn't believe he deserves to find happiness.

* * *

In the garden around my cottage, the first snowdrops come into flower, their petals translucent in the sunlight, and as I finish writing my book, I think of the new chapter that lies tantalisingly around the corner.

Finding my phone, I call Lucy. 'You better sit down.'

'Oh God.' Lucy sounds horrified. 'The last time someone told me that, they followed it with news that they were pregnant.'

'It's hardly going to be that,' I tell her. 'Anyway, it's way better. I've finished my book!'

'That's fantastic, babe! What happens now?'

'I'm sending it off to literary agents! And I've almost finished packing... It won't be long before I'm with you...'

* * *

* * *

Poring over road maps, I start from Calais, plotting my drive through France, circling places of interest along the way. Fitting in a stop en route at Charley's house, it comes together effortlessly.

When Millie comes for a weekend, I show her my plans. She gazes at the map in disbelief.

'I wish I could come with you.'

'Why don't you?'

She looks regretful. 'We're already short-staffed at the café. I don't think I could get the time off. But seriously, Anna, this is cool. I swear, one day, I'm going to do something just like this.'

Spurred on by Millie's approval, I finish going through my possessions. But what I keep to take with me amounts to relatively little, while getting rid of physical clutter is liberating.

As I pack my last few things, I play loud music, revelling in the sense of freedom I feel as I imagine the life I'm going to make for myself. It's why I've no idea where the sense of finality comes from. Like a heavy wooden door set in an old brick wall, it's cracked tantalisingly open, so that if I peer through, I can glimpse the sun shining on a garden where the childhood ghost of Millie is playing with her friends. But as I glance away, it feels like a door I'm closing forever.

I make the most of the days I have left here, and after sending my book out to half a dozen literary agents, I see more of Millie than I have in ages. Taking time off when she can, she spends it with me and Yippy. One day she brings her portfolio, opening it and spreading it across the kitchen table.

'I've been working on these. I wanted to show you.'

She leaves me to leaf through a series of sketches and paintings that take my breath away. Then she pulls out one of Yippy, in which she's captured his air of defiance perfectly. 'This is for you.'

'I love this.' I gaze at it. 'I'm going to frame it, Mills, and take it with me. And every time I look at it, I'll think of you.'

* * *

Just before I leave, I start the blog I've been planning to write.

My last few days before I leave the UK, my mind is filled with many things – that I could stay here – and it's a good life. But... What drives me on is the sense that there's a different way to live. I don't have time to waste – none of us do. What we have is this moment, and all the moments that will follow. What matters is making them count.

So that's what I'm going to do. Take these moments and have an adventure with them.

Watch this space.

After packing up my car, I post a photo of an empty room. Outside, the garden is coming to life, the daffodils starting to flower. Photographing the clematis that trails over the front door, I write another post:

As human beings, some of us are hardwired to be nostalgic, full of regret, held by a past that can't be changed. It can take a meteoric shift to let that go.
I could feel sad right now, about what I'm leaving behind, nostalgic about the past. But the new lies ahead, and I can't wait to see what that brings, while the important stuff will come with me – in my heart.

Then the day is here – and I'm ready. But saying goodbye to Millie is hard.

'I'm excited for you!' She smiles through her tears, but her voice wavers. 'It's a long way to drive. You will be OK, won't you?' A look of anxiety passes across her face.

'Oh, Mills.' I hold her, trying to stop my tears, not wanting to let her go. 'Of course I will. You must come and stay. Whenever. Forever, if you want to. There's a room for you. Not a spare room, your own room,' I emphasise. 'Lucy will be next door! And you know how long I've dreamed of doing this.' This road trip is possibly my greatest adventure. 'You should go,' I say gently. 'I've a few more things to do, but I have to leave soon, too. I'll call you every day – I promise.'

As she hugs me again, we're both in tears.

'Look at us.' It's a bittersweet moment, but in spite of the emotion surging inside me, I can't help laughing. 'I'm only going to be a couple of hours away!'

Wiping her eyes, Millie tries to smile. 'I know. I'll just miss you!'

'I'll miss you too. But we can talk every day, Mills – and we're still part of each other's lives – we always will be.'

I walk out with her, watching as she gets in her car, waving as she drives away, before it's my turn. Taking a last look around the house, I whisper a *thank you* to these walls that have held me safe these last months.

Then all that's left to do is post my key through the letter box for Jessica's friend to pick up later. Badly wanting to hear her no-nonsense tones, I call Lucy.

'For fuck's sake, darling, where are you?'

It's exactly what I need to hear. 'I'm just about to leave.' I take a deep breath. 'I just said goodbye to Mills.'

'Good. So you're ready then! Well, get going. Ring me when you get to Folkestone.'

'OK.' Suddenly, I'm properly excited. 'Talk to you soon, Luce!' Closing the door for the last time, I post the key, then without looking back, head for my car.

As I start the car, I hesitate for a moment, thinking of Will, knowing he would love what I'm doing. But maybe it's his destiny to live a life that's joyless. He won't notice, though, because he'll have shut down, so that he's back to how he was when we met up again. Being half of Will, instead of the whole glorious technicolour human he used to be.

As I drive, he stays in my mind. I wonder if it's the same for him, as my mind grows silent, the universe whispering to me.

This changes nothing. Whether you are together or not, he loves you. He always will.

PART IV

40

WILL

Since the party she'd been to on New Year's Eve, there'd been a distance between him and Darcey. Will had put it down to his emotional detachment from her, but he was starting to wonder if there was more.

With Flo upstairs doing her homework, Will was flicking through TV channels, trying and failing to find anything that interested him.

'Will?'

Looking up, he hadn't noticed Darcey come in. 'Hi.'

Coming over, she sat down beside him. 'Is everything OK?'

The question startled him as suddenly he was wary. 'Yes. Fine,' he said briefly.

'It's just that...' She hesitated. 'You seem quiet. Distant.'

Looking at the wedding ring she'd started wearing again, he frowned. 'I suppose this isn't ideal, is it? I mean, it is for Flo. But not so much for us.'

Sadness crossed her face. 'I really hoped things might go back to the way they used to be.'

Looking at her, Will tried to remember how he used to feel,

when they first met, when they decided to get married; feelings that had been extinguished by the fighting between them – irrevocably, it seemed to Will. 'Don't you think that's asking too much?' he said softly. 'I don't think anyone can go back – only forwards.'

She shrugged. 'Couldn't we make a fresh start then?'

He sighed. 'Isn't that what we're doing?'

She hesitated. 'I'm trying... But I'm not sure you are.'

Will's head was starting to thump. He couldn't believe she'd switched allegiance so suddenly; that moreover, she expected him just to turn his feelings back on. 'It isn't that long ago you were going to marry Eric. We were about to be divorced. After all the rows and disagreements we had, you can't just forget what's happened and conjure old feelings back.' Too much time had passed. And a whole load of shit between them, too. 'We're not the same people any more.'

But she wasn't giving up. 'That doesn't mean we can't make this work.'

Seeing tears glitter in her eyes, Will cynically wondered if she was acting. 'Look, the way I see it, we're making the best of this – for Flo's sake. She's the only reason we're together,' he reminded her gently.

She glared at him. 'Talk about brutal.'

When the tears vanished instantly, Will knew his hunch was right. 'I didn't mean to be. I was trying to be honest.'

As Darcey got up, any softness about her had vanished. 'You've made it clear enough how you feel. Just so you know, I'm planning to spend more time in Bristol.'

Will stood up. He absolutely could see this for what it was – yet more of her classically manipulative behaviour. He'd had enough. 'Just so you know, we're in this together, Darcey. If we're living under one roof, we play by the same rules.'

'Or what?' she taunted. 'If you want me here, you need to be more of a husband, Will.'

Will was rigid with anger. It was Darcey at her absolute worst, resorting to blackmail to get what she wanted. The sound of Flo's bedroom door opening came from upstairs as Will glared at her. 'Remember why we're doing this,' he said quietly.

* * *

That night, Will lay in bed, unable to sleep. The conversation with Darcey had felt like the last straw. But at some point in the early hours, a new clarity had come to him. It wasn't right to go on with this sham of a marriage, to live with this apathetic resignation to a status quo that deep inside, left him empty.

But as he lay there, his mind was racing. It wasn't just about him and Darcey. It was the fact that the weeks and months were drifting past, time he was wasting in a marriage that was over, when he should be filling it with more of what excited him, such as music, travelling; with a job that fulfilled him.

He was going to have to pick his moment and talk to Darcey again. He wasn't sure what they were going to do, but he needed her to understand they couldn't go on like this.

41

ANNA

After calling Lucy from Folkestone, I leave England behind. Then, emerging from the train in Calais, I drive towards the sun. Avoiding lunatic French drivers and playing music, I find the small cottage near Evreux I've booked for tonight.

After checking in and picking up my key, I whistle to Yippy and walk through hazy fields in the afternoon sunlight. Then back at the cottage, after pouring a glass of wine and checking my emails, I start to write.

Day 1 of my road trip to Ibiza… A few hundred miles, yet so far away from where I woke up this morning! I've always believed that a door closing means another opening; that endings lead to new beginnings. Never has it felt clearer that I'm meant to be doing this.

Already I feel different. I post a photo of Yippy sitting in the middle of my antique bed, ears pricked as he watches me. Then, after climbing into my pyjamas, I sleep blissfully.

Still slightly euphoric the following day, I set off along roads bathed in mist that burns off in the early morning sunlight. As I drive, I'm thinking about writing, in particular the book I told Will I was going to write. *I'm giving our story an ending.*

I think about giving it the ending it should have had, the happy-ever-after one which brings us together, but as I know too well, real life isn't always like that.

Now and then stopping to jot down thoughts, I make a pact with myself that when I get to Ibiza, whatever else is going on, I'll find the time to write it, the entire story of Will and me, set against the countryside we both love; the times it flowed, the times it felt impossible; an end that has no closure. But for all of that, it's a story of love – for life and for other people; for this beautiful world; for the one person, if you're lucky enough to find them, who is your soulmate.

As I drive further south, France turns warmer, lighter, the colours more vivid, England already feeling a lifetime away. I take my time, and, when I reach the vineyards and tiny villages around Gascony, I make a detour, enjoying the unfamiliar countryside, stopping for delicious food, warmed by the unexpected friendliness of strangers.

Day 2… My room is simple – a wooden bed, soft linen, a tiled floor; has blue shuttered windows that look out onto green fields, pots of geraniums on the balcony, silence that's only broken by the breeze. Taking a meandering path through woods, Yippy and I walked to the village to buy a baguette and a beer, which we had sitting on a riverbank. I'm in the full throes of an uninhibited wanderlust! In love with this adventure I'm having. Whatever's next, I'm ready! Bring it on!

Adding a close-up photo of the reeds fringing the river, on impulse, I post a link on Facebook.

I've started a blog! #RoadtriptoIbiza.

In the village, I buy a postcard with pictures of markets, wine and sunflowers, to send to Ron and Grace, my old neighbours, before writing another to Millie.

Wish you were with us. Love you xxx

Then with that done, I set off for Charley's house.

It's another glorious day of driving through a landscape of lush green fields and pale stone houses, as I start to get an idea of how much Charley's life has changed. The small village she lives in consists of grandly proportioned houses in various states of decay on either side of streets lined with plane trees.

Eventually, I find her wonderful old French farmhouse, set back behind a square of neatly mown grass. As I turn up her gravel drive, even before I've parked, she throws open the door and runs towards me.

'It's so good to see you.' Charley hugs me. 'I can't believe you're here!'

'It's so great to be here!' I've already forgotten how tired I am from driving. 'This is stunning, Charley.' I gaze at the house, with its large windows and typically sloped French roof, hardly able to believe my friend lives here.

'It wasn't always like this. I've worked my arse off, not to mention my fingernails.' But Charley looks proud. 'It's been worth it, though. I love this place... Come on! Give me your bag... I'm dying for you to meet Freya!'

After letting Yippy out, I follow her towards stone steps that lead into a cool, tiled hallway, then through another door into the sitting room, where Freya is asleep in a huge old-fashioned cradle. I gaze at her, taking in how petite she is, with hair the colour of Charley's, her fingers curled into tiny fists. 'She's beautiful, Charley.'

'Isn't she?' Charley's voice is quietly proud. 'Come through to the kitchen. I'll make us a drink.'

Tiptoeing away, I follow my friend further along the hallway into a large, light kitchen, with an original tiled floor and distressed units that look as though they've been there for a hundred years. 'This is heavenly.'

'I'm glad you like it,' she says. 'I thought I was a bit nuts buying somewhere so vast, but the first time I saw it, I fell in love. And now... with Jacques, and Freya, everything's fallen into place.' She hunts around the fridge, then pulls a bottle out, holding it up. 'We need to toast your adventure! Champagne?'

After pouring a couple of glasses, we sit at the bare wooden table. 'Jacques will be back soon. He's working on another house – that belongs to another crazy Englishwoman, as he puts it. There are a few of us around here. It's really nice.'

'It's great how you have a whole new life.'

'And soon, you will too!' She studies me for a moment. 'So it didn't work out with Will?'

'No.' The champagne is cool and crisp. 'I guess it wasn't to be.'

'I'm so sorry, Anna.'

'Don't be. Honestly, I'm getting so much out of doing this on my own.' However much I'd love Will to be here, it's true.

'Empowering, isn't it? To decide, then just get on with it?' Charley raises her glass. 'To strong women everywhere!'

'I'll drink to that!'

We're on our second glass when Jacques comes in. With twinkling eyes full of kindness, it's easy to see what Charley sees in him. When Freya wakes up, he goes to get her. Charley catches my eye. 'He's great with her. I'm lucky.'

That evening, Jacques babysits while Charley and I go to the single restaurant in the village.

'There's not a lot of choice,' Charley warns me. 'And the menu is different pretty much every day.'

The restaurant is sparse yet homely, the food simple and tasty, the wine free flowing. 'One of many things that are different that I love about here.' Charley seems so at home. 'And in Ibiza, it'll be tapas bars and cocktails at sunset.'

'You should come to Lucy's,' I suggest. 'There's loads of room for the three of you. She'd love to see you!' I pause. 'Do you ever think back to how our lives were just a few years ago? We all seemed so settled. None of us could have imagined what's happened since.'

'No.' Charley looks thoughtful. 'It's been a real mix of the highest highs and shittiest lows... But where we are now is good, isn't it? And who knows what's around the corner?'

* * *

My two days at Charley's pass too quickly. Our farewell is emotional, as she and Jacques make me promise to visit again – soon.

Climbing into my car, Yippy and I get on our way. As I drive, my sense of freedom is back. It isn't just being able to choose where I go, it's the absence of expectation by myself or anyone else; of being ruled by time. A feeling that's amplified by being anonymous. It's a theme that continues when I reach the southernmost part of France and cross the border, driving through the mountains into Spain.

That night, I stay in a hotel in a small Catalan village. Taking Yippy for a walk, I explore steep, medieval streets that are barely wide enough for a single car; take photos of weathered shutters and rusted balconies; of olive trees, faded grandeur, flaking terracotta paint.

This is what it's about. Vast roads cutting across France. A wide sky, an endless sun. Precious days with one of my oldest friends, meeting the baby she nearly lost, seeing her beautiful new home, the new life she's made, that's fallen into place only because she's brave enough.

One day, vineyards, rocky ground, where the trees are scrubby; the next, twisting tree-lined mountain roads, far-reaching views, a tiny medieval village, a hotel steeped in Moorish charm.

A simple sign strung overhead: 'Espagne'.

My feeling of excitement.

In my room, after updating my blog, I go on Facebook, posting a single photo of me and Charley, with a link to my latest post. Just before I log off, for the first time in ages, a message from the universe flashes onto the screen.

Breathe…

Everything is happening the way it's meant to.

There's a funny feeling inside me, because that's exactly how it feels. But ever since I drove away from my cottage in Marshfield, every second of the way, it's felt like that.

In the sumptuous bed, I sleep undisturbed, waking early the following morning before creeping outside to walk Yippy. Outside the hotel, the sloping street leads to a stony path that winds through olive trees, the light changing as the sun rises.

After breakfast, I start the last leg of my trip. As it has been all the way, the blue sky is cloudless, the traffic light on the wide road that runs parallel to the coast, as mile by mile I make my way south towards Dénia.

As I draw closer to the port and the mountains come into sight, I think of the many times I've seen them from the terrace at

Lucy's finca, statuesque peaks flaring into view briefly when the sun sets.

With hundreds of miles behind me, it seems almost unbelievable that there are only these last few to go. But every mile of this road trip has felt effortless, as though the universe has had my back. Arriving with a couple of hours to spare before the ferry leaves from Dénia, I find the port.

After a walk with Yippy along the beach, sitting in the sun, I wait. But it isn't long before we start boarding and once my car is on the ferry, Yippy and I make our way up on deck.

As the last cars board, I breathe in the sea breeze, a surreal feeling filling me as at long last, the ferry pulls out. It's another moment I commit to memory and as we leave the mainland behind, I watch the town of Dénia grow smaller, behind it the mountains looming larger as I briefly think of Will, knowing he would have loved every second of the last few days. But I give him no more thought than that.

The sea is millpond flat, dusk falling by the time we're halfway across. Thrown into relief by the setting sun, the Spanish mountains stand out sharply before fading into the darkness. Sitting on the deck with Yippy curled up next to me, I reach for my phone and post a photo of the sunset, listening as the ferry chugs closer to the island I love, as I write the last blogpost of this road trip.

Ever since I've left the UK, there's been not a single obstacle in my way – and there could have been dozens. Instead, there's been a flow. A seamless journey from the old towards the new; one that's been effortless. I take that to mean I'm in the right place; doing what I'm meant to be doing. Every step along the way, the universe has had my back.

By the way, it has your back, too.

Over one thousand miles later, I'm nearly here.

As we get nearer, the bright lights of San Antonio Bay come into view, then more of them scattered around the coves towards the south. I gaze at the smaller lights blinking amongst the hills, knowing one of them is Can Mimosa.

A rising moon lights the jagged spine of Es Vedrà, before further on, Ibiza town comes into view, the stone walls of Dalt Villa more impressive from the sea. Reaching the port, as the town's lights grow brighter, my heart starts to race.

'We've done it, Yippy,' I whisper to my dog. '*We're here*.'

It takes another hour after our arrival before I disembark, heading out of the town and leaving the traffic behind as I take the almost deserted road towards San José. Passing landmarks I know, pride swells inside me that Yippy and I have made it here. I think about calling Lucy, but instead I drive slowly through the darkness, savouring these last few moments of this magical journey, along the twisty roads that have become so familiar to me.

Then as I turn up the dusty track to Can Mimosa, I'm home. Even before I stop the car, Lucy's shriek of excitement reaches me. As the light comes on outside the finca, I hear her call out, as she runs towards me. '*Anna!*' As I get out, she pulls me into her arms, hugging me tightly. Sensing our mood, Yippy bounds around us. 'Welcome, babe! I can't believe you're here!' she whispers fiercely, her eyes bright with tears.

I can't speak. Utterly exhausted, I feel lighter than I've ever felt, as the biggest smile plasters itself across my face. 'It's been the most bloody brilliant trip,' I tell her. 'I will be talking about it forever!'

'I want to hear about it forever! Leave your stuff in the car. We can unload it tomorrow.' She links her arm through mine. 'I'm so excited! There's champagne in the fridge – the proper stuff. You must tell me about Charley and Freya, too.' Going into the kitchen, Lucy hurries to get the bottle and glasses.

'Two minutes, Luce.' Leaving her, I head into the bathroom, where I splash my face with cold water, gazing at myself in the mirror for a moment. As a sense of achievement fills me, in a moment of quiet pride, I smile at myself.

When I go back to the kitchen, Lucy's waiting for me. 'Come on. Let's go outside.'

We head to the terrace where the fire pit is lit, two chairs pulled up close to it. Sitting down, I gaze across where the hills are, at the lights glittering in the darkness.

'Here.' After pouring the champagne into two flutes, she hands one to me. 'Are you warm enough?'

'I'm fine. Everything's fine.' Looking at her, I burst out laughing. 'I've had the best time ever, Luce. I'm so happy to be here!'

'So am I. And I'm so bloody proud of you, Anna... Cheers!'

I gaze at this amazing woman – my touchstone, who, whatever happens will always be here for me, then at the night sky twinkling with stars, the icy bubbles tingling on my tongue. As moments go, it's a perfect one. One I wouldn't change for the world.

42

WILL

So far, Will's attempts to inject vitality into his life had failed. After contacting his old band mates and his efforts to resurrect anything had fallen flat, Will had approached a local after-school music club, and started teaching guitar to a couple of teenage boys whose parents couldn't afford lessons. One of them reminded him of himself at that age – a bit of a comedian, with a talent Will found impressive. *Don't let this go,* he wanted to tell him. *Don't make the same mistakes I did.*

For the first time in months, he was walking through Dyrham Park again, his hands firmly in the pockets of his jeans. Finding the fallen branch where he used to sit with Anna, Will perched on it, gazing out across the countryside. Closing his eyes, he could almost feel her presence. Hear her voice. For several minutes, forgetting everything, he lost himself in the memory.

One day... Maybe fate or whatever there was out there would intervene so that their paths crossed again. At least, he hoped it would. But today, at least, there was no sign of her.

So far, Will had bloody-mindedly resisted the temptation to investigate Anna's whereabouts. But for reasons he couldn't explain, today was different. Once he was home, he couldn't stop himself. Finding her profile picture, his heart was racing. It had changed. In sunglasses, her skin was tanned and she was smiling. Within seconds of scrolling, he realised Anna had moved – to Ibiza.

A feeling of shock washed over him. In his mind, he always imagined her not that far away – a thought that up until now, had remained comforting. But it clearly wasn't the case. Photos and posts traced her journey from England, through France and Spain, telling the whole story in colourful detail. He stopped at a photo of her sitting on a deserted beach. Framed by blameless blue sky and golden sand, she looked tanned and serene.

Touching the image, he felt deeply unsettled. Scrolling back, a link to a blog caught his eye. Clicking on it, as he started reading, an uneasy feeling hung over him. In a few paragraphs, she'd cut to the heart of what was important.

Scrolling down, he continued through every picture, searching for the smallest sign that she was missing him, but she looked relaxed, content – everything he wasn't. But she was living her life, chasing her dream.

* * *

The following morning as Will was about to go out and pick Flo up, Darcey's voice came from the kitchen. 'Will? You won't believe this.'

'What?' Will went to find her.

'It's Flo.' Sitting at her laptop, Darcey looked dazed. 'That scholarship she told us she was going for... She's only been offered it – on the strength of her swimming. I've just had an email from her school.'

Will was stunned. He'd known Flo was good, but not this good.

'It could be brilliant for her.' Darcey's eyes were bright. 'Academically as well.'

'Where's the school?' He was trying to take it in.

'Kent. Here. This is it.'

Going over, he looked over his wife's shoulder at the website on her laptop, as Darcey went on. 'Apparently, she can start this term if we can get organised in time.'

He looked at Darcey. 'We need to talk to her, don't we?'

Assuming she wants to go... After moving from Glasgow, Flo might not be up for more change. But if she was, there was the potential for more to change than just her school.

* * *

'Oh my God.' Flo looked thunderstruck when they told her. 'Do you know how cool this is?'

'I have an idea! You want to go?' Will looked at her uncertainly.

'Duh, YES!' Flo's eyes were wide as she stared at him. 'It's the best thing ever for my swimming.' She hesitated. 'If it's OK with you?'

'Of course it is. It's an amazing opportunity, Flo. Things like this don't come along too often, but when they do...' Will paused. 'Believe me, you have to grab them.'

Flinging her arms around his neck, Flo hugged him. For a moment, Will was taken back to when she was small and used to hug him all the time. His little girl was growing up so fast. Coming in, Darcey watched them.

'You've done so well.' Uncharacteristically, she held out her arms.

Flo hugged her, not quite the way she hugged Will, he couldn't help noticing. But that was because of Darcey rather than Flo.

* * *

Later that evening, Flo came to find him.

'Dad?' She came over and sat on the sofa next to him.

'Hey, superstar.' Will ruffled her hair.

She gazed at the TV. 'What are you watching?'

'Some boring rubbish about corrupt politicians.' Switching it off, Will turned to look at his daughter. 'I'm so proud of you – getting that scholarship.' He paused. 'Things are going to change a bit, aren't they?'

She looked troubled. 'That's kind of what I wanted to talk to you about.' She hesitated. 'I know why you and Mum are back together. It's because of me, isn't it?'

Will frowned. 'Your mum and I did what we felt was right – for all of us.'

'I know.' She gazed at the sofa. 'But I don't want you to be sad.'

Will was taken aback. He hadn't known it was so obvious. 'Don't you worry about me. I'm fine, Flo.'

She looked upset. 'I thought if I got the scholarship, you wouldn't have to worry about me...'

Will was startled. 'I thought you wanted this.'

'I do,' she said fervently. 'I really do. But if you and Mum don't want to be together, I suppose what I'm saying is, I'll be OK.'

As he looked at his daughter, he felt a weight lift as suddenly he couldn't speak.

'Thank you,' she said quietly. 'For being here.'

A rush of emotion took him over. 'You know wherever you are, I'll still be here for you, don't you? Always?'

Flo nodded. 'I know, Dad.'

Reaching out her arms, Will's heart was full to overflowing as she hugged him. Letting go of her, he tried to lighten the mood. 'Let's go out tonight – the three of us. I mean, it's not every day you get a scholarship to one of the best sports schools in the country... We should be celebrating!'

In the two frenetic weeks that followed, they bought everything on the school's extensive list, before the Saturday morning arrived and Will drove Flo over there.

'Are you sure you have everything?' Will was joking. The car was piled with stuff.

'Yes, Dad.' Flo rolled her eyes.

'And you will call us? Let us know how you're settling in?'

'*Yes, Dad.*' This time the eye-roll was more exaggerated. 'And don't forget I'm coming back in a month for half-term.'

'I'll pick you up earlier if you want to come back for a weekend.'

'Dad. It's miles. You're going to be busy, anyway. I'll be fine.'

* * *

Flo wasn't a child any more, Will thought as he drove away. But, as he joined the motorway, a mixture of feelings assaulted him. He'd expected her to go away to uni, at some distant point in the future, not get a scholarship that meant going away now.

When he got back, Darcey was in the kitchen, the aroma of cooking filling the house.

'Was she OK?' She looked uncharacteristically anxious.

'She was fine.' He hesitated. 'Weird, isn't it? Her not being here?'

Hesitating, Darcey nodded. 'I've made a cottage pie for

tonight. I thought we could open that nice bottle of red. It's a while since it's been just the two of us.'

'Sounds great.' Will forced an enthusiasm he didn't feel. Staying together for Flo was one thing – she was the glue that held them together. And she'd still be back, he reminded himself. It was important Flo knew her parents were there, that home was always here to come back to.

Halfway through the cottage pie, Will was onto his second glass of wine, a rich, velvet-smooth red. He raised his glass. 'A toast – to our wonderful daughter.'

Darcey clinked hers against his. 'To Flo.' Putting her knife and fork down, she was quiet for a moment. 'Can I say something? I've wanted to say this for a while.' She paused. 'I wanted to say thank you. For being here with me, for Flo.'

Will was taken aback. 'What else could I have done? Flo needed us.'

'I know.' Darcey looked troubled. 'But I haven't made it easy for you – the thing with Eric? And I'm sorry about what I said the other day – about spending more time in Bristol. I know we're far from being back to how we used to be. Right now, it's enough that Flo's OK.' She paused. 'I suppose what I'm saying is, I have no expectations – of us. What's meant to be...' She shrugged.

Will was flabbergasted. But Darcey had always had the ability to surprise him. 'Things have changed, haven't they?' It was a relief to be able to say what he was thinking.

Darcey looked sad. 'They have. To be honest, if your feelings have changed, I'm not sure what we do, going forward.'

Will was silent for a moment. 'Nor am I.' He looked at his wife. 'After Flo found out about the scholarship, she said something to me.' He left out the bit about Flo noticing he wasn't happy. 'She knows we're only together because she ran away. She also said, that if we separated, she'd be OK.'

Darcey looked shocked. 'Are you saying you want to move out?'

Will shook his head. 'I'm not suggesting we do anything in a hurry. But maybe we both need to think. Flo's in a good place. She's come a long way, hasn't she?' But they all had. He hesitated. 'Do you ever speak to Eric?'

A cloud crossed Darcey's face. 'We've spoken a couple of times. But that's all.'

Will was curious. 'Do you miss him?'

Darcey sighed. 'I suppose I miss the fun – seeing new places, travelling first class, the grand hotels... I know.' She looked at Will. 'Shallow, aren't I? I can't say I miss Eric as much as I should. Anyway... It all dwindled into insignificance after Flo ran away.'

It kind of summed it up in Will's mind. But the change in her outlook, from needling him to quiet resignation, had astonished him.

Darcey's eyes met his. 'What do you want, Will?'

It was his chance to be honest, to tell her how he really felt, about his frustrations, but once the words were out, there'd be no taking them back. And he needed to know for sure that Flo was settled at school. For now it was enough to have clawed back some kind of friendship out of the wreckage of their marriage. But he couldn't imagine it ever being any more than that. 'We've agreed, haven't we, that for now, we put Flo first? Let's see how she settles at school and go from there.'

* * *

Will couldn't get the image of Anna out of his head. For now, it sufficed to read her blog posts. He was almost sure he was meant to see them, dreading finding images of her holding hands with a bronzed Adonis, fears that, so far, remained unfounded. Mostly they were about her life and the landscape she loved. Anything from the sea to flowers, wild dogs, sparkling wine, orange and lemon trees that made him think of her teenaged list, shuttered windows, goats, geckos, sunsets – the list went on, with occasional selfies of Anna looking sun-kissed and beautiful.

Staring at the screen of his laptop, there were so many things he wanted to talk to her about. He wanted to ask her not to give up on him, to save him a place in her heart. To tell her that Flo would be OK; about the feeling he couldn't ignore that they should be together.

Needing to put it into words, he started typing a letter, hesitantly at first, until suddenly it was pouring out of him, incoherently, over-effusively, until several rewrites later, after reading it back, he deleted it. It wouldn't be fair to contact her now. Until he extricated himself from Darcey, he had no right to ask anything of her.

43

ANNA

Having sent my book out, I wait with trepidation as the responses come in. The first two are brief and to-the-point rejections, followed by a third that's more detailed – still a rejection though. It's a blow, but as I keep reminding myself, I only need one agent to say yes.

Meanwhile, I carry on writing the blog that started out about the road trip, as it becomes a blog about my changing life in which I write the kind of posts I would have wanted to read last year, had I found them.

A little while back, I remembered a list I made. I was fifteen at the time. It was ten things to do before I die. Remember Jackie magazine? The idea came from there. And when you're fifteen, anything is possible. I wanted to jump out of a plane, go to Australia, dye my hair blonde and I haven't done any of them. Happiness was on my list, too – that deep-rooted sense of joy from which to wonder at life. The way you feel when you follow your heart, when you're with those you love, when you're standing in the place where you want to be.
As time passes, some of our dreams change, while we lose sight of

others when life gets in the way. But dreams are not trivial things. They're what life is about, what inspires us to go after what we most want. It's never too late to dream a new dream...

But beneath it all, happiness comes from inside. We are not defined by the past. We are prepared by it, a past that we should accept, embrace, love everything about – then let it go as life carries us forwards.

This time I post several photos – of Lucy's finca, of soft purple rosemary flowers that grow on the hills, the long sandy beach at Salinas, a bar crowded with people listening to live music. So very different to how I lived in Bath... but there's more than one way to live a life.

As the casita becomes my home and I talk to Lucy about finding work, it brings a whole new sense of settledness.

'A friend of mine has an agency that rents out ridiculously priced villas,' she says thoughtfully. 'She's always looking for help with the outside spaces. Leave it with me, but I reckon you'd be the perfect person.' Lucy's already hunting around for her phone. Seconds later, she's talking in perfect Spanish of which I can't understand a single word.

That's how I come to spend the following day driving to the north of the island to meet Larissa. Near the sleepy town of San Joan, the villa is tucked away up an uneven track that disappears between pine trees, before opening out in front of a white-painted villa with heavy wooden doors set into the wall.

After parking next to the small Fiat abandoned there, as I get out, one of the doors opens and Larissa appears, gravel scrunching under her feet as she walks towards me. She's tall, with dark hair and olive skin and as she holds out her hand, her eyes light up.

'Hi, Anna. I'm Larissa! Come on in.'

As I go inside and the gate closes behind me, my jaw drops. The villa is beautiful. Like Lucy's finca, it's old, with original timbers and exposed stonework, but as Larissa shows me around, as I soon see, it's much bigger.

'We get all sorts pitching up here once the season starts – large families, hen parties – it sleeps up to twelve. The pool's this way.' She leads me around a corner, where a shimmering pool is surrounded by sunbeds. 'The chaos began on the first of May, but this one's empty until the end of next month, so we have time to tidy up the garden. Some parts need new plants – it gets so hot, not everything lasts. There's other stuff, like a bit of painting, that sort of thing... Still interested?'

In the event, my new job encompasses much more. Once she has the measure of me, Larissa leaves me to source new plants and decorative items in keeping with what's already there. I find driftwood containers – filled with tropical plants, they bring colour to the courtyard, then I strike gold when I find a photographer who sells large, vintage prints of seventies Ibiza. Taking a risk, I buy several of them. When Larissa sees the finished result, she's impressed.

'I've got a couple more villas that need a facelift, if you're interested. I don't have time for bloody shops,' she says breezily. 'Cheers, Anna. This is great.'

But Ibiza is an island of contrasts and as I drive to and from work, as well as the luxurious villas that nestle amidst the hills, there are isolated pockets of traditional Ibicencan life – small farms where the rust-red soil is turned and cultivated; where chickens roam and a few animals are kept.

Often, I pass an elderly woman, who from under the shade of an olive tree watches her herd of goats, as she probably has, I can't help thinking, most of her life. Then one day, I notice her walking along the road, laden with shopping bags.

Pulling over, I get out. 'Would you like a lift?'

Shaking her head, she stops suddenly and puts down her bags. Going over to her, I point to my car, then in the direction of where I've seen her with the goats, cursing that I don't speak Spanish. '*Si*? Yes?'

Up close, she's small, her skin lined. Her face is expressionless as she nods. Picking up her bags, we load them into my car. Then as I start to drive, I notice how short of breath she is. But it's too hot to be dressed in dark clothing.

Feeling her hand on my arm, I glance at her as she points towards a stony track. Turning up it, I try to avoid the worst of the potholes as we head towards the house up ahead.

On reaching it, she turns to me. '*Gracias.*'

As she slowly gets out, almost immediately the air fills with the sound of goats bleating, almost as though they know she's here. Picking up her bags, I follow her into the cool of a small kitchen, neatly arranged around a traditional oven.

After putting the bags down, I'm about to leave when I hear a car pull up outside, followed by footsteps as a voice calls out.

'*Hola?*'

The woman who comes hurrying in looks about my age, with brown eyes and dark hair. When she sees me, she stops short.

'Hello – *hola*...' Not sure what to say, I glance at the goat lady.

The woman's face lights up. 'You speak English? Thank God.'

'I gave her a lift,' I explain. 'It's so hot and she was struggling with some shopping. I drive past here every day and I've seen her with the goats.'

'It was kind of you to stop. I'm Isabella. Sofia is my grandmother. She was supposed to wait for me to pick her up, but she isn't very patient.' Turning to Sofia, she says something in Spanish before turning back to me.

'I'm Anna.' I hesitate. 'I should probably get back.'

'Oh, no. Stay, Anna... for a drink? You've no idea how much I'd *love* to have an English conversation.' She glances at her grandmother. 'She doesn't speak a single word of it. Are you staying near here?'

'I live with a friend in San José.'

'It's your home?'

'For a few months, but maybe for longer.' I watch as Isabella fills three glasses with ice cubes and lemon slices, before topping them up with sparkling water.

Giving one to her grandmother, she passes another to me. 'Let's sit outside.' Leaving her grandmother to put her shopping away, she leads me through the house to the shade of a terrace.

Pulling out one of the chairs arranged around a large table, I take in the view. It's not dissimilar to the one from Can Mimosa, of hills and valleys, the single road twisting through them; the sea only slightly more distant. 'How long have you lived here?'

'I don't. I live in England. It's a bit of a story.' Pausing, Isabella sips her drink. 'I was adopted. I've only recently found out Sofia is my grandmother on my mother's side. She didn't know anything about me. She's quite distrusting.' Isabella shakes her head. 'She refused to believe who I was, until she saw my birth certificate.'

'Is your mother here?'

'I never knew her.' Isabella looks sorrowful. 'She was on her way back here in 1972, but her plane crashed. I didn't know until Sofia told me. There is a memorial where the plane came down, in the hills above San José, where it happened. It has an atmosphere. You can feel what went on there.'

I'm shocked. 'That's so sad.'

'Yes. Ibiza's only plane crash.' She's quiet for a moment. 'Not the best reason to go somewhere. But I'm glad I'm here. What brought you here?'

'My friend Lucy moved here years ago. I've visited a few times but I fell in love with the island. I suppose, it was a question of timing and things falling into place – or not.' I hesitate. Then because there's no reason not to, I tell her about leaving my marriage and meeting Will.

As I finish, her eyes are warm. 'It's why you're here. When we experience pain… it changes us, doesn't it? It makes you look for meaning, I think. And that's different things for different people. Sorry,' she breaks off. 'I don't mean to sound personal, but when we go through trauma, I'm interested in what helps us heal.'

But so am I. 'Here has always felt a good place to be. I think it's the peace – and the sun.'

'Nature, too, I think… And the vibe.'

'You're right though. Meeting Will felt like it was a part of something more profound.' I shrug. 'Then losing him… It's changed the way I see so many things.'

'Suffering is the other side of happiness, I think?' Isabella looks at me questioningly. 'But we're not very good at it. We expect to feel good all the time, and when we don't, we fight it, when perhaps instead, we should just accept it.' She shrugs. 'You can't have one without the other, can you? Suffering can be good for us. It reminds us not to take things for granted. To be empathic and stay humble.'

I can't believe how closed my life in Bath had become, because this is how I used to make friends – easily, with openness. Before I leave, Isabella and I arrange to meet for a drink, while in between everything else that's new in my life, I start on the book I was always going to write. It dredges up memories, good and bad, but as my road trip did, it seamlessly comes together, as I write about what started that first morning Will and I met.

* * *

Spring... but only just. Mid-March, the trees still winter-bare, the air cool on my skin. The early light and crisp mornings bringing a sense of optimism. After all the times we'd met before, that's where you were – in my mornings.

The years since we'd seen each other seemed to fall away that day. We talked, or rather, you talked... There were hundreds, thousands, millions of words. You'll laugh if you ever read this! You've often joked about how much you've talked, shared, confided in me; at the sheer volume of what you had to tell me.

Things you've never told anyone else.

The beginning of a hundred years of talking.

When we'd known each other so long, why hadn't it happened before? But I think more of life had to unfold, for us to become the people we were, that day, when we met at the top of the hill.

* * *

From the quiet of Lucy's terrace, I write another blog post.

I love the idea of serendipity... Even when things don't seem to be going to plan, it's all part of the journey. There's a reason the route twists and turns. It's teaching you what you need to learn; leading you where you're meant to be. And that's the point. The journey. When the time is right, doors you've never seen before will start to open in front of you. Here's a photo of one of mine:

I post a photo of the wooden gates into the villa I've been working on, cracked open, affording only a glimpse of what lies beyond.

If I'd stayed in England, I never would have found that door. But it's symbolic of so much more, of the heat and flaming sunsets here. The barometer of cicadas; a sea that sparkles. New friends. Peace, but it's no ordinary peace here. It's tangible, gets right inside you.

* * *

Now and then, Lucy and I meet Isabella in one of the locals' bars, far enough off the beaten track to avoid the holiday crowd, drinking cocktails and whiling away the sunset hours.

'I really don't want to leave here,' Isabella says one evening.

'Then don't.' Lucy is matter of fact. 'Pointless going back to England, darling. It has nothing going for it. And you have a home here. Sofia will leave you her house, now she knows about you.'

Yet again, I'm grateful I have no reason to leave here. 'You're not going yet, are you?'

She looks uncertain. 'I'm supposed to be going back next week. My job is there. And there's Mike – that's a whole other question.' Mike's her boyfriend. She pauses. 'I have decisions to make. Maybe I have to go back before I know for sure, but my heart tells me I should be here.'

* * *

When Isabella flies back to England, I think about the sequence of events that have brought me here; how at any point, a different fork in the road might have led me somewhere else. Then the universe gives me a prod, as another message appears in my Facebook feed.

Time flies.

That call you were going to make, that friend you were going to see

That book you were going to write…

Do it now.

I know exactly which book it's talking about. On and off, I've started. But this time, I move a table in front of a window that looks across the hills. Then I start to write undistracted, trying to put into words how it isn't just dreams that spur us on in life; how grief and loss teach us just as much in our eternal quest to find happiness.

* * *

It was a spring that blessed us with sunshine, so that we walked miles together. Quite a few hundred miles, hours passing fleetingly, both of us swept along by an unstoppable force.

We shared our dreams, our sadness; moments of uncontrolled laughter, our entire lives overheard only by the whispering trees, our dance unchoreographed, uncontrived, in big jumpers, well-worn boots; with windswept hair. But it was never superficial between us. It was about eye contact, energy, skin.

* * *

When my book is rejected by all the literary agents I sent it out to, I try a new tack and submit it to a couple of digital publishers, holding my breath as I type the emails and press 'send'. Then I do the only thing I can – I keep working on the next book.

'You're sure you should be doing this, hun?' One late afternoon, while I'm writing in the shade of the terrace, Lucy comes over clasping gin and tonics. 'Wouldn't it be better to write something new?'

'If there's a book I have to write, it's this one, Luce,' I tell her. 'When it's finished, I'll start something else.'

Lucy's quiet for a moment. 'Do you ever hear from him?'

'No.' I take a sip from my glass.

'I'm quite annoyed with him, Anna. I know what you're going to say... that he had his reasons...'

But it isn't for me to judge what he's done. 'He did have reasons – and I'm fine. And I've often wondered if I hadn't met him again, whether I'd still be trudging along with James, only half awake, doing the same old.' Settling, instead of living. 'You'll probably think I'm mad, but I'm going to say it anyway.' I pause for a moment. 'There's something between us that goes way beyond anything else I've known. I think we're soulmates. I never used to believe in them, but even when we were teenagers, it was there – and every time we met after that.' I look at her, wanting her to understand, but I don't think you can unless it's happened to you.

She looks uncertain. 'In that case, shouldn't you be together?'

I shake my head. But the more I've thought about it, the more convinced I am, that there was a purpose to Will and I meeting, regardless of how things worked out. 'I used to think that it was just a question of us finding our way back to each other. But now I think that we were each other's wake-up call. I think you said as much, before I left James.' I glance at Lucy, wondering if she remembers. 'Neither of us were happy, and we reminded each other what we'd both lost sight of. We showed each other what needed to change in our lives. It was always going to be painful, no matter what happened. He didn't mean to hurt me. When it came to Flo, he didn't feel he had a choice.'

Lucy looks puzzled. 'Yes, but you could have been part of both of their lives.'

'I know.' That's what makes it hardest to accept, but I think he was too scared of what it would do to Flo. 'Sometimes there are no answers, Luce.'

44

WILL

Under unbearable pressure at work, at home Will was acutely aware of what Darcey wanted from him. He knew what the answer was – an honest conversation – one that would lead to him and Darcey going their separate ways. And he knew what he wanted: for Flo to be happy, for Darcey to accept it was over between them. For them to maintain their relationship as united parents, but beyond that... Will ached for the freedom to follow his heart, leave his job, get away from the hideous mundanity of his life.

Maybe he needed to go away for a bit, broaden his horizons, break the routine of the everyday. Feeling his heart lift, he knew it was exactly what he needed. Getting out his laptop, he started searching for somewhere wild, off the beaten track, a tall order at this time of year, when most people would have already booked their holidays. Scrolling through lists, his eyes settled on a tiny cottage on the banks of the River Fal. Off grid, a hundred metre walk from the nearest road, it looked perfect. Quickly he sent off an email.

'It's a bit remote.'

Will hadn't heard Darcey come in. He turned to find her looking over his shoulder. 'It's exactly what I'm looking for.'

She looked put out. 'You're going alone?'

Will nodded. 'For a few days, if it's free.'

She sat down next to him. 'Maybe we could look for somewhere – for the three of us.'

'Maybe.' But knowing all it would do is prolong the pretence, Will couldn't help but feel half-hearted about it.

It clearly wasn't the answer she was hoping for. Getting up again, he heard her go to the kitchen and pick up her keys, before opening the door and closing it loudly. Listening to her car start, Will sighed.

When the email came through confirming availability, he hesitated briefly before booking. But he owed himself a few days away. Work wouldn't miss him and going out of his mind wasn't going to help anyone. Already, just knowing he was escaping on his own, the pressure was lifting.

He'd fully expected Darcey to come back and challenge him about going away. But later, when she still wasn't home, he was starting to get worried. After sending her a text, when she didn't reply, he knew he'd upset her.

His frustration was back. If he did something she didn't like, it was ludicrous how guilty he felt, even more so given how she'd treated him when she met Eric. Getting up, he paced over to the window, suddenly seeing it differently. All this was just another manifestation of Darcey's selfishness, of her attempt to control him, as she had when she'd been with Eric, expecting Will to take care of Flo when it suited her rather than anyone else. Always on her bloody terms.

It was much later when the sound of a car outside distracted him, before a door slammed and the car drove away. Guessing she'd had too much to drink to drive herself home, Will steeled himself.

He heard her key fumble in the lock, before she stumbled inside, slamming the door shut. Coming into the sitting room, she looked surprised when she saw Will, before a nasty look crossed her face.

'Don't pretend you bloody care, Will. I'm not an idiot.' Instead of her usual immaculate appearance, her face was flushed and her eye make-up smudged.

He ignored her. 'Where have you been?'

'Out,' she said. 'With people who like me.'

'I'll get you a glass of water.' He started towards the kitchen.

'Don't bother Mr Holier-Than-Fucking-Thou. I'm having a whisky. Then I want to talk to you.'

With Darcey in the state she was in, any conversation was going one way only – into an abusive, drunken ramble. Will headed towards the stairs. 'It can wait until tomorrow. I'm going to bed.'

* * *

When he came downstairs the next morning, he was greeted by silence. He went through to the kitchen where Darcey was sitting at the table. She didn't move.

'Darcey?' he said quietly. When she didn't answer, he went over and sat next to her. 'What's going on?'

As she turned to look at him, her face was stained with tears.

'Why are you so upset?'

'It's everything.' Her voice was muffled as she rested her head in her hands. 'You and me – and Flo going away... I know it's amazing for her. But for a while, I could pretend I had a family again. And now...' As she broke off, more tears rolled down her face.

Will shook his head. After last night's performance, this was ridiculous. 'Not so long ago, you didn't want anything to do with me,' he reminded her.

'It's different now.' She wiped her face. 'And it doesn't help that you'd rather go away without me.'

Will felt exasperated. It was impossible to tell if she was genuine or not. 'I've told you I need some time away. Surely that isn't unreasonable.' He got up. 'I'm going to pack a few things. I'll stay in a B & B until the cottage is ready.'

* * *

As soon as he drove away from Hinton, he felt his mood lift. It was a glorious late summer day, and as he headed west, a sense of freedom filled him, expanding the further he drove. Turning up the radio, he sang along tunelessly.

The cottage he'd booked wasn't available until Tuesday, but with Darcey the way she was, he couldn't have stayed at home. Anyway, as he reached the outskirts of Falmouth, he struck gold in the form of an old country pub. With its cosy bar and rooms to rent, Will dropped anchor.

After a couple of days of chatting to people he'd never see again and a pit stop for some food shopping, he was ready for the solace of the cottage he'd booked. And it didn't disappoint. It was off the beaten track with no neighbours in sight. After parking in the lane, he walked the hundred metre path carrying his bags, his heart lifting as the river came into view, then the cottage.

It was tiny, with a hot tub outside, decking with a table and chairs. After finding the key, he unlocked the door and went inside, finding himself in a large room with a double bed in one corner, a sofa and wood-burner in another; a tiny, beautifully fitted kitchen.

Feeling pleased with himself, Will put his shopping away and went outside. The views of the river were glorious. There was something about being close to water. About being alone, too, with no one to worry about other than himself.

Had he been selfish coming here? But he'd done it to still the incessant chatter in his head, the push–pull of emotions, the demands of a job he was disenchanted with. He gazed towards the water, taking in its rippling motion. It was the kind of place he would have loved as a child, that fuelled the imagination, with trees to climb, dens to make; fish to attempt to catch with a makeshift fishing rod.

Sitting there, he felt the breeze on his face as he listened to the leaves rustling, a few birds here and there. Closing his eyes, he felt himself relax, as at last his mind started to calm. This was everything he'd been craving. Not just this feeling of peace, but of being at one with the world.

He could never have shared anything like this with Darcey. Only with Anna, who'd love it here for the same reasons he did. Thinking of Flo, he wrestled with familiar conflicting emotions, before letting them go. There was no rush. He had three whole days of walking, star-gazing, nature-watching, while he figured out what he was going to do next.

* * *

The solitude, the being surrounded by nature, had unblocked his logjam of thoughts the way he'd hoped it would, leading to the clarity he'd been seeking. After leaving the cottage and driving home, when he reached Hinton, the house was empty. After dropping his bag at the bottom of the stairs, he went into the sitting room. Sitting on the sofa, he waited.

He'd wondered if when he got home, familiarity would cause him to question his decision. But as he sat there, looking around at the photos, the shelves of books, Will wasn't faltering.

An hour passed before he heard Darcey's car pull up outside. When she came in, she looked at him uncertainly.

'Hi,' he said. 'Can you come and sit down?'

'That sounds ominous.' Coming over, she sat at the other end of the sofa. 'I take it you've been thinking about things.'

He nodded. 'But probably not in the way you hoped. Look...' he said gently. 'What I want to say is that I don't think this is working – for either of us. You must want more than I can give you.'

Darcey looked uncertain. 'I really hoped that we could patch things up – enough. But it isn't what you want, is it?'

'I wanted to – for Flo's sake.' But Will had a question. 'When you left me for Eric, that was a fairly major decision. What's changed that suddenly you want me back?'

Darcey gazed at him for a moment. 'Don't you remember how good we used to be together? We're still married, Will. Is it really so strange?'

He didn't want to upset her but she was ignoring the elephant, the one that dominated not only this room but every aspect of their lives. 'Darcey, there's only one reason we're together.'

'I'm aware of that, but it doesn't have to be the only reason.' She sounded hurt. 'So what are you suggesting?'

He hesitated. 'I'd like us to find a way to live independently – not acrimoniously, like before, but as parents who live apart, but who can be united for their daughter's sake.'

Darcey brushed away a tear. 'I know the last few years, I haven't made it easy for you. And we're far from being back to how we used to be. But do you think there's any chance that could change?'

'I really don't know.' It seemed kinder, less brutal, than the truth.

'I'm guessing that's your way of saying no.' Darcey looked sad. 'So what do we do, going forward?'

Will had thought about this, too. 'It depends what you want. You can have the house, or rent somewhere, in Bristol, maybe, if that's where you'd rather be. I'll fit around what you decide. But however we do this, we have to be mindful of Flo.'

'Agreed,' Darcey said quietly. 'Don't worry. It won't be like before. She can spend as much time with you as she wants to.'

'I don't think she'll feel the same without the sheep.' Will tried to lighten the mood. He looked at her. 'We could really do this, you know. Stay united as parents.'

She nodded. 'I think Flo will be OK. Sad, obviously.' Her voice wavered. 'But she knows you sleep in the spare room. I don't think she'll be surprised.'

After the conversation they'd had before she started at her new school, Will didn't think she would, either. Prepared for more opposition from Darcey, for another angry outburst, he was filled with relief. Reaching out, he took one of her hands. 'Thank you,' he said quietly.

She looked surprised. 'What for?'

'For not fighting me.' It was an achievement in itself if they could maintain some kind of friendship.

'I can't force you to stay with me.' She shrugged. 'Anyway, I don't want to, any more. I've had enough of battling with you. Life's too short.'

45

ANNA

As the summer goes on, more and more, the island gets under my skin. If places exist in this world where there is magic, no question this island is one of them. Meanwhile, with the villas occupied, my work for Larissa dwindles, and under the August sun, I write relentlessly, obsessively, driven by something I can't explain as something incredible happens.

Elated, I run to find Lucy in the kitchen. 'Luce? You'll never believe this!'

Lucy looks up from making lunch. 'What's happened?'

'My book! Someone wants to publish it!'

Coming over, Lucy flings her arms around me. 'This is so, so amazing, babe!'

'It really is. I've some work to do, but it's going to be out in the world! I can't believe it!'

'We need to celebrate!' Going to the fridge, Lucy gets out a bottle of champagne.

* * *

It's another dream come true as while I wait for my edits to come back, I set myself a deadline to finish my next book, still undecided how it ends.

Me without you... It was never how I saw us. Maybe somewhere out there is a whole parallel universe where we are together. A vivid, brilliant world where we make a difference.

There's something else I've learned since coming here, and that's how little any of us really need. It puts me in mind of one of Will's stories.

When your friend moved to France, he sold his house and got rid of everything. All he had in the world were two bin bags, you told me. One contained the few possessions he'd decided to keep, the other was full of rubbish. It was only after arriving, he realised he'd thrown away the wrong bag.

You loved that story. You imagined the sense of liberation at being unencumbered by possessions. It hadn't remotely bothered your friend.

Life isn't about stuff. At this point in time, I have fewer possessions than at any other time, but my life is richer than it's ever been.

* * *

As I continue to write my blog, what started as a handful of followers has steadily grown in number. More than once, I've wondered if Will has read it. But I've no way of knowing.

When Millie comes to stay, from the moment I meet her at the airport, I know she gets why I've come here. From the light in her eyes as I drive her to Can Mimosa, I watch her fall in love with Ibiza the same way I have.

As she stares outside at the olive groves and palm trees scattered across the arid landscape, she looks amazed. 'I thought it was mostly clubs. I'd no idea it was like this.'

She's seeing it at its hottest, dustiest, busiest, but it's still breath-taking. 'It's what everybody thinks, but most of the island is like this. Gorgeous, isn't it?'

When I tell her about my book, she's as excited as I am. 'It's so cool, Anna. I mean, a book out there with your name on it...'

'I know. I still can't believe it.' I hesitate. 'But tell me your news. Have you seen your dad lately?'

'He seems good. I've been to see him and he came up to London last weekend.' She sounds puzzled. 'He was really enthusiastic about the painting I'm working on. He seemed different, Anna.'

'I'm pleased.' When I've worried that he wouldn't be, that it would damage my relationship with Millie, relief fills me.

When we pull up outside Can Mimosa, Yippy reaches us first, with Lucy not far behind. She welcomes Millie with open arms. 'Hello, lovely girl! How was your flight? Here... let me take that... Come inside! There's a bottle of champagne chilling.' She grabs Millie's suitcase and starts walking towards the finca.

I turn to Millie. 'There's always a bottle of champagne chilling around here!'

But Millie just stands there, looking around at the hills. 'This is paradise.'

'I'm so glad you think so. Come on, let me show you around.' After giving her a tour of the casa, when I lead her to my casita and show her the second bedroom with its soft linen sheets and huge vase of flowers, her expression is blissful. 'I'm not going to want to leave.'

'Then don't,' I tell her, watching her eyes light up, only half joking as I add, 'Stay here.'

Over a lazy afternoon, in the shade of the terrace, with the bottle of champagne, I catch up on Millie's life, before we all go out for tapas at a nearby bar. There, surrounded by the buzz of life, we drink cocktails and watch the sky erupt into glorious colours before the sun goes down.

The next day, I take her on a tour of the island, avoiding the tourist spots and showing her some of the small towns in the north, as well as one or two of the villas I've been working on. That evening, we go to a restaurant on the beach where we sit at a table shaded by palm leaves, feet from the sea, listening to the water lapping on the sand.

'I need to paint here.' Millie looks mesmerised. 'Next time, I'm bringing my stuff with me.'

'You should. I'm so pleased you love it here.' It matters more to me than anything that the Ibiza magic touches her too. When Millie lives and works in London, I don't want it to swallow her.

'You could flog your paintings to the villa owners, darling. Most of them are loaded.' Lucy takes a slug of wine. 'You should seriously think about it.'

By day, we find off-the-beaten-track beaches, while another night, I take Millie to an open stretch of rocky hillside where a meditation group is meeting. As a dozen of us sit on mats, she embraces it just as I do. While we're there, the first stars appear, the sliver of a crescent moon, and after, as we walk away, I see a peacefulness in Millie that wasn't there before.

'I need this.' She looks slightly dazed.

I smile at her. 'Told you you'd love it here!'

Our feeling of Zen lasts until we get home, where Lucy's already making drinks.

'Take these, girls. And get your glad rags on.' When she hands us each an enormous gin and tonic, my heart sinks slightly. I'd imagined a quiet evening on the terrace, just the three of us. But Millie's face lights up as Lucy goes on. 'Is an hour long enough? We've a party to go to! Isabella called while you were out – she's back!'

Thoughts of the quiet evening I had in mind evaporate, but I can't wait to see Isabella – and this is Ibiza. Anything goes, from meditation on a solitary hillside to partying around the clock, and everything in between.

When we see her, Isabella looks excited – and Spanish, as though her life in England is already far behind her. But I know how that feels. When she tells us she's moving here for good, it's another reason to celebrate and we party on the beach until the sun comes up.

In a million years, in as many lifetimes, I would never have done this with James. But there is no place here for the fleeting sadness I feel. Letting it go, I imagine it floating away on the breeze.

One evening, before we go out, Millie asks about Will. Seeing the worry on her face, I try to reassure her. 'I'm over him, Mills. Life is really good here.'

'I know it is.' But her eyes are anxious. 'It just seems such a waste.'

'Mills,' I say gently. 'Some things are not meant to be. And that's OK.' I smile at her. 'I'm really happy.'

Lucy's voice interrupts us. 'Hurry up, you two... We're going to be late!'

* * *

Millie's stay is over too soon. 'Two weeks are nowhere near long enough,' I tell her as I drag her suitcase out to the car. 'It suits you here.' The sun has lightened her hair, given her skin a honey glow.

'I know.' Her high spirits are dampened by her imminent departure. She's silent for a moment. 'I don't want to go.'

'Then don't,' Lucy says. 'There's plenty of room if you want to stay.'

'I don't want you to go, either.' I inject the words with a brightness I don't feel, because it goes against everything in me to let her leave.

We're both quiet as I drive her to the airport. As she gets out of the car, I pull her case out of the back, then hug her tightly. 'I'll come over and see you very soon, and promise it won't be long before you come back.'

After she goes into the terminal building, an unfamiliar sense of loneliness comes over me, before I remind myself that she has her own life in London – for now, at least.

And I'm where I need to be, on this island she can visit any time, for as long as she wants to. Pondering the workings of the universe, I send a silent prayer of gratitude into the ether, for having Millie in my life; for James, too. It may have all gone wrong between us, but if it wasn't for him, I wouldn't have her.

* * *

With Millie gone, I could easily feel sad, but instead, I focus on the beauty of this amazing life I have.

The big house, new cars, endless stuff, none of it's important. What matters is being true to your own heart. That's what I want to write about now, because it's what the world needs more than ever. The abundance of kindness in all our hearts.

No one can tell you how to live. Only you can decide that. For me, it's about living my best life: inhabiting moments, quiet gratitude. Not so quiet gratitude! But most of all, love.

Meanwhile, winter has arrived, a season of storms and fallen leaves, of streams carved into the earth by heavy rain. Here, even on cooler days, there can be blue skies and bright sunlight. The return of green to summer's bleached shades, tiny wild flowers in unlikely places; then, as spring arrives, acres of trees festooned in almond blossom and mimosa flowers, before the first swallows arrive.

I post a photo of myself with Lucy and Isabella, sitting at a beachside restaurant which even at this time of year draws crowds. So many people I've met here have come to do what I've just described – live their best lives on this beautiful island.

I soak up the feeling as I lie in a scented bath that night, a candle Millie gave me flickering on the windowsill. It's a blissful moment, one that's brutally shattered as under the skin of my breast, my fingers find a lump.

46

WILL

Since Darcey's acceptance that their marriage was over, Will had been aware of a momentum gathering pace. With no desire to live in Hinton, Darcey had gravitated back to Bristol, finding somewhere to live in no time.

'This is amazing.' Will looked around the apartment. Light and airy, freshly painted white, it had views of the water. 'Flo is going to love this.'

'You think?' Darcey looked uncertain.

'Near the shops and nightlife? What's not to love? Especially as she gets older – plus a number of her old school friends live in Bristol.' When they'd told Flo – together – that they were separating, she'd been slightly upset, but Will had seen relief there, too. But Flo had known she was the reason he and Darcey had got back together. And she was growing up, with her new life at this incredible school she loved.

Looking at his wife, he paused. 'Do you think you'll be happy here?'

Darcey was silent for a moment. 'Yes,' she said quietly, turning towards Will. 'To be frank, we both know I was never a country girl. I tried, though.'

'This is the start of a new chapter.' Will was determined to keep things upbeat. 'But I can't help thinking, that in a way, it's been worth everything we've been through. At least we can talk without yelling at each other.'

Looking more like the old Darcey, she rolled her eyes. 'I was pretty vile for a while, wasn't I?'

Will didn't comment. 'So when's your mother coming to stay?' He would forever be grateful to Darcey's mother for buying the apartment, instantly resolving their most urgent problem.

'As soon as I invite her – she can't wait. She's already checking out theatres and galleries. I'm going to be busy.' Going over to the new sofa, Darcey plumped the cushions that had just been delivered.

Going over to his soon-to-be ex-wife, Will hugged her lightly. 'Maybe you should think about giving Eric a call.'

Pulling back, she shook her head. 'I thought about it, but it feels like a step backwards. Right now, I think I'm happy just to be me.'

As he went out to his car, his phone buzzed with a text from Flo.

Are you OK Dad? xxx

Will shook his head. She needed to stop worrying about him.

I'm fine. Just seen your mum's new place. Really cool, you'll love it. How's school? Xxx

She texted back straight away.

School's awesome, we're training for a national competition, my biggest so far!!!!!!!

She followed it with celebrating emojis.

Will smiled.

Can't wait. Will be there.

He paused.

We both will.

When Flo texted back a smiley face and heart emojis, Will's heart warmed.

* * *

When half-term came, he drove Flo over to Bristol, watching her as she rushed around the apartment, squeaking delightedly at how perfect it was. Darcey had clearly been shopping – it had changed since he'd last been here, unfamiliar artwork adorning the walls, the addition of ornate bookshelves and other pieces of furniture he didn't recognise.

'Don't think you need to worry,' Will said to Darcey. 'Just wait till she discovers the shops.'

Darcey looked at Will. 'Are you rushing off or would you like to have dinner with us?'

Just then, Flo came bounding into the room. 'Stay, Dad! It will be cool!'

As he smiled at his daughter, he couldn't think of a reason not to. 'OK. Why not?'

Watching Darcey poach fillets of salmon, Will looked around

the room, his eyes settling on a photo of the three of them. Sipping his glass of wine, with Flo chattering incessantly, suddenly it struck him that this was working, that they could still spend time together; that in time, maybe there would even be new memories to make.

Later that evening, as he drove back to Hinton, grateful for the peace between him and Darcey, he felt a new sense of calm. However hard the last few months had been, it had been worth all of it to reach this point.

Could they have got there sooner? He'd never know, but for the first time in his life, having shaken off the need to please everyone else first and leave his own needs to last, he'd learned a lot about himself.

Turning off the busy roads into the quiet lane that led to Hinton, Will felt the tension leave him. Outside, the sky was dark, scattered faintly with stars. On reaching the house, he switched the engine off, and sat there in the silence, savouring the moment; knowing that after everything he'd been through, somehow, at last, he'd reached a turning point.

47

ANNA

That night, sleep is impossible. Instead, I sit in the middle of my bed, a blanket around my shoulders, the windows and shutters open to the night, as I google lumps, before my imagination takes over and I google breast cancer. It's probably benign, I try to convince myself, but I can't shake my fear that it won't be.

At some point the breeze picks up, its restless energy filling the room as I consider every possible scenario; tests, followed potentially by surgery, then maybe chemo or radiotherapy; more tests to establish whether my cancer's spread. For this to be happening now, just as my new life is underway, seems to me the ultimate injustice.

The following morning, I've barely slept when I go out to the terrace. Sitting under the ancient vine held up by the oldest timbers of Can Mimosa, above my head are bougainvillea flowers, the leaves turning shades of red, now and then floating to the floor. I look across the hills to the sea, which even in the early October sunlight is a clear azure; its beauty so exquisite it's almost painful.

As the sun swings around, I hear Lucy clattering in the kitchen. Getting up, I go inside. 'Luce? Do you have a moment?'

'Coffee?' Turning around, when she sees my face, she frowns. 'Are you OK?'

Guessing Gianluca's still in bed, I glance towards the terrace. 'Can you come outside?'

There's a quizzical look on her face as she follows me out there. 'Beautiful, isn't it? Remember when we first came here all those years ago? It was before you married James. Who'd have thought we'd end up living here?'

Standing beside her, I wait for her to fall silent. For a minute, neither of us speaks, as I etch each detail into my mind. Lucy's sun-streaked hair, the green of the scrubby pine trees, the scent of rosemary; the stillness, that indefinable magic I've always felt, ever since the first time we came here; Lucy's friendship, so constant in my life. Suddenly I'm scared, that everything's about to forever change.

'I've found a lump, Luce.'

Her face turns pale, before she rallies, doing her best to reassure me. 'It's probably nothing, Anna. Loads of lumps turn out to be benign, hun. But you need to see someone straight away.'

After spending most of the night researching on the internet, her words do nothing to take away the fear I feel. 'I'm going to contact James – we used to have private health care. If I'm still covered, it makes sense to use it.'

'Absolutely it does. Call him now,' Lucy says firmly. 'Then we need to look at flights.'

When I speak to James, he's curt but helpful. After calling the healthcare company, he gets back to me with their direct number.

'Thank you, James. I know you didn't have to do this.'

'It's not a problem. We are still married – if only officially,' he says abruptly. Then his voice softens. 'I hope everything turns out OK.'

I'll let you know what happens.' I hesitate, because right now, I can't face telling people. 'There is one thing... Can you not tell anyone? Especially Millie? She'll only worry. If I have to tell her, I'd rather she heard it from me.'

After hanging up, I call the number James has given me and take the first available appointment in two days' time. But my relief that it's done is short-lived, and as I contemplate what lies ahead, my fear is back.

'There's a flight tomorrow morning.' Lucy looks up from her laptop. 'It gets into London City at midday. Book it, hun. There's a hotel around the corner from the hospital.' Looking at me, she pauses. 'I can come with you, Anna. There's nothing going on here that can't wait.'

'Thanks, Luce. But you stay here.' I need to do this alone – I also need to see Millie. 'We don't even know if it's anything to worry about yet.'

'If you're sure.' But she doesn't look convinced. 'As long as you know I'm here if you need me.'

The following day, both of us say little as Lucy drives me to the airport. Parking in the drop off zone, she turns towards me. 'Now listen to me, Anna. You're going to be OK,' she says fiercely. 'I refuse to allow myself to think even for a second that you won't be.'

'Thank you.' I hug her tight.

'Let me know when you're on the plane... And when you get there... And when...'

'I'll keep you posted, Luce,' I say softly. 'Go and walk in the hills and send me good vibes. Please... You mustn't worry about me.'

After checking in and going through security, I text Millie.

Hey, Mills, are you busy this afternoon? Xxxxx

Seconds later, she gets back to me.

Anna! I didn't know you were in London!!! Xxxx

I decide it's easier to call her. 'Hi Mills!

She sounds excited. 'Why didn't you tell me?'

'It's a last minute thing... How are you? Are you free later on?'

'I was supposed to be covering someone's shift, but they've just called and told me they don't need me – so yes! Definitely!'

'That's brilliant, Mills. This is where I'm staying.' I give her the name of the hotel. 'How about I meet you there around three?'

'I'll be there.' She sounds excited. 'I can't wait!'

'Me neither. Mills, I have to go. My flight is boarding. See you later!' There's plenty of time, but I end the call before she asks any questions.

The airport is oddly busy for the time of year, yet the flight is half empty. I have a window seat, from which I stare down at the sea until we reach Barcelona, then at the Pyrenees and France, remembering the tiny twisting roads I'd followed on my road trip not that long ago; as the same distance that took days of driving takes little more than a couple of hours.

Thinking of the uncertainty I face, I'm suddenly light-headed; gazing out of the window as we descend over the English Channel then cross the coast, a layer of cloud washing the sky a milky blue that turns to grey. As the plane banks and I glimpse the London skyline, my stomach turns over nervously.

* * *

The pace of London contrasts sharply with the sleepiness of winter in Ibiza. After hailing a taxi, I check in to my hotel and change, before going downstairs, timing it perfectly to meet Millie as she walks through the revolving door.

'Anna!' As Millie runs into my arms, I hold her tightly, breathing in cold air and her trademark perfume, then push her slightly away, so that I can look at her. She's wearing a patterned coat over black jeans. The subtle gold strands in her hair are new. I stroke one of them behind her ear. 'You look fabulous, Mills! How about we hit the shops, then catch a bite to eat?'

She nods happily, linking her arm through mine as we walk outside and along the street. 'How long are you here for?'

'A few days,' I tell her, trying not to think about what lies ahead. 'But not much longer. Larissa has a villa she wants me to look at.' My voice sounds too bright and I watch Millie to see if her lie detector has kicked in, relieved when it appears it hasn't.

Her face falls. 'I have to work tomorrow.'

I touch her arm. 'It's OK. We have today! We'll make the most of it! Who knows – maybe I'll stay a little longer.'

I stay silent about my worries, wanting this time with Millie to be happy, untouched by fear of the unknown. It's an afternoon in which we talk, about the past, the present, the future; create memories that will always be there, no matter what. We try on ridiculously high-heeled shoes and belly laugh at each other, then I buy Millie a beautiful dress she'd never have bought for herself. All the time I'm soaking up how she has everything I'd ever wanted for her: loving her life, painting when she can, secure in her job; clearly happy in herself.

Early evening, our feet sore from walking, we go to the Shard for cocktails and dinner. As we sit looking at the jaw-dropping view, Millie tells me James has met someone.

'Oh my God. You mean, it's serious?' She'd told me some time ago that he was dating a number of women. Even so, I'm astonished.

Misinterpreting my reaction, Millie looks anxious. 'He told me after I got back from Ibiza. You don't mind, do you? I thought you'd be pleased.'

It seems even more miraculous that he was prepared to help me – or maybe this woman is the reason. I find my voice. 'I'm really pleased. You know I want him to be happy. Is she nice?'

Millie nods. 'I like her. I know you and Dad didn't get on, but he's different with her.'

Which is even more astonishing. 'It's the best news, Mills. I'm happy for them.'

And I am. I want James to share his life with someone, to be happy. If I'm surprised, it's because it's happened so quickly.

All too soon the evening is over and I walk Millie to London Bridge to catch her train.

'I miss you,' she says, slightly tearfully, as we stand on the platform.

It takes all my strength to swallow the lump in my throat as still I can't bring myself to tell her why I'm here. 'We can catch up again over the next couple of days – if you have time?'

She's nodding. 'Definitely! I'll check with work and text you.'

She blows me a kiss, then the doors close and I watch her train pull slowly away. Filled with nostalgia for a carefreeness that's gone forever, a sense of foreboding hangs over me.

* * *

My consultant understands how terrified I am, patiently talking me through the ultrasound and biopsy I've been dreading. But it's no worse than the limbo I've been caught in. With it all done, I face the surreal prospect of having to wait.

That evening, I walk along the South Bank, trying to get my head around what's happened in just a few days. Stopping beside the Thames, I lean my elbows on the wall, gazing at the lights reflected in the water, thoughts churning relentlessly in my head.

How long will I have to stay in England? How am I going to tell Millie? If my diagnosis is the worst kind, what comes next?

I spend another sleepless night, tossing and turning. By the time the sun rises, my hotel room feels claustrophobic, and getting up, I go out.

Compared to last night, the streets are quiet, an undercurrent of life going on even at this hour. Finding a café, I order coffee. Then, as I sit there, I think of the plans Will and I once made. The fictitious dates we dreamed up, the future we imagined together. After the losses he's suffered, maybe, if I have cancer, it was for the best that we didn't end up together.

As the shops start to open, I task myself with finding a present for Millie. Heading for Covent Garden, I have another memory from years ago – of the time I arranged to meet Will, when he arrived there late and having given up that he was coming, I'd left. Another of those insane missed chances our relationship has been defined by.

A timely text from Millie distracts me.

I'm free tonight. Will buy you pizza? Xxxx

I text her straight back.

Perfect xxx

Shortly after, I stumble across the perfect gift. A tiny moonstone bracelet that reminds me of the one Will gave me when we were teenagers. I loved it at the time, because he'd chosen it for me, but since, I've forgotten about it – until now.

Waiting outside Millie's favourite restaurant, my heart lifts when I see her walking towards me. In jeans and a leather jacket, when she sees me, her face lights up.

'Hi!' Millie hugs me.

'Hi, Mills! How was your day?' I study the brightness in her eyes, the fair hair that's slightly untidy. 'I've booked a table.'

'I'm famished.' Millie pushes the door open. 'I'm sorry I couldn't see you last night. It was something we'd planned weeks ago.'

After following her in, we're shown to a table over by the window.

'So was it fun?'

'Hilarious – too much wine and this amazing Chinese food.' She smiles. 'After today, I won't be able to eat for at least a week.'

'Prosecco?'

The restaurant is about half-filled. I order a bottle of Prosecco and a jug of water, while Millie peruses the menu. Then, after ordering, I pour us both a glass.

'How come you're over here? I completely forgot to ask you!' Her eyes widen. 'It's your book, isn't it! Have you found a publisher?'

The Prosecco is suddenly too celebratory. Hating what I have to tell her, I shake my head. 'It's probably nothing to worry about, Mills.' I hesitate. 'Before I left Ibiza, I found a lump.'

The colour drains from Millie's face. 'Where?'

I touch where they took the biopsy yesterday. 'I'm still covered by your dad's private health insurance. He's been really good. I got in touch with him and he got things going. Yesterday, I had a scan and they've done a biopsy.' I pause, watching her take it in. 'I have to wait a couple of days before I know whether or not it's malignant. It probably won't be,' I add hastily. 'Most lumps aren't. But it's always best to check these things out.' I deliberately underplay my concerns. 'I get the results early next week.'

But I haven't fooled her. From her face, I can see she's frightened. 'Are you staying here until you find out?'

'I think so. It makes sense. If I need surgery, hopefully they'll do it quickly. And if not... Maybe you and I can spend more time together.'

As I mention surgery, Millie looks terrified.

Our food arrives and as we pick at it, suddenly I realise, whatever happens, I have to find a way to put a more positive slant on this.

'Even if it's malignant,' I tell Millie. 'Treatment has come so far, Mills. I've been reading about it. I know it's scary, but there's every chance it's curable. Until I know more, that's what I'm focusing on.'

'Yes.' My brave stepdaughter looks defiant. 'Whatever this is, you're going to get over it.' She tops up our glasses. 'Let's drink, Anna – to good health.'

'And to life,' I add.

After, we walk across London, and as I put my arm around Millie, she leans her head against my shoulder.

'Let me come with you – when you get your results.'

'You don't need to do that. Honestly.'

'Someone should be with you,' she says obstinately. 'If it was me, I'd want you to be there.'

I'd want to be there, too. But it's how it's always been – with Millie closer to me than either of her parents. I understand why she wants to be there with me. 'If you're sure.' I give in gratefully. 'Thank you.'

48

WILL

Back at home, as Will glanced around the house, even without what Darcey had taken with her, he had an overwhelming sense of feeling at home. He stopped himself. Maybe the feeling was more about him, that sense of being at home coming from this point he'd reached.

Tomorrow he was resigning from his job. Having made the decision, he'd felt a weight lift. What with Christmas coming up and the leave he was owed, with any luck he'd never set foot in there again. Then he was going to look around for some consultancy work. Rather than be tied to an office, he wanted to be free to work from anywhere.

Sitting on the sofa, as he opened his laptop, it was the moment he hadn't stopped thinking about. The moment he could write honestly, from his heart.

Tentatively, he started typing, then deleting, line by painstaking line, until eventually he stopped. Reading the end result, he gazed at the screen.

Dear Anna,
You have no idea how many times I've wanted to get in touch with you, how I've thought about you every day… How I've never been able to give up on the idea of us. I know I let you down – but things have changed.
Please don't delete this. Darcey and I are getting a divorce. We're amicable and it's calm. Flo is OK. Darcey's moved to Bristol, leaving me living alone in Hinton. These last months have been hellish if I'm honest, though I think at last I've done what you said I should and let go of the past.
I'm only now realising just how influenced I've been by what everyone else expects of me. But knowing everyone else is OK, I'm free to think about what I want from the rest of my life – which is where you come in. Even from when we were teenagers, it's always been you. All those times the universe brought us back together, I think it was meant to happen, each time cementing what I knew deep inside, that you and I are meant to be together. But I got it wrong.
I'm sorry, so sorry, that I hurt you. I've felt so empty without you. I think you know I reacted on impulse because of Flo. But going back to Darcey wasn't the answer. It just took a while for us to realise that and find another way.
So now, if there's any room in your life for a somewhat jaded but devoted man who loves you with all his heart, who always will, say the word and I will be there, through whatever life brings our way, whatever ups and downs we face, unfaltering, supporting, loving you. I've worked that out, too – that the only thing that really matters in this world, is love.

Signing off, about to send it, he hesitated. What if Anna really had moved on? If she sent a negative response, he'd have nowhere to go with that. After all their missed chances, no way could he afford to risk this going wrong. An idea came to him. There was only one way to know for sure. Christmas was coming up and he owed it to Flo to be here, but once it was over, instead of sending an email, he was going to get on a plane and go to find her.

49

ANNA

Millie and I are silent as we wait together for my appointment, only one thought in my head. *What if I'm dying*?

When the consultant tells me my lump is malignant, suddenly I'm numb, listening to her words, unable to take them in. *Stage two* registers somewhere. *Surgery – gene expression profile testing.*

'We've caught it early.' She sounds quietly positive. 'We'll carry out more tests but depending on the results, we'll probably be looking at chemo or hormone therapy.'

For the second time in my life, being faced with a potentially life-threatening diagnosis brings the horizons of my world closer. Time is no longer a given, life suddenly fragile; while far from definite, I can only see my future as tenuous.

As we walk away from the hospital, I'm still in shock as Millie and I go over what the consultant told us. 'If they're only removing the lump, that's a good sign, isn't it?'

'I think so, Mills.' I cross my fingers, trying to hide my fear from her.

'And it's just the one lump?' Like she used to as a child, she takes hold of my hand.

'That's what they said, isn't it?' I should have written everything down, but then it comes back. 'She definitely said it was just in the one place.'

Her fingers tighten around mine. 'It's still scary though.'

It's terrifying; the last hour redefining what normal is, as I try my hardest not to let fear run away with me. 'We have to look on the bright side. I may not even need chemo. I should call Lucy. I promised I'd let her know.'

Finding a café, as we sit outside, Millie orders drinks while I call my friend.

'Luce? I've got the results.' I hesitate. 'It's malignant.'

Her voice is sharp. 'What else did they say, babe?'

As I repeat what the consultant told us, I can almost hear her brain ticking. 'When are you going in?'

'They're going to call me – but probably soon. The results of the genetic profile testing may take a couple of weeks or so – at least, I think that's what they said.'

'Are you staying in London?'

'For now. It depends how long I have to wait.'

'How's Millie?' Lucy sounds concerned.

'Millie is wonderful.' I glance across as she comes back with our drinks. 'A tour de force of positivity and optimism.' Catching Millie's eye, I know how lucky I am to have her.

'She's a superstar, isn't she? I'm so glad she's with you. Give her my love.' Lucy pauses. 'And keep me posted.'

The call from the consultant that comes later that afternoon catapults me into the next stage. They can fit me in the day after tomorrow.

* * *

Time becomes surreal, events picking up speed when I'm admitted, then taken for surgery. After, relieved it's behind me, I feel tired and sore, but I'm lucky that it doesn't amount to much more than that.

Fear stays with me, but through the uncertainty, there is much to be grateful for – the urgency with which I've been treated, the kindness of the hospital staff; for Millie when she arrives the following morning when I'm discharged.

'I've taken a few days off, and I've borrowed an airbed. You're staying with me,' she tells me.

'I have the hotel room. You don't have space, Mills. And you have to work – or paint.'

'I really don't.' She refuses to budge. 'Not for the next couple of days. Don't argue, Anna! You've done so much for me. Let me do this.'

After picking up what's in my hotel room, I check out. Her flat is a taxi ride away and when we go inside, it's cosy and welcoming.

Showing me into her bedroom, there's a jug of colourful flowers on the windowsill.

'You're sleeping in here,' she tells me. Before I can protest about taking her bed, she adds, 'It isn't up for discussion! Now, I've got loads of herbal teas. What would you like?'

It's as though our roles have been reversed. But in truth, I'm where I want to be, her quiet company everything I need while my body heals. As we wait for more results, it cements the relationship Millie and I have while I try to stop my imagination running wild with worst-case scenarios. *This is just life,* I keep telling myself. *Another of its down slopes, before invariably it hits the bottom and comes up again.*

When I feel better, we walk in a nearby park, one of those unexpected spaces London is known for, where the constant background noise makes me long for the peacefulness of Ibiza. Millie takes me to a little eco café around the corner from her, a friendly place with great coffee and home-made cakes, that's clearly a hub for those who know about it.

After a check-up at the hospital, at last I'm free to go home.

'You must tell me when you get your test results.' Millie is uncompromising as I get ready to leave. 'And any time you have to come back, you know you can come here.'

'I know, Mills. Thank you... Being with you has made all the difference.'

Though I'm looking forward to flying home, my diagnosis has opened a different window onto the world. More than once, I contemplate if it's true that in adversity we find our strength, and as I sit on the train to the airport, I consider the extremes of human experience that have been condensed into the last five days. Fear, love and ultimately the sense of hope I'm holding tightly to; all of it amplified, crystallised, by what I'm going through.

The flight is quiet, a feeling of relief filling me as the plane takes off. As it bursts through the clouds into blue skies, though I still don't know what lies ahead, I'm grateful that this part of the process is behind me.

As the plane lands in Ibiza and taxis in, I feel the familiar sense of coming home. The airport is quiet and I'm through arrivals in next to no time. When I walk outside, Lucy waves at me from her car before getting out, she hurries across the road and hugs me.

'I'm so pleased you're back. I haven't been able to stop thinking about you.' She grabs my case. 'I want you to fill me in on everything.'

As we get in her car, Lucy glares at the driver hooting behind us. 'Arsehole.'

'We are blocking the road,' I remind her, as he shouts something in Spanish through his open window.

'Bloody wanker. It's the kiss and fly zone.' As she sets off, she fires questions at me. 'What happens now? How long before you get your results? Have you looked into having treatment here? The hospital's bloody good, you know.'

'One thing at a time,' I tell her. 'The tests will give them an idea how likely or unlikely it is that my cancer will recur. If it's low enough, they'll put me on hormone therapy.'

'And if not?'

'Chemo,' I say quietly.

'Let's hope it's the former,' Lucy says quietly. 'When will you get the results?'

'Any time in the next three weeks.'

'Right. In the meantime, you're going to rest. But we're bloody going to make the most of it.'

* * *

Lucy is everything I need – strong, bright, doing her best to buoy me up; listening to me when I need her to, even though I know she's scared, too. I see it in her face when I catch her unawares. But however determined I am to stay positive, the shadow of my illness hangs over all of us.

It's a while since I've written a blog post, and sitting at my laptop, I try to channel the last few weeks into words.

I've been telling myself it's OK to not always have the answers. To feel scared, unsure; to know you have no control. At times like this it's about taking small steps, about small acts of courage – that mean nothing to anyone else. But other people don't know what you're going through. And your life isn't about anyone else. It's your precious, wonderful, unique life that you want to wholeheartedly live each extraordinary day of.

And, for now, while I'm still here to watch another sunrise, I have this day and all the magic it holds, knowing that tomorrow will bring another.

It's a time of extremes as in the midst of this, my editor comes back with her comments on my book. Immersed in working on it, it's the distraction I need, while in between, I carry on with my next one.

I'd never watched a sunset before – not the way we did, sitting on a fallen tree, listening to the birds as we saw out the last hour of daylight, waiting for the split second the sun slipped out of sight. I remember the coldness of the air, the scent of damp earth.

You didn't speak, not because your mind was somewhere else. It was one of those moments that didn't need words. But we could both feel it, in the movement of air that felt alive around us, the energy that flowed tangibly between us.

How it ends? I don't know yet. No one does. But if there's a blessing that comes with the uncertainty I face, surrounded by the beauty of this island, by friendship and love, it's the reminder of just how rich my life is.

* * *

Two weeks pass before I receive a phone call from my consultant. It isn't the news I'm hoping for. My cancer isn't one of those which is unlikely to recur. Listening to what she says, the bottom falls out of my world.

I go to find Lucy. 'My consultant just called. She wants me to start chemo.' Tears blur my eyes as I swallow the lump in my throat.

'Oh, babe…' Lucy looks startled. 'When?'

'Next week.' Shaking my head, everything catches up with me. 'I have to think about booking a flight. And a hotel.'

'You know Millie will want you to stay with her.' Lucy's silent for a moment. 'There has to be a way for you to be treated here. I know you don't have residency yet, but maybe you can find out if James's policy will cover you. You don't want to go back to London for weeks on end.'

Feeing my hopes rise, they sink just as quickly. 'If they find out we're not together, it will probably invalidate the policy. I need to talk to him again.'

Knowing how she's going to feel, I call Millie to tell her. I know from her voice she's frightened.

When I call James, Millie's already spoken to him. He agrees to talk to the insurance company. But some time later, when he eventually calls me back, I see a side of James I've never seen before.

'The insurance company won't go for it, Anna. So I've found a hospital in Ibiza – I'll text you their number. You need to call them and give them permission to contact your consultant in London. It would probably help if you call the consultant first so that they know what's coming. There will be nothing to pay – they're going to bill me directly.'

I'm stunned. 'You can't do that, James – it's going to cost thousands.'

'Not as many thousands as you might think, and I've just been paid a bonus. Look, it's not like I can do anything else to help,' he says gently. 'I'd like to do this for you.'

I'm astonished. But knowing he means it, relief flows over me. 'I can't thank you enough for this.'

'I hope it makes it a little less complicated… I don't suppose it's going to be an easy time. At least this way, you can stay with Lucy.'

As the call ends, I wonder if this is the influence of the new woman in his life. I go to find Lucy. 'You're never going to believe this. The insurance won't cover my treatment here, but James is paying. He said he's been paid a bonus. Everything's set up – all I need to do is call my consultant.'

I watch Lucy's look of disbelief, before she shakes her head, incredulous. 'I never in a million years thought the day would come I'd say this, but thank fuck for James.'

* * *

With another layer of support from the most unexpected place, it fuels a new resolve in me as I pick myself up, determination filling me to do whatever it takes to get over this.

Lucy comes with me for my first appointment, where they explain the treatment schedule, before what feels like another huge, very real step in my cancer journey when I'm taken to have a port inserted.

I'm numbed and I try not to think about what's being done, reminding myself how grateful to James I am that I can stay here; that I haven't had to travel to London.

Then as December arrives, I start chemo. I try my hardest to stay positive, to be grateful for Lucy coming to the hospital with me; even for the sickness I feel, envisaging an army of drug molecules pitched in warfare against my cancer cells.

But the weekly cycle that gets under way is challenging to say the least. There are days when all I can do is rest, while on the better days before the next treatment, I feel well enough to continue working on my book, looking forward to Christmas when Millie's coming.

* * *

In the run-up to Christmas, I face another reality check as my hair starts falling out. As it gets more noticeable, I bite the bullet and ask Lucy to cut it for me.

After, she produces an armful of scarves. Selecting one of them, she ties it turban-style around my head.

'Very Ibiza,' she says admiringly. 'You look gorgeous, Anna.'

'I look bald, you mean.'

Lucy gazes at my reflection. 'It'll grow back. A year from now, all of this will be a distant memory.'

Hopefully... But as I know from experience, even if cancer disappears, you never quite cast off its shadow.

The week before Millie flies out, the weather takes a turn for the worse as a series of storms arrive and winds lash the island. Meanwhile, Lucy and I decorate the house with a huge tree and dozens of candles.

'Millie's going to love this.'

Lucy smiles. 'I'm so pleased she's coming. Isabella messaged me – she and Sofia are joining us, too. Don't worry, they know it's going to be a quiet one – and you're not doing a thing by the way. And if at any time it's too much, Anna, everyone will understand you need to rest.'

Fortunately, Millie's arrival coincides with one of the better days in my chemo cycle and I drive alone to the airport to meet her. The tail end of another storm is blowing through, the wind still gusting, flattening the palm trees, the landscape unfamiliarly green after so much rain.

In the terminal building, for a moment, I forget about the uncertainty my future holds; I'm just like any mother waiting for her daughter. When she walks into the arrivals hall, Millie's excitement is unrestrained.

'Anna!' She jogs towards me dragging her case behind her.

'Hi, darling.' I run to meet her, then hug her tightly.

Pulling back, she gently touches my scarf and I see the love in her eyes. 'You look beautiful.'

'It started falling out. Lucy cut the rest off – it will grow back.' But I don't want to dwell on this when she's only just got here. 'The car's this way.' We start walking towards the door. 'How was your flight? We've had ongoing storms the last week or so. I was worried you wouldn't be able to land.'

'It was awful.' She rolls her eyes and I notice the pallor of nausea that's yet to leave her face. 'It was bumpy for the last hour. I nearly threw up.'

'At least you're here... I'm sure Lucy will have a fortifying drink waiting for you. She can't wait to see you!'

Reaching the car, we load her case into the back before climbing in.

'So how are you?' Millie looks at me anxiously. 'Really? I wasn't sure you'd be up to coming, to be honest.'

'Today's a good day,' I tell her. 'There's a pattern of feeling rubbish the first three days after chemo then I start feeling better until the next one.' Glancing across at her, a smile spreads across my face. 'But having you here makes all the difference.'

* * *

After the storm, the skies clear and the weather settles to spring-like days and chilly nights. With the house stocked with food and wine, by day we walk on deserted beaches, by night we light the fire and play music.

For the most part, my illness stays in the background, though Millie wants to know where I am with it.

'After I finish chemo, I'll just need check-ups going forwards.

But as far as they could tell, there was no sign of it anywhere else.' I tell her about James paying for my chemo.

'I'm so pleased he's done that,' she says quietly. 'He came to London and took me out for dinner last week. He asked me if I was interested in exhibiting some of my paintings. Someone he knows has opened a gallery.'

'That would be amazing!' The new James gets more surprising by the day. 'You said yes?'

'I'm thinking about it.' She hesitates. 'He kept saying he was really proud of me.' Her voice wavers slightly.

Christmas arrives, a day we drink champagne and fill Lucy's kitchen with the smell of delicious food. It's a truly multicultural occasion, from Gianluca's favourite Italian seafood soup on Christmas Eve, to the tapas Isabella has made, while Lucy adds a Spanish twist to a traditional English roast.

Sofia is oddly quiet as she sits taking it all in, a distant look on her face.

'Is your gran OK?' I ask Isabella.

Isabella frowns. 'I'm not sure. She isn't herself, but she refuses to see a doctor – you know how stubborn she is. I'm keeping an eye on her. But if she doesn't pick up soon, she's going to have to see someone.'

Our worries aside, it's a day of laughter, love and friendship of the best kind, as it makes no difference that none of us are related by blood. In every other sense, we are family.

50

WILL

'Dad!' When she opened the door to Darcey's apartment, Flo's eyes flashed with excitement. 'It's brilliant you're here! I have a present for you!'

For all her growing up, Flo's excitement about Christmas hadn't changed. As he went in, Will was gratified to see the lengths that Darcey had gone to. The place was lavishly decorated, a tall tree installed in the corner of the sitting room, hung with glittering baubles, a garland of fir draped across the mantelpiece.

'Hi.' Going over to Darcey, Will kissed her cheek. 'It looks lovely in here.'

She looked pleased. 'Seeing as it's our first Christmas here, I wanted to make an effort.'

He passed a carrier bag to an exuberant Flo. 'Could you put these under the tree?'

As Darcey served up a sublime Christmas lunch, it was kind of weird – and kind of nice, too, Will reflected, only taking a surreal twist when as they finished eating, the doorbell rang. When Flo opened the door, Eric was standing there.

Actually, all you could see was a bouquet of flowers of ridiculous proportions, Darcey looking flustered as he passed it to her, before glancing awkwardly at Will.

But there was no need for awkwardness. Times had changed; Darcey had her own life to live. Will got up and walked over to them, holding out his hand. 'Good to meet you, Eric. Are you joining us?'

'Thank you. Er, if that's ok?' Eric looked slightly wrong-footed.

Will winked at Darcey. 'Of course.' Out of the corner of his eye, he caught a look of relief on Flo's face. 'It's Christmas, isn't it?'

* * *

It was early evening, Eric on his second brandy, by the time Will got up to leave.

'Good to meet you.' He shook Eric's hand. 'Bye, darling.' He hugged Flo tightly.

Her eyes were on his. 'Can I come and see you tomorrow?'

'Absolutely you can. As long as you're up for a really long walk.' Teasing her, he knew she shared her mother's aversion to the long muddy walks he loved.

Flo rolled her eyes at him. 'If we have to.'

'Cool. I'll pick you up around ten?'

When Darcey walked him to the door, he kissed her on the cheek. 'Thank you for today.'

'I'm sorry...' She nodded behind her to where Eric and Flo were flicking through TV channels together. 'I didn't know he was coming.'

'It's fine.' Will looked at her. 'He seems like a nice guy.' He paused. 'You have to do what makes you happy.'

As her eyes held his, Darcey looked as though she was about

to say something, before thinking the better of it. 'Happy Christmas, Will,' she said softly.

***

It was a Christmas he'd been dreading, that had actually worked out better than he'd hoped. Back at home, Will arranged Flo's present in pride of place on the chest in the sitting room. Standing back, he studied the montage of photos taken at various swimming competitions, feeling ridiculously proud, not just for what she'd achieved, but for who she'd become. He was proud of Darcey, too, for maintaining her dignity, for realising that in fact, she had made life hard for them all, but was doing her best to make amends.

After Darcey's proclamation that she was going to spend some time alone, he hadn't realised Eric was back on the scene, but actually, he wasn't so bad. A bit of an old duffer, perhaps, but when he seemed kind hearted enough and he'd cottoned on to Flo's sense of humour, Darcey could do a lot worse, he mused.

As his mind turned to his own life, Will was aware of an emptiness that Christmas with Flo and Darcey had briefly stuck a sticking plaster over. He knew where it came from, and what he needed to do. But having waited this long, he wasn't doing anything rash. This time, it was important to get it right. And that started with talking to Darcey. OK, so he didn't have to explain himself to her, but for Flo's sake, he wanted her to know what his plans were. He should talk to Flo, too. After that... He had no idea what Anna was thinking, but as he thought of seeing her, he felt his heart lift.

51

ANNA

Between Christmas and New Year, when I return from the hospital after more chemo, Millie is determined to look after me.

'It's how it works,' she says firmly when I tell her she ought to go out with Lucy. 'You looked after me for years. Now it's my turn. I've been studying reflexology – not for long, but I've read it can help when you're having chemo. Would you like me to try?'

Sitting on the bed next to me, she gently takes off my socks. Closing my eyes, as she works on my feet, the sensation is relaxing. More than that, she's right. It does help. Half an hour later, I feel a lot less nauseous.

'I'll do some more tomorrow.' She looks at me anxiously. 'Is there anything I can get you?'

When I shake my head, Millie leaves me alone, closing the door quietly behind her.

As I lie there, I think how for all the fear and uncertainty in my life, my eyes have been opened to the kindness of the people around me, the love I'm surrounded by, as I see my life in a way I haven't before. The past stretching out behind me, a trail of dark and light, Millie being the high point, the blazing star in my world; my book another; my divorce a stretch of black, Will, a transient ray of sunlight, suddenly grateful they're all part of my life, a life that's the way it is because of millions of synchronicities. Change one, and going forwards, everything else changes too. It's happened the way it did, because it was meant to.

* * *

By New Year's Eve, even with Millie's care, I'm feeling unsettled. Putting it down to the side effects of chemo, I spend the afternoon resting. But when I get up, the feeling intensifies.

Determined not to put a downer on New Year's Eve, I keep it to myself. Getting changed, I cover the pallor of my skin with make-up, gazing uneasily at my reflection. But given the cumulative effect of the chemo I'm having, it's not surprising.

When I go to join the others, the fire is lit, the fireplace freshly garlanded with rosemary from the hills, filling the room with its scent.

'Right. You wait here, Anna. And drink this.' Lucy passes me what looks like a mojito. 'It's non-alcoholic. Now, don't come out until I call you.'

Wondering where everyone else is, I do as she says, watching the flames flicker as music drifts inside.

A few minutes later, Lucy comes back. 'Put this on.' She throws me a huge jumper, standing there as I put it on. 'OK. You can come out now.'

I follow her out to the terrace, where Millie and Isabella are standing with Gianluca. The fire pit is burning, the whole terrace lit by what looks like hundreds of candles.

'Millie and I have been talking,' Lucy says. 'We thought New Year's Eve is a good time to close the door on the past in some way. The idea is we each write down things we don't want to take forward, and then throw them into the fire. In your case, that's your illness... And in my case, that's your illness, but that's the point. We can write things for ourselves or other people. There's three pieces of paper each. Here.' She passes some to me, then to the others. 'There are pens on the table. You have three wishes.' She picks one up. 'Use them wisely!'

Sitting down, the first one is easy. *Cancer*. So is the second. *Anger with James*. But the third is less obvious. I could write *Will*, but something stops me. However much I should, even now I can't bring myself to close the door on us – forever. In the end, I settle for *regrets*, because life is far too short for them – and it applies to all of us.

One by one, we throw our wishes into the flames as Lucy turns to me. 'All of us have written "cancer", just so you know,' she says quietly. 'The universe better be bloody watching.'

Tears blur my eyes as I turn to these wonderful people in my life: Millie, Isabella, Gianluca, all of them watching me. 'Thank you.'

Lucy kisses me on the cheek. 'You're welcome. Right. We need to get this party started. Champagne anyone?'

I'm tired, but I make it until the New Year begins before creeping away and leaving them to it, in my casita, listening to the sounds of voices and laughter drifting across the garden.

My thoughts turn to Will. I used to be so sure that he would break away from Darcey, but sadly, he never will. Instead, he's one of those people who'll always find reasons *why not* to do something. In short, he's one of those who'll have regrets.

Whereas I've learned to follow my passionate, occasionally reckless, heart. I regret just two things – that I didn't learn to do it sooner and not being able to share my life with him. *In another lifetime, I can see us together...* Will said that once. So in my quieter moments, I imagine another lifetime when we are all together –

me, Will, Millie and Lucy. It's a beautiful image that I hold tightly to me, not caring that it isn't real, picturing us here, in Ibiza, knowing that it's what should have been; feeling the love between us; knowing there's still so much that will forever remain unsaid.

* * *

Having finished working on my edits, over the next couple of days, I write the last chapters of my next book, or at least, I think I have, until that night, I wake in total darkness, filled with a sense of urgency, knowing I've forgotten something important. Glancing at my phone, the time is 4.10 a.m., but if I don't do it now, I know I'll forget.

Getting up, I fumble around my room, looking for the manuscript Luce has carefully printed off for me, finding the page at the beginning, with the single line that says it all:

Only love is real

Then I find a blank sheet of paper to insert directly after it, writing two words, a dedication:

For Will

However it's ended, it feels right. Then on another piece of paper, I write him a letter. It takes me the rest of the night, each word painstakingly chosen, because I know exactly what I want to say. Only then, can I rest.

But my sense of peace is short-lived. The next morning, I wake up struggling to breathe. Getting out of bed, my legs almost give way as I go to Millie's door. Opening it, when she sees me, she turns white.

Leading me into her room, she sits me on the bed. 'I'll be right back. I'm going to get Lucy.'

Terrified the tests I had must have missed something, without enough air in my lungs, dizziness overcomes me and I start to panic. *This isn't supposed to happen. I can't die. I need more time.*

Lucy comes rushing in. 'Anna? What's happening?'

The pain in my chest is vicelike, speech impossible, my breath coming in gasps.

I think I hear the words, *calling an ambulance.* Above me, Millie's face blurs, fear is taking me over, as suddenly it's as though my life is slipping away from me.

52

WILL

A few days into the New Year, while Flo had been otherwise occupied, Will had gone over to talk to Darcey.

'Are you going to be OK to take her back to school once the holidays are over?'

'Of course. I was going to suggest it.' Clearly picking up on something, Darcey frowned. 'Is everything OK?'

'There's something I need to talk to you about.' Will sat on one of the plush new sofas.

Sitting next to him, Darcey looked quizzical. 'Go on.'

'Before we moved back in together, I met someone. Her name is Anna. We've known each other since we were teenagers. Our paths have crossed a few times over the years – but this time, we were going to be together.' He watched the look of shock on Darcey's face. 'But when Flo ran away, I ended it with her. I haven't mentioned her to Flo, yet. I will, but I wanted you to know first. Tomorrow morning, I'm flying to Ibiza to try and find her.'

Darcey looked stunned. 'Why haven't you told me before?'

He shrugged. 'It wasn't going to help us when we were trying to live together. I don't even know if she'll want to see me – she doesn't know I'm coming.'

'I hope she does,' Darcey said softly. "Don't worry about Flo. I'll explain – that you've gone to see someone you love.' She paused. 'That's right, isn't it? You love her?'

Will found his voice. 'Yes.'

'Then you must go.' She held his gaze for a moment. 'I didn't realise you'd made such a sacrifice.'

But Will didn't see it like that. 'Flo came first. That's all. And don't forget, you gave up Eric.'

'His money, you mean,' Darcey said cynically.

Will was surprised. 'I thought you and he were together again.'

Darcey was quiet for a moment. 'He keeps asking me to go away with him. But I think it's like you said. You can't go back, can you?' she said quietly. Then she rallied. 'I've decided to get involved with the drama school here. I need something new in my life.'

Just then, Flo came in. Darcey looked at him. 'Shall I give you a moment?'

* * *

Flo took it well, especially when she knew he'd told Darcey. When he'd told her he was going to Ibiza, seeing her face light up, he'd had a flicker of hope that if all this worked out, one of these days maybe Flo would be going there with him.

But first things first. Having handed in his notice, he'd taken the leave he was owed and booked a flight. It felt like a step in the right direction – with or without Anna in his life, he couldn't go on like this.

He'd worry about money later. He'd been offered some freelance work, and he'd never planned to keep the house. With just him there, he rattled around in it, if he was honest. He pictured a tiny cottage somewhere, with enough land for some sheep – *with Anna in it.* God. If that was possible, he'd be the happiest man alive.

A few hours... That's all there was, now. There was still the small matter of finding her. He'd remembered Anna telling him the name of Lucy's house. *Can Mimosa.* The only problem was he wasn't sure what part of the island it was. Hopefully it would be like in the UK and taxi drivers would have encyclopaedic knowledge. If not... He still had her mobile number – he'd have to call her.

He went upstairs and checked he'd packed everything before zipping his bag shut. Back downstairs, he picked up his passport, checked for the last time he'd closed all the windows, before locking the door and going out to his car.

As he drove to the airport, a sense of trepidation filled him. For the first time, he was free to imagine they could be together – if that was what she wanted. If she didn't... Will didn't want to go there.

After parking his car in the long stay car park, Will got on a bus to the terminal building. It was a beautiful day, perfect for flying. It was the same in Ibiza – he'd checked. After dropping off his bag, he made his way to security where he was through in no time. There was a brief delay to the flight, but no more than that. All he had to do was wait.

Only as the plane took off did Will allow himself to relax. As he watched England grow smaller, he thought of the list he'd made of all the Can Mimosas he could find in Ibiza – with sea views – he'd remembered that too.

Through the window, he watched the English Channel disappear behind them as they reached the coast of northern France, gazing out at the patchwork of fields, growing paler in colour as they flew south. *South...* He liked how that sounded, the suggestion of sun, blue sea, the orange and lemon trees on Anna's teenage list.

After ordering a Coke, he closed his eyes. At last, instead of just dreaming, he was doing something.

In what seemed like no time, the aircraft was starting its descent. Will watched the coast come into view, before the sea came closer. As the aircraft banked, he glimpsed sandy cliffs, the dusky green of pine trees, before the wings levelled out, the landscape racing past them as the wheels touched down.

As the aircraft taxied in, Will's heart started to race. He barely registered the cabin crew, managing to mutter a *thank you* as he disembarked. As he stepped outside, the air had a warmth to it, an unfamiliar softness. He followed the other passengers into the terminal, and handed over his passport before claiming his bag. Glancing around for the exit, he followed the crowd – something he'd sworn to stop doing, he reminded himself.

As the electric doors opened and closed, he found himself in the arrivals hall. Walking along to one of the rotating gates, he then went in search of a helpful, English-speaking taxi driver.

53

LUCY

Seeing Anna unconscious in a hospital bed brings a clarity that's blinding. Only one thing matters in this life – and that's love. The rest is a crock of shit. Swearing to myself that I'll never lose sight of that, I leave Millie with Anna and drive home to pick up some things for us.

Alone, I no longer have to hide how terrified I am, that the doctors have missed something; that Anna isn't going to come through this, and my emotions take me over, until wiping my tears away, I tell myself, *she has to.*

When I reach the house, there's an unfamiliar car parked outside. Imagining someone lost, or a satnav blip, as I start walking towards the driver, a voice calls out from behind me.

'Lucy?'

Turning around, I look at him incredulously. '*Will?*' I stand there for a moment, then suddenly I'm running towards him, hugging him as though I've never been so pleased to see anyone. 'I can't believe you're here.'

'It's so good to see you.' Will glances towards the housed. 'Is Anna here?'

Tears fill my eyes as I gaze at him. Of all the times for him to arrive, it has to be now. Swallowing, I shake my head. 'Anna's sick, Will. She's in hospital.' I watch the colour drain from his face. 'I've just come back from there. She collapsed last night –she's still unconscious. She's been having chemo...'

Will's face turns pale. '*Chemo?* She has cancer?'

'It came back – last autumn. The doctor's think it's possible she's picked up an infection. Either that, or it's a reaction to the drugs. Until they do more tests, we don't know.' Seeing his shock, I pat his arm. 'You'd better come in.'

'I need to pay the taxi driver.'

I wait as he walks back to the taxi, wondering what the chances are that he's come here when Anna needs him most; how it's the strangest fucking timing.

An hour later, when we go back to the hospital, as I lead Will to the ward where Anna is, he hangs back. 'You go. She might not want to see me.'

I stare at him in disbelief. 'Oh, hush, Will, for Christ's sake. Of course she will.'

As our eyes meet, an unspoken understanding passes between us, because when we both love her, being here is all that matters.

I touch his arm gently. 'Millie's with her. Come and meet her.'

At Anna's bedside, Millie's where I left her. 'Hey, hun,' I say quietly. 'This is Will.'

Millie's eyes widen, flickering towards his as she whispers to Anna, 'Will's here.' She gets up. 'Thank you so much for coming,' she says to Will. 'Do you want to talk to her?'

Taking Millie's place next to Anna, Will takes her hand, then leaning down, gently kisses her cheek before murmuring something to her.

I glance at Millie. 'Shall we give them a moment?'

***

That evening, Will comes back to Can Mimosa with us. When we walk in, Gianluca is in the kitchen creating one of his pasta dishes.

Going over, I kiss him. 'Smells incredible, hun.' I lower my voice. 'Will's here.'

His look of shock morphs into approval. 'This is good,' he says quietly. 'And Anna?'

I shake my head. 'No change.'

***

Whether it's Will's presence or the medication starting to take effect, over the next couple of days there are signs of Anna starting to come round. On the third day, while Will takes Millie out to get some lunch, she opens her eyes.

'Hey,' I say softly. 'Welcome back.' Watching her eyes come into focus, I bring her up to speed. 'You're in hospital, babe.'

'How long?' she murmurs.

'A few days.' I take a deep breath. 'You haven't been so good.' I hesitate again. 'There's something else you should know. Will's here.'

Incredulity flickers in her eyes before they close again. I glance around for a nurse. Seeing one, I wave across the ward.

'She opened her eyes just now,' I tell her joyfully. 'It's a good sign, isn't it?'

***

As we walk this precarious line together between life and whatever's next, Millie, Will and I surround Anna with a love that's palpable. Slowly, her skin takes on more colour, her periods of wakefulness lasting minutes rather than brief seconds.

I watch Will and Anna, his head bent over hers, in moments she's dreamed of, moments that only he can give her. What exists between them is magical, beautiful, timeless; the kind of love that's remained beyond my grasp, maybe beyond the grasp of most of us, as I start to understand why she held out for so long; why it hurt her so much that they couldn't be together. But it's as she said. Real love doesn't end. It's infinite.

When at last Anna grows stronger, we take an evening away from our vigil to drive to the beach to watch the sunset.

'We need a laugh.' I take Millie's arm, leading her towards Es Saphira. 'This is the only bar in Ibiza where they serve hot food cold or try not to serve you at all. Don't say I didn't warn you.'

True to form, we order a tray of mojitos, waiting thirty minutes for them to appear, even though we're the only customers. Then as the sun sinks below the horizon, we drink a toast to Anna – and to friendship.

* * *

Starting to imagine Anna coming home, I pack some clothes for her to take to the hospital. But this morning when we get there, instead of sitting up, Anna's lying down.

'Anna?' When she doesn't respond, I gently shake her arm. 'Hey, babe, it's us again.' Taking in how deathly pale her skin is, I start to panic.

Suddenly her eyes flicker open and she tries to speak, but instead of words, it's an indecipherable sound.

Turning to Millie and Will, I start to panic. 'I'm going to find a nurse.' I try to keep the worry out of my voice. 'Can you stay with her?'

I hurry towards the nurses' station. 'It's Anna. Something's wrong – can one of you come?'

We make it back to her bedside just as Anna's eyes seem to roll up before her body slumps. At that moment, an alarm sounds on one of the machines she's hooked up to. Looking at the trace, instead of peaks and troughs, it's a steady flat line.

My blood runs cold. 'What does that mean?'

'I'm afraid you have to leave.' The nurse glances at us. 'Now, please,' she says briskly as another nurse comes over and pulls the curtain around Anna's bed.

Millie's face is white as a sheet. Every fibre of my being is screaming at me to stay with Anna, but I also know I need to get Millie out of here.

Mercifully, Will takes charge. 'Come on. Let's wait outside.'

As we wait, I hold tightly to Millie's hand, thinking of what Anna's always said, about how life isn't about longevity. It's about intense bursts of brilliance; that more meaning can be condensed into a few days than into an entire lifetime. She'd tried to explain it to me. It wasn't about the length of time she and Will had together. It was about the strength of the connection between them, the meeting of minds, hearts, souls. Having watched them together, I know everything she said is true.

Meanwhile, it's as though time stops, restarting briefly when Anna's wheeled away to ICU, before one of the nurses comes to find us.

'Her body has gone into shock,' she tells us quietly. 'It happens when sepsis isn't treated.'

Suddenly I'm petrified. 'But she is being treated – she's on antibiotics.'

'I know.' The nurse looks anxious. 'For whatever reason, she isn't responding to them.'

'So what now?'

'We're doing what we can...' She pauses. 'We just have to hope she turns a corner, but...'

I stare at her. 'But what?'

'She isn't at all well,' the nurse says quietly.

She walks away, leaving us alone together, while next to me, feeling Millie's body start to shake, I put my arm around her.

'She has to get better,' I whisper, unable to stop the tears pouring down my face; terrified from what the nurse just said, that she isn't going to.

54

WILL

Back at Lucy's house, Will glanced at Anna's book. Lucy had given it to him when they came back from the hospital. As he'd slowly unwrapped the paper, underneath were loose pages tied together with ribbon, with a single folded piece of paper slipped underneath it. A letter.

He'd known immediately what it was. It was the book Anna had always said she was going to write. *Their story*. He'd been filled with the need to read her words here, at Can Mimosa, where she'd written them; breathing in the same pine-scented air that she had, under the clear skies she loved, surrounded by vibrant blues, dusty greens, shades of earth and sand.

Taking the path up the hillside, he reached a large rock. Sitting on it, he'd put the manuscript on the ground, and opened the letter.

Dearest Will,

Remember that day I called you? I told you I was giving our story an ending. After the highs and lows we've been through, if it's only on these pages, in these words, we're together the way we talked about when we fell in love.

So, this is our story. It doesn't matter how little time we had. Meeting you again changed my life. Ever since, I've wanted to share what it taught me about myself. Too many people don't understand the power love has, so that's what I've tried to write about.

It's because of you I know what love is; that it has no boundaries, exists beyond the constraints of our small lives. It's unconditional, beautiful, all-encompassing. The time wasn't right for us, was it? But I have a feeling I'll be seeing you, Will. Maybe our paths will cross again, in another lifetime, when we'll recognise each other, just as we did this time round. Maybe that will be your moment for brilliance… You'll take a deep breath and come to find me. The beginning of the rest of our lives…

Until next time, Will. I love you. Forever. Never forget that.

As he sat there, an echo of Anna's voice came to him. *We're so lucky, Will... How many people never feel this?* They'd been walking, the early morning sunshine filtering through the trees. What he'd give to have that moment back, even for a second. It was followed by another memory of something he'd said to her: *I wasn't looking, but then I found you.*

They had been lucky. And he hadn't been looking, but then he'd found her again, and in his turmoil, let her go, let her down, too many times.

But now, it was about what Anna had said – making it count. There would be no more procrastinating, no more excuses... it started now. He picked up the manuscript.

For Will... He stared for a moment at the dedication, before reading on: *I called you one morning. It was early and I'd gone for a run. Reaching the top of the hill, the sun was bursting through the trees, the air vibrant with the sound of birdsong.*

For a moment, I stood there, as suddenly everything was falling into place, answers coming to me, answers that had evaded me for weeks, if not forever. I reached into my pocket for my phone and started texting you.

I have an idea for another book!

God, he remembered that morning vividly – living with Darcey at the time, he hadn't been expecting to hear from her. He carried on reading.

Stories don't exist in isolation. They all come from somewhere, their beginnings traced back to chapters that we bury deep in our subconscious; entwined with other stories. Yours and mine began long before we met, moulded by all the things life had thrown at us, the storms we'd weathered, the people we'd met along the way, all of which had played a part in making us the people we'd become.

All those missed chances over the years... Maybe the scene was still being set; the final chapters in the stories around us still being drawn, the last pen strokes barely dry when events contrived to lead us to the same place at the top of the hill.

We were part of the way back then. Still caught in our old lives but aware of what had been missing; awakening to life, to joy, to love. We had no idea what the future held, but life was carrying us along, ready or not, on a tidal wave of highs, lows, synchronicities and heartbreak, as inevitable as it was unstoppable.

But that's what love is. A force like no other.

Real.

As he sat there, suddenly he was replaying his life, imagining a million different scenarios that might have followed, if his mother hadn't died so young, if he hadn't lost his brother; if his problems hadn't scarred him. Maybe he'd have had more self-belief, a greater sense of self-worth. But he'd never know.

55

TWO WEEKS LATER

Will

Sitting near the front of the church, the scent of flowers reached Will – the rosemary that grew wild on the hills, mixed with lavender and the fragrant white roses. Blended with incense, it made him think of his mother's funeral, before he thought of Simon's. Will felt a pang of sadness. There had been too many people he'd loved for whom life had been cut short.

It was a typically Spanish church, set into a hillside and surrounded by olive trees. White painted, its interior was simple and unadorned.

He'd come here early today, wanting a few minutes to just sit undisturbed in the quiet, imagining echoes of the sadness and desperation of the people who had come here over the centuries. Apart from the old man who'd wandered in and knelt down to pray briefly, he'd been alone.

It was only a matter of time before the congregation would

begin drifting in – he'd no doubt the church would be packed. Weddings, funerals, it was always the same. A wave of emotion washed over him. It seemed a complete paradox that our desire to survive was so strong when under it all, life was so fragile.

The last month had underlined that in a way he'd never seen before. He'd never known such love – from Lucy and Millie. There was his unexpected friendship with Gianluca, too. He felt his heart swell with gratitude for them.

Will didn't turn around as he heard people file into the church, his gaze staying firmly fixed on the flowers beside the altar as someone slipped into the pew beside him.

'You OK?' she whispered.

As he turned to look at Millie, her eyes were anxious. She worried too much about other people, Will had quickly learned that about her. There was so much of Anna in her it defied belief that they weren't related by blood. Nodding, he reached for her hand.

Hearing the door open at the back of the church, as the organist started playing, he heard the congregation stand behind them. Will stood up. Far from being a celebration of a life, to him funerals always felt like an endurance test.

In a few steps, the pallbearers were parallel with him, before laying the coffin on the bier at the front. He watched them stand back as Lucy laid the flowers she was carrying on it, then Isabella kissed the photo she was carrying before placing it carefully among them.

Will took a deep breath. Holding a simple posy of the pine, rosemary and thyme that grew wild here, Anna placed it in front of Sofia's photo.

Tears filled his eyes. He still hadn't shaken off the fear he'd felt when she was in hospital. He'd honestly thought he was going to lose her – watching her grow weaker, they'd been warned to prepare for the worst. But then, against the odds, to the amazement of the medical staff, she'd fought back.

She was still weak, and his heart overflowed with love as he watched her turn towards him, catching his eye, smiling at him. As she, Isabella and Lucy filed into the pew in front of him, beside him, Millie squeezed his hand.

The service was simple and understated, befitting of Sofia and a life well lived. In spite of the sadness of losing her daughter, he hoped she'd felt blessed to have discovered she had a granddaughter.

It kind of summed up life – the people who came and went in our lives; the sorrow and happiness you felt along the way; how in such a short time, so much could change. But one fundamental never would. As Anna had always said, it was about how you loved. *Only love was real...* If you could see the beauty in this world we live in, if your heart soared when your eyes met those of the one person who was meant for you, if you were loved and loved back in equal measure, you had it all. You were blessed.

You'd found magic.

POSTSCRIPT

On the terrace at Can Mimosa, as she glances at Will, Isabella nudges Lucy. 'That man coming here, now... Pretty amazing timing, isn't it?'

'Fucking weird, if you ask me.' Lucy looks uncertain. 'Let's have another G and T. I've been meaning to ask you something.'

'Oh?'

'About your goats,' Lucy says cryptically. 'Will's been talking about them. I've always rather liked them, actually. Couldn't sell me a few, could you, darling?' As Millie joins them, she smiles at her. 'We're going to buy some of Isabella's goats.'

'Cool.' Millie hesitates. 'Actually, Lucy? I wanted to ask you something.'

Lucy looks surprised. 'Ask away.'

'OK.' She takes a deep breath. 'Well, I've been wondering if it would be possible for me to stay? For a few weeks, maybe? I thought I'd see if I can sell my paintings here.'

'Oh my God, I can't believe this, babe.' As she looks at Millie, there are tears in Lucy's eyes. 'Not just for weeks, though. Stay forever.'

Going over to the sofa at the far end of the terrace, Millie sits down next to Anna. 'Anna?' Her face is flushed with excitement. 'I have to tell you something.'

As Anna looks at her stepdaughter, her eyes widen. 'Tell me what?'

'I'm leaving London.'

Anna looks shocked. 'What will you do? What about your painting? And your job?'

Millie smiles. 'I can paint anywhere, can't I? I just feel it's time for a change.'

Anna looks incredulous. 'So where are you moving to?'

Millie's eyes are bright as she gazes at the woman she loves more than anyone. 'Here.'

Holding out her arms, there are tears in Anna's eyes as she hugs her. 'I've dreamed of this,' she whispers.

There's concern in Will's eyes as he comes to join them. 'How are you feeling?'

'Tired. But otherwise...' Anna's eyes rest on his as Millie gets up and leaves them alone together. 'I just feel lucky.'

'Me, too.' Sitting next to her, they gaze across the hills, splashed yellow here and there with the first Mimosa blossom.

'So, what now, Will Anderson?' Anna says softly, leaning her head against his shoulder. 'I know it's complicated. When you go back to England, I'll be fine. I was fine before. Chemo will be over soon. Oh – and did you know Millie's moving here?' Sitting up again, she looks at him. 'She's only just told me – I still can't believe it.' She pauses. 'Whatever happens, I'll always be so glad you came here.'

'So will I.' He pauses. 'But you know, I don't think it's complicated at all. In fact, I think it's quite simple...' Pausing again, he looks at Anna. 'After all our missed chances. don't you think now, maybe this is our time?'

She looks stunned, before an anxious look crosses her face. 'I'm not out of the woods yet. You know that, don't you?'

'I know. But I want to be here for you,' he says quietly. 'Through whatever life throws at us. For however much time we have – and hopefully it's loads of time – because I love you.'

'You're really sure?' she whispers.

Unable to speak for a moment, he takes her hands. 'I've never been more sure about anything.'

ACKNOWLEDGMENTS

Many people are involved in a book being published and I'd like to say a huge thank you to everyone who makes up the fabulous team at Boldwood. You've made me feel so welcome, and your creativity and hard work make you a joy to work with. Thank you so much to Nia Beynon and Claire Fenby. And to my editor, Tara Loder – from the start, you homed in on the heart of this book, and helped me to rediscover it... I know it wouldn't be the book it is without you.

A massive thank you also to the brilliant team at Mushens Entertainment, especially to Juliet, my agent, one of the loveliest and most brilliant people I've had the pleasure of working with.

Then there's you, my readers. It never stops being a privilege to know other people are going to read my words. Thank you from the bottom of my heart to all of you, for buying my books, for writing wonderful reviews and for sharing them with other people.

One of the themes of this book is the way life has of sending us the unexpected. Never has that been more so than in the last few years, when we've been travelling in France and Spain, and living fairly nomadically. It's inspired more book ideas than I could ever have imagined and we've made wonderful new friends, which is another of the themes of this book: the importance of the people in our lives. It bringing me on to my family: Dad and my sisters. I love you loads. Thank you for always being there – and for being such great supporters of my books.

To my friends, too... your support is so much appreciated.

Thank you and much love to Martin, for sharing this amazing adventure. Here's to the next chapter, wherever it may take us.

And much love to my wonderful children, Georgie and Tom, who constantly inspire me. I'm so incredibly proud of both of you.

MORE FROM DEBBIE HOWELLS

We hope you enjoyed reading *The Girl I Used To Be*. If you did, please leave a review.

If you'd like to gift a copy, this book is also available as an ebook, digital audio download and audiobook CD.

Sign up to Debbie Howells' mailing list for news, competitions and updates on future books.

https://bit.ly/DebbieHowellsnews

ABOUT THE AUTHOR

Debbie Howells' first novel, a psychological thriller, The Bones of You, was a Sunday Times bestseller for Macmillan. Four more bestsellers followed, including most recently The Vow, published by Avon. Fulfilling her dream of writing women's fiction she has found a home with Boldwood.

Visit Debbie's Website:

https://www.debbiehowells.co.uk

Follow Debbie on social media:

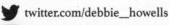

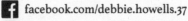

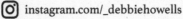

- twitter.com/debbie__howells
- facebook.com/debbie.howells.37
- instagram.com/_debbiehowells
- bookbub.com/authors/debbie-howells

Lightning Source UK Ltd.
Milton Keynes UK
UKHW042254221022
410896UK00006B/147

9 781804 150160